ABOUT T

Elizabeth O'Roark spent many years as a medical writer before publishing her first novel in 2013. She holds two bachelor's degrees from the University of Texas and a master's degree from Notre Dame. She lives in Washington, D.C. with her three children. Join her on Facebook at Elizabeth O'Roark Books for updates, book talk and lots of complaints about her children.

ALSO BY ELIZABETH O'ROARK

THE SUMMER I SAVED YOU

ELIZABETH O'ROARK

PIATKUS

PIATKUS

First published in Great Britain in 2023 by Piatkus

1 3 5 7 9 10 8 6 4 2

A CIP catalogue record for this book
is available from the British Library.

ISBN: 978-0-349-44069-9

Printed and bound in Great Britain by Clays Ltd, Elcograf S.p.A.

Papers used by Piatkus are from well-managed forests
and other responsible sources.

Piatkus
An imprint of
Little, Brown Book Group
Carmelite House
50 Victoria Embankment
London EC4Y 0DZ

An Hachette UK Company
www.hachette.co.uk

www.littlebrown.co.uk

THE SUMMER I
SAVED YOU

PROLOGUE

LUCIE, 2002

My great-aunt wasn't happy.

I'd only met her once before, this woman who'd raised my father, but as she waited on her front porch, watching me tug a beat-up suitcase behind me, she looked no more impressed than she had the first time.

I wasn't all that happy either. I'd seen my father before, in magazines and on TV, sitting on a yacht with other famous tech guys or showing off his mansion—his model wife and kids beside him. I'd had high hopes for his aunt Ruth's lakeside cottage, but her house was barely any better than *ours*. And Elliott Springs, which sounded like the name of a resort to me, had turned out to be a crappy town far to the south of San Francisco. There weren't even *stoplights*.

"Didn't even shut the engine off," Ruth muttered as my mother drove away. "*Work emergency*, my ass."

My mom doesn't even have a job. She's going to Disney with her boyfriend. Somehow, I held the words in. It helped that my mother had promised to take me with them next year if I kept it to myself.

My aunt sighed, grabbing my suitcase. "Well, come on,

then," she said, walking into the house and leading me up a flight of stairs, explaining things I already knew: that it would be very dull here for a six-year-old, that I'd need to stay inside.

"No one can know you're here," she warned. "Having a kid around is not what I need right now."

I nodded. I was used to both things—keeping secrets and not being wanted. My father had refused to ever meet me. My mother's boyfriends complained about me all the time, and when they weren't complaining, my mother was. It was a bruise I'd become so used to I barely noticed when it got poked.

Ruth led me into a room that faced the neighbor's house, but I could see the lake to the left, with a dock jutting out onto it and a bunch of boys who looked a few years older than me standing on its edge. I walked to the window, drawn to them, barely listening as Ruth told me she had to get back to work.

They were flipping into the water, one after the other, howling and yelling and so...free. They were *all* tan and happy and handsome, but for some reason my gaze landed on just one of them and refused to stray.

The sight of him called to me. As if he was saying, *"Lucie, find me, you belong here,"* though he had no clue I existed.

I decided to watch him carefully, whenever I could. If he was drowning, I'd go save him, like Ariel saved Prince Eric.

I was weirdly certain that one day he'd need me to do it.

1

LUCIE

2023

There are logical things to think about when you call your husband to tell him your marriage is over, but the boy next door—a boy you haven't even seen in thirteen years—is not among them.

I could blame it on the fact that I'm back in Elliott Springs... that I'm at the lake and standing on the same dock where Caleb once executed perfect flips and dives. But that would imply I ever *stopped* thinking about him in the first place, which I did not. Not entirely.

"How exactly do you think you're going to leave me?" Jeremy asks. "Your only skill is being hot, and you've barely got that anymore."

It's telling that he hasn't mentioned our twins—asleep in the house just past my shoulder—once during this conversation. He's been too focused on his outrage—first that I'd dare to accuse him of cheating, then that I actually had proof and was doing something about it.

"No smart comeback?" Jeremy asks. "Oh, wait. You'd need to be smart in the first place for that."

I look over my shoulder at Caleb's old house looming dark

and lifeless behind me. It sold years ago, so I'll never get to see who he grew into—if he became a man who cheats on his wife and then blames her. If he tells the mother of his children that her only skill is *being hot*. I can't imagine he does, but I bet he didn't marry someone like me. Someone who stands here listening to it.

I hit the button to end the call and drop the phone in the pocket of my robe. Jeremy will make me pay for that—hanging up on him—but I feel like a different person here. The girl I used to be, with different fears and different desires.

I'd just wanted one person to want me, back then. Perhaps I latched onto the idea of Caleb simply because he was my opposite, surrounded by people who adored him...but it felt like more. I'd been a dirty secret my entire life, yet I was certain it would change—that I'd eventually be down here by his side, jumping off the dock, trying to balance on an inner tube.

And now I'm back, over two decades later, and I've still never jumped in the lake. In some ways, this is the first time in my life I've actually been free.

So jump, says a voice in my head. A crazy, illogical voice. I'm a grown woman with two children asleep inside. I don't even have a towel. But already I'm shedding my robe.

I bend my knees and spring off the balls of my feet.

This will be my clean break, my fresh start, and—

Fuck, fuck, fuck.

I'm gasping as I reach the water's surface, flailing in my frantic attempt to get to the ladder.

The water is *so fucking cold*, and if I'd hoped this would help, would prove to be *transcendent*, I could not have been more wrong. I'm an idiot who somehow forgot a lake in northern California would be cold in late March, and there's nothing transcendent about that at all.

I scramble up the ladder in panties and a camisole that are soaking wet, wishing I'd at least considered bringing a towel for this fresh start of mine. I blot my eyes with my robe, but as I straighten to wrap it around myself...there's movement.

Someone or some *thing* is standing behind the kitchen window inside Caleb's abandoned house.

I could have imagined it, but no. There it is again, shifting shadows behind the glass doors. And whatever it is just watched me climbing semi-nude from the lake.

My new beginning was already off to a rough start. Now it's the opening scene of a horror movie.

JEREMY

> Don't know who the hell will hire you. Turning on the TV and putting chicken nuggets in the oven seem to be your only talents.

HE'S DELIVERED a near-constant stream of insults since Saturday night. You'd think he'd be too busy sleeping with our teenage babysitter to find the time, but he's good at multitasking.

Unlike Jeremy, I don't have the luxury of crafting pointlessly cruel texts. I had two kindergartners to get to school one town over, before hustling fifteen minutes down the highway to Technology Solutions Group, my new employer.

The massive brick building a bit north of Santa Cruz looks a lot more impersonal than it did when I came for my interview, but I doubt I looked at it all that carefully. Back then, I was more worried about Jeremy finding out I was job hunting than anything else.

Wiping damp hands on my pencil skirt, I walk to the front doors and head into the lobby, where a receptionist actively ignores me until she's done taking pictures of her coffee.

"Hi—I'm Lucie Monroe, the new hire. I was told to ask for Mark Spencer?" She stares at me as if I'm still speaking, still boring her, and hits a button. "Mark, someone's here to see you." She returns to photographing her coffee without missing a beat.

I've been hired to improve morale—a job I convinced myself I was perfectly suited for, because if you spend your days trying to persuade young children to bathe, eat vegetables and go to bed, you've got more experience enhancing morale than anyone alive.

If this girl is a typical TSG employee, it may be more of an uphill battle than I anticipated.

"Lucie, welcome," Mark says, walking toward me. "Looks like you've met Kayleigh already. Let's find you an office."

He turns down the hall opposite the one he came from, and I follow.

"I know you've just arrived," he says as we walk, "but the board is excited to hear your ideas and we happen to have a meeting tomorrow. I'd love it if you could swing by and tell them where you'll be starting."

My nod of agreement is weak. I came in for my interview spouting research about employee programs I'd found online, but that hardly means I'm ready to present a *plan* to the board.

He comes to a stop in a large room full of empty, silent cubicles. "You've obviously got your pick of offices." He winces as he laughs at his own joke. "With all the staff turnover, we consolidated most of the teams and put them on the next few floors."

"Turnover?" I repeat.

He shrugs. "I think I mentioned in the interview that a number of our employees have gone to competitors. Everyone wants to work from home since the pandemic, and the CEO is avidly against it. That's where you come in...We're hoping you can stem the tide."

Mark never mentioned even once that they were *losing* employees. He said, *'We want to be a place where people love their jobs,'* which is pretty different, and the insanity of what I've done is becoming clearer by the second.

He gestures to the nearest cubicle, and I step inside. My first office. It's three felt walls—probably an eighth the size of the offices my half-siblings have, working for my father—but it's mine.

Mark follows, perching on the edge of the desk. "Look, this isn't the greatest way to kick off your first day, but I feel like I need to level with you. The CEO's been out of town and he was never a fan of creating this position in the first place. But I only became aware this morning of how *strongly* he was opposed to it."

Oh, God. Oh, God. Oh, God.

I put three grand into a new checking account before I left, but it won't last long, and then what? Jeremy said I'd be crawling back in a week. Maybe he was right.

I sink into a chair. "So he could just...cancel this whole thing?"

Mark's gaze flickers to mine and away. "Well, as you know... the initial contract is only for three months. I suppose if it doesn't go well, he could conceivably decide to eliminate the position. But it won't come to that. Why don't we go say *hi*? I'm certain he'll change his mind once you talk to him."

I'm not certain about that at all, especially if he decides to look carefully at how much of my resume involves volunteer positions at the twins' old preschool and realizes this is my first real job. But Mark's already rising, already leading me back past the unfriendly receptionist and on to his boss. There was no mention of the CEO on the website, but it's easy to imagine the sort of miserable old man who awaits us, a guy who doesn't want to spend a dime on his employees but probably flies by private plane.

I follow Mark inside an office ten times the size of my cubicle...and stare, open-jawed, at the man sitting behind the desk.

He is, in no way, a miserable old man.

It's Caleb, all grown up. He was in college the last time I saw him, but I'd know his face anywhere. It featured prominently in every innocent and *not* so innocent fantasy I had through adolescence, after all, and it's twenty times more handsome now—all hard angles and soft mouth, a jaw in need of a shave.

I have kids to support and more shit to manage than I can possibly handle well, but something stirs to life in my chest anyway—tiny, baby butterflies whispering that perhaps this is fate. Because how else do I explain the fact that my childhood crush has reappeared in my life just as I've become single?

He tugs at his tie, scowling at me. "I really hope this is a joke."

2

CALEB

The girl I watched prancing around my backyard all fucking weekend is in my office, and my buddy Liam's got to be the one behind it.

He saw her outside yesterday afternoon babysitting someone's kids and didn't stop talking about her rack for a minute. I'm not sure how he convinced her to walk in here in a skirt pretending she's the new hire, but I'm not amused.

I wait for the two of them to start laughing, for Liam to pop out from around the corner to slap Mark on the back.

"Caleb—" Mark's voice is wary, uncertain, and if he's acting, he's better at it than I thought. "This is Lucie Monroe, our new director of employee programs. Lucie, Caleb Lowell, our..." He looks at each of us in turn. "Do you...know each other?"

It's not until he says *Lucie* that something clicks.

It can't be.

There was a kid named Lucie who stayed next door at the lake occasionally when I was a teen. Big, gray-green eyes, talking a million miles a minute when she got the chance. It can't possibly be the same girl, can it?

I study her more carefully. Everything about her has changed, but not those eyes, the color of a stormy sea.

"We used to be neighbors," she whispers to Mark. Her voice is nearly mute with surprise, which makes *neighbors* sound like a euphemism for something much, much worse: an ex or someone she took a restraining order against.

Holy shit. It *is* her, and I don't know who I want to punch more—Liam, for what he said aloud, or myself, for silently agreeing with some of it.

Mark's mouth falls open. "*Neighbors?* Where?"

"It was ages ago," she replies, biting her lip.

"We're *still* neighbors," I correct, and she winces. Maybe she's wondering if I saw her swimming in her fucking underwear on Saturday night.

Yeah, Lucie, I definitely saw. You grew up. Jesus, did you grow up. And I need to know why I suddenly can't seem to get away from you.

She appears to be surprised to find me here, and I guess it's possible—I've had my name scrubbed off everything online— but there's too much overlap for this to all be a coincidence.

I glance at Mark. "Can you give us a minute?"

My tone is more a demand than a request, yet Mark hesitates, shooting me a look that asks what the hell is happening before he complies.

The door shuts, and Lucie slides into the chair on the other side of the desk. Her hair is lighter than it used to be, still dark but shot through with streaks of honey and caramel, perhaps because she's finally allowed to go outside during the summer. Robert Underwood's illegitimate child. I guess it's still a secret since I've never heard anything about it, and he's famous enough in my field that I would have. I'd have hoped she made the bastard pay for her silence, if nothing else, but she's working here...so probably not.

"This is a surprise," I begin. I clear my throat. "I didn't even realize it was you until I heard your name. It's been, what, fifteen years?"

"Thirteen," she says, blushing. She blushed a lot as a kid, but it hits different now. I want to punch myself in the face again. "I thought you'd sold the house."

"I bought it back last month. I had a place down in Santa Cruz but I needed a change of pace. I guess Miss Underwood left you her cabin?"

She nods, her eyes fixed on her lap. "I haven't really come out much, but I'm going through a divorce, so we needed a place to stay. I've got twins. They turned six last week."

"*Twins?* You don't even look old enough to be married."

She laughs. "Caleb, I'm only four years younger than you. I'm definitely old enough to be married. So are you."

"I *am* married," I reply. I'm not sure why I say it. Reflex, perhaps. Or maybe I simply sense a threat here in Lucie with her curves and her big eyes and her lip-biting.

"That's...you're..." She fiddles with the hem of her skirt. My gaze catches on her long legs and veers away fast. "The house has been so quiet. I didn't think there was one person in there, much less two."

I lean back in my chair. "I've been traveling for a few weeks and Kate's been away too." *Kate's been away too.* As if she's shopping in Paris with her mom or down at Canyon Ranch getting facials.

She nods. "No kids?"

I swallow. It's time to curtail this walk down memory lane. "Kids are the last thing I need. Anyway, about the job...I'm sorry if you were misled during the interview, but this was never intended to be a permanent position. Even if I could swing the cost of another salaried employee who isn't bringing in dollars, I can't swing a bunch of expensive programs to increase morale."

She goes pale beneath her tan, and no wonder—she's got

kids to support, and I just told her the job isn't going to last. I silently curse Mark for not being more upfront when he hired her.

"What if the programs aren't expensive?" she asks. "If employees are leaving because they want to work from home, it must cost you thousands to hire new people and get them up to speed, right? Stopping the flow would pay for the programs right there."

I sigh heavily. I know for a fact that pizza parties and posters that say 'Believe in yourself' aren't going to keep someone here if he wants to sit on his couch playing video games and jerking off. But the board needs to see it for themselves, which is why I agreed to three months. "It's not going to work, Lucie. But look...stay for the next few weeks. Take the salary and spend every minute you're here sending out resumes and interviewing. When you meet the board tomorrow, rattle off some bullshit and keep looking for a job."

She's staring at me as if she doesn't understand what I'm saying. "Rattle off some bullshit?"

I shrug. "Whatever. Tell them you want to host a blood drive or get everyone to wear a lapel pin or something. The lamer your ideas are, the better, as far as I'm concerned, because I need the board to realize it's not going to work."

Her shoulders sag. "Why are you so sure I won't make a difference?"

"I just am. Take the next two weeks to job hunt. You can even stay three if you must."

She appears to hear the finality in my tone and rises, smoothing her skirt. "Maybe I'll surprise you," she says as she turns to leave.

"I don't want to be surprised," I reply.

Surprises are the last thing I need.

Especially surprises who swim naked outside my window.

3

LUCIE

S*hit.*
   Shit, shit, shit, shit, shit.
   I march out of the office and wince once the door shuts behind me. What a complete disaster this is.

Does he really believe I can get another job that will support a family within two to three *weeks*? I spent *months* applying for jobs before I got this one. I spent months saving enough money to get us by until that first paycheck.

How long will that last us if I'm unemployed? Not all that long. I could conceivably sell my aunt's house, but I doubt it's worth much and I assume I'd have to split that with Jeremy. I could never buy a new place with what would be left over.

I collapse into the desk chair and bury my face in my hands. God, I'm foolish. There I was, wondering if it was fate that we met and eager to find out where his life had taken him, while he was simply trying to figure out how to get me out of his company as soon as possible.

But if he told the board he'd give me three months, he'll have no reason *not* to give me three months as long as I can impress them tomorrow. I just need to create a *miraculous* program by the end of the day, despite having no idea what the budget is and no real-world job experience. *Great. Super. No problem.*

I always think of Ruth during moments like this, panicked moments when I'm not sure I have what it takes. She'd spend the day on conference calls while I sat by quietly, and between each of them she'd give me advice—all these sayings that were utterly meaningless to a little kid who just wanted to go outside: *Work smarter, not harder; don't recreate the wheel.*

Those meaningless phrases of hers have helped me out of more than one situation and—because I have to pick up the twins in seven hours, and that's not nearly enough time to come up with an idea of my own—not recreating the wheel is decent advice.

I start looking at what larger companies offer their employees, and though every idea seems like a terrible one when it has to be perfect *or else*—'*Perfect is the enemy of good*' Ruth says in my head—by the time I leave to get the twins, I've at least chosen something and started to pull together a presentation.

"*Finally*," my friend Molly says, picking up on the first ring. "I texted you a million times."

I look both ways before I take a left out of the parking lot. "I couldn't text. I couldn't do anything. I'm already about to get fired."

She laughs. "That can't be true."

Molly is the one person who knows everything about me. She knows who my dad is, she knows about Jeremy's cheating and overall ugliness. But she is endlessly confident and competent, at least where work is concerned—as the only Black supervisor at a research lab, and one of only three females, the nonsense she hears is endless, so she'd have to be. I'm not sure she can even imagine getting fired because she's too damned good at what she does for anyone to want her gone.

"My boss—there's a whole story there too—basically told

me he needs me gone. He said he's giving me a couple weeks to find another job and that's it."

"Shit," she whispers. "Have you met with the divorce lawyer yet? You need child support if nothing else."

The lawyer, who is booked out for weeks and wants five hundred for the first meeting. "It's next month."

"I still think we should just poison Jeremy. It would solve so many problems."

I laugh wearily. "That's a pretty bold plan coming from a woman who can't even tell her boss she likes him."

She hasn't been on a single date during all the years I've known her. There was an ugly break-up in grad school, and ever since she started at her current job, it's been *Michael, Michael, Michael*—the boss she lusts after from afar.

"Here's what we do: apple seeds," she says, ignoring my point. "They contain arsenic. We crush them up and put them into his food. Nothing ever gets traced back to us."

"Unless they test for arsenic and someone wonders why I recently bought ten bushels of apples. I'm not ready to turn to murder *yet*." I pull into the parking lot of the twins' school and let her go, as St. Ignatius doesn't allow cell phones to be used on the premises, and it's the kind of place where you follow the rules, because we need them more than they need us. I'm still not sure how Jeremy got the twins in when we're pretty much the only parents here who didn't attend St. Ignatius ourselves and couldn't afford to build the school a new stadium if necessary. Jeremy comes from money, at least, but me? I spent my entire childhood moving from one guy's trailer home to another guy's apartment, and now—broke and soon-to-be-divorced—I don't see myself fitting in any better.

Fortunately, the halls are empty this late. I rush back to the aftercare room, where Henry is waiting for me, sitting at a table alone. My heart pinches hard at the sight. He never plays with anyone but Sophie, and I've been hoping it would change, but they've nearly got an entire year of kindergarten behind them and it hasn't. One day, Sophie will move on—to new friends and college and a career. Who will Henry have then?

Both twins run when they see me but it's Sophie, happily occupied at the play kitchen only a moment ago, who's outraged. "Where *were* you?" she demands. Like my mother, she's never one to let the opportunity to complain pass quietly, but in her, it's a good thing. No one pushes my mother around, and no one will ever push Sophie an inch either.

I offer an awkward smile to the teacher as I shepherd them out. "I had to work, sweetie. I told you."

"I-D-L-T," she announces.

It's a game I made up last year, to help the twins learn the sounds letters make. ILY is *I love you.* TFB is *time for bed.* I created it mostly for Henry, who doesn't have Sophie's ease with words nor her love of stories, but it's Sophie who uses it, mostly to express her disapproval. Today's is easy to figure out because I hear some version of it quite a bit.

"I didn't like this?" I guess.

"I didn't," she says. "I still *don't.*"

If today had gone better, I'd probably laugh. But I just don't have the capacity for laughter at present.

I wanted to give my children everything my mother did not give me. Now I'm worried I'll be giving them even less.

THE PRESENTATION CONSUMED MOST of my evening and I've only gotten two hours of sleep when it's time to wake the twins the next morning. I felt sorry for Caleb when I saw his truck pull up late last night—I assume, based on his stress level, he was just getting home from work—but I feel sorrier for myself. When Sophie cries about how unfair it is that we have to get up so early, I want to agree.

I get through the school drop-off then rush past scowling Kayleigh the receptionist and work frantically until it's time to go to the conference room.

When I arrive, it's Caleb I notice first, sitting at the end of the table like a king. A lovely king, his tie askew, jaw still in need of a shave, offering me a forced, reluctant smile.

No, not a lovely king. A married one who wants to fire me and who may be furious in a minute.

And yet, even now, I can't shake this lingering feeling from childhood, this certainty that he's mine. I'd better figure out how to shake it soon.

"Welcome, Lucie," Mark says, gesturing to a guy my age and an older female. "You've met Caleb, of course. Debbie is the head of HR and Hunter is our VP of sales. Our board members will be watching your presentation online, so we're ready whenever you are."

I take a deep breath as I move to the front of the room, doing my best to ignore the random sounds coming from the video attendees I can't see. Sweat trickles down my back as they watch me fumble, trying to get my laptop to connect. I entered every beauty pageant that offered scholarship money as a teen, so parading in front of three people should be no big deal, but my dress feels too tight, my heels too high, and I've only used a smart board once in my life. The odds of this going well are diminishing by the second.

"It's not..." I mumble, flushing, clicking the *connect* button again and again.

Hunter walks over to help, thank God.

"Ah," he says after a second. "Not your fault. The conference room is on a different network and this laptop they gave you is ancient. Here—"

With two clicks of the mouse, my presentation goes up on the board and I beam at him like he's a nurse handing me my newborns for the first time. "Thanks."

"Can we get going?" Caleb asks. "We have a whole lot to discuss today."

I stare at him. What the hell happened to that infinitely sweet boy who was so kind to me as a kid, so patient? Because there's no sign of him now.

"My idea is a walking challenge," I begin, and Caleb's eyes narrow. "Employees would divide into teams and compete to get the most miles. It's healthy, obviously, but it would also foster some fun, friendly competition between departments."

A disembodied voice—one of the board members, I assume —says, "What a fabulous idea."

Caleb clearly does not agree. "I don't understand why anyone would choose to participate in this," he says, his eyes dark.

I forward to the next slide. If he hated the idea before, he's about to hate it even more. "Prizes. The winning team would get a party and an extra day off, but there'd also be tiered incentives like a grand prize to the person with the most miles. A trip for two, with TSG paying the hotel and airfare."

"Jesus," he groans. "Do you have any idea how much that would cost?"

I'm sure if I got more sleep, I'd handle his criticism better. But I didn't get more sleep and he's kind of being a dick. My aunt was a brutal critic of any plan presented to her and even *she* wasn't this bad. "Well, according to your corporate travel policy," I reply tartly, "the company is keeping the miles accrued when people travel for work, so you could use those to cover both travel and hotel."

Caleb rattles a pen against the table. "What are these other tiers?"

I flip to the next screen, fighting the mounting sense that I've failed miserably. "Restaurant gift cards—that kind of thing. Overall, there's very little cost to the company for these prizes compared to the amount of goodwill they'll generate."

Caleb pushes away from the table. "Listen, the whole purpose of this is to retain employees, not generate goodwill—you really think you can keep everyone at their job because they have a quarter of a percent chance at winning a prize?"

I'm too irritated for diplomacy. "Everyone? No. I figure at least five people in the building have already accepted positions elsewhere and just haven't given notice. But if you're asking me to prove it works, all I really need to show is that *fewer* people have left, don't I?"

There's quiet laughter from the video participants, but all my attention is focused on Caleb, staring at me balefully from beneath those dark brows. Such a lovely face, wasted on such an irritating man.

His gaze shifts from me to the smart board. "There's no way you came up with this so fast on your own."

"BP oil did something similar." Really, *really* similar. I offer him a saccharine smile. "I can be more creative, but not when I've only had twenty-four-hours' notice."

"Wonderful work, Lucie," says a video attendee somewhere. "You're exactly what we needed."

"Yes, Miss Monroe," Caleb growls. "Thanks for being so *helpful*."

I stare at him. This is the man about whom I crafted elaborate fantasies for a decade of my life, fantasies in which I somehow proved my worth. I wanted to save him—like Belle saved the Beast, like Mulan saved Shang—because how else does a girl no one wants win over the boy beloved by everyone?

I should have focused more on how I'd save myself.

4

CALEB

The look Mark gives me as he walks into my office is asking the same question it often does: *Why?*

Why did you cancel the holiday party?

Why can't employees keep their airline miles?

Why did you close the seventh floor?

He sinks into the chair across from my desk. "Why were you so rude to her this morning?"

Because I thought she understood the assignment, and she clearly didn't.

I slam my laptop shut with a sigh. "I asked a handful of entirely reasonable questions about a program that will cost way more than she's indicating it will. The *better* question is why you hired her in the first place. She didn't even know how to work a fucking smart board."

"I liked her enthusiasm."

I roll my eyes. "Yeah. I bet a lot of men like her 'enthusiasm.' Hunter was so smitten by her *enthusiasm* he could hardly function today." Fucking MBA from Harvard and she reduced him to a lovesick teenager in a matter of seconds. If he'd seen her Saturday night—miles of bare skin, nipples pebbled tight under a soaking wet tank top—he'd have written her a blank check.

Mark runs his tongue over his teeth, struggling to remain patient. "Caleb, she did an amazing job, and you were borderline rude the entire time."

"I don't especially enjoy getting to know people who will soon be *former* employees, especially when they live next door to me. And we both know she isn't going to last. I told you I was only keeping this person on for three months and you led her to believe it was permanent. That's on you."

"I hired her for a permanent position because this *should be* a permanent position and I assumed you'd come to your senses." He climbs to his feet. "Based on what she just did today, you already should have."

I can't even argue. She knocked it out of the park, but that changes nothing. She still can't stay.

I head to my friend's bar a short time later. I'd prefer to skip the weekly get-together, but I've been out of town for weeks and it's easier to get it over with than having my friends harass me by phone for the rest of the week.

Once I'm there and have a beer in front of me, I'm glad I came...until Harrison tells us his dad is putting their beach house on the market.

That house was a staple of our childhood, the place where we surfed from dawn to nightfall, fooling ourselves into believing we were the next Kelly Slater, the next Andy Irons. I thought we'd teach our kids to surf there, our grandkids too, but I think we've all avoided it since our friend Danny died during a trip in college.

"Did you ever go back, after that weekend?" I ask Harrison.

He shakes his head. "I intended to. It was just—"

We all know what he means.

"That was the weekend shit started to fall apart," Liam says. "It's like we were fucking cursed."

None of us argue. We all held so much promise back then, but after Danny's death...we withered. Maybe that's how adulthood is for everyone, but it's nothing I foresaw for us, back when Liam and Beck were the star athletes at Gloucester Prep and Harrison and I were vying for valedictorian.

"Maybe we should go surf there, one last time, before it sells," Beck adds. "Break the curse."

Liam shoots a wary look at the corner of the bar, where a group of women are gathered—and scowling at him. "I'm not sure I'll live long enough to join you."

Harrison reaches for the pitcher. "You wouldn't have this problem if you'd attempt something that lasts more than two minutes."

"Two minutes? No wonder your wife looks so unhappy," Liam replies, which would be funnier if it wasn't true. "I think I'm finally ready to settle down, however, now that I've laid eyes on Caleb's hot new neighbor."

I set my beer down with a thud. "She's got kids and she's going through a divorce, so leave her alone."

"All I heard was '*She's getting divorced,*'" Liam replies. "Was there something more?"

Harrison laughs under his breath as he turns to me. "What neighbor? I thought you were the only idiot who'd buy a house on the north end of the lake. Not a single place there was built after 1950."

"I have no idea who she is." That she's Robert Underwood's kid obviously isn't public knowledge, and I'm sure as shit not about to admit she works for me. It's a situation I plan to change, ASAP. "She moved in next door."

Beck leans back against the far side of the bar. "Why aren't *you* interested if she's so attractive? I mean, have you slept with anyone since Kate left?"

If I tell him it's none of his business, I'll look like I've got something to hide. And I, unequivocally, do not. "Of course I haven't. She's been through a lot. I'm just trying to do the right thing."

Harrison looks at the others briefly before clearing his throat. "She's been gone for nearly a year, Caleb. You've waited long enough."

I look between them and sense this was all pre-planned. Intervention for the guy who refuses to cut the cord. They see me as the victim when they look at us, but when I look in the mirror, I see a villain.

Because everything that went wrong with Kate began with what was wrong with me.

5

LUCIE

My mother's name lights up the phone mere seconds after I've gotten dressed in the morning. Calls from her are rare and visits even rarer. I'm okay with the infrequency: I don't need my kids lured in by the same false promises she always made me.

"I can't believe I had to hear about this from Jeremy," she says. "Are you insane?"

Her reaction is not a surprise—she's spent her entire life looking for a golden ticket, which she erroneously thought she'd found when she got knocked up by my father. The one thing I've ever done right, in her estimation, was marrying Jeremy, and now I've thrown it away.

I walk to the kitchen and get the eggs out while she continues.

"You've got mouths to feed, Lucie. Or did you think your pageant experience and a degree you've never used set you up to take over the world?"

I reach for the matches. My aunt was frugal and refused to accept help from anyone, including my father. I'm wishing, now that *I'm* the one who has to light the stove by hand, that she'd accepted just a *little* help. "I've got a job. I'm the director of employee programs for a software company."

"No job *you're* qualified for will bring in the kind of money Jeremy makes. You realize you can forget about the country club membership and skiing in Tahoe and your Christmases in Palm Springs, right?"

I pull open a cabinet door and the whole thing snaps off the hinges. "I never cared about any of that in the first place." I hated the big, soulless house Jeremy chose without my input. I hated those trips he'd take us on, constantly jostling to be seen by the *right* people, putting on a show of his parenting only when there was an audience.

"Yeah, that's easy to say until you realize what it's like to live without it. And your *kids* might have liked those things you claim you don't care about. Whatever. I just hope you aren't under the impression that I'm going to help you out when it falls through."

I give a small, bitter laugh. "Have no fear, Mom. I never thought for a minute you'd be helping us." She doesn't lift a finger for anyone but herself, which is, no doubt, why my aunt set up her will to keep the house in trust for me until I became an adult—so that it would remain out of my mother's reach.

"You think you're so smart, Lucie, but mark my words: you're going to regret what you're doing here."

No shit, Mom. I've only been gone for five days and I'm already full of regret.

I end the call and get on with the process of getting the kids ready. Sophie cries about having to go to aftercare the entire way to school and Henry is unusually pensive, staring out the window. They barely say a word as they walk to class, and my phone is already buzzing with incoming texts from Jeremy, the ones he sends every morning, intended to ruin my day.

JEREMY

> Your mom told me about your job. You couldn't even remember to buy toilet paper, so I hope their expectations are low.

This is his specialty, finding some stupid mistake I've made and throwing it in my face endlessly. And it's hard to argue when I'm about to leave my children miserable at school, am nearly out of gas, and may well lose my job today. It's barely eight in the morning and I already want to give up.

I arrive at work on fumes and smile at Kayleigh as I walk in. She looks at me blankly, as if I'm a ghost or perhaps simply an employee she knows won't be back tomorrow.

Turn this around, Lucie, I command as I walk to my cubicle. *Yes, things look bad, and your mother has taken your cheating ex-husband's side, but...turn this day around.*

I'm still saying it when I open my laptop to find an email from Caleb:

See me as soon as you get in.

There is no greeting, no signature. It's the email you send someone who has really fucked up or is about to get fired, and every ounce of determination I had seconds before fails me. I rise slowly from my chair, forcing my feet forward. I looked at jobs online last night but was too tired to send out resumes. It appears I should have.

The phone in my hand chimes just as I reach Caleb's door. I'm certain it's Jeremy telling me I'm stupid or losing my looks, and whatever it is, I've no longer got the energy to fight. My mother, Jeremy, Caleb—I officially concede to any or all.

I enter Caleb's office, and his gaze moves over me, head to foot, before he swallows and looks away.

Go ahead, Caleb, fire me. I give up.

"I'm approving the walking program," he says.

What?

It's shocking enough that I'm not in here to be fired, but did he *like* the idea? I straighten. "That's—"

"Have it ready to present to the executive committee on Friday and I'll need some results for an interview the following week."

I freeze. *Results?* What he's asking is impossible. I need Molly to create the software that will track the miles. I need to arrange the prizes, figure out how the hell to divide up teams when employees are leaving in droves, and promote it to the entire freaking company. Even with a staff at my disposal, I couldn't have results in a week.

Yet…it doesn't take away from the thrill of having succeeded at something, and I want him to admit it because he was kind of a jerk yesterday. "So you were impressed?"

He shifts a folder in front of him and releases a sigh. "This was the board's decision, not mine. I thought you understood the assignment, which was *not* to come in with something they'd be wowed by."

If he was a stranger, I'd be intimidated by this conversation. I might *apologize*. But this is the same boy who used to *whoop* as he raced down to the water, the same boy who used to stand on a floating inner tube and beat his chest like an ape until his friends made him capsize. The same boy who was consistently kind to me at a point in my life when no one else was. He doesn't scare me, even if he should.

I grin. "It still sounds like you were impressed."

He waves me away, but there's a ghost of a smile pulling at the side of his mouth. "You're a pain in the ass. Go create your expensive fucking program we don't need."

"I'm eager to do so."

His not-really-a-smile fades. "Lucie, this doesn't change anything. We've got stuff going on with the company that I can't discuss, but…we need to be as streamlined as possible. So no matter how much the board loves your dumb little walking program, in three months, you're going to need a new job."

Except forty-eight hours ago, he was telling me I only had two weeks. Now I potentially have *months*.

Three months is enough time to change my entire life.

I'm up late again Wednesday night, working on the web page for the walking program. As a kid it kind of stunk to sit next to Ruth all summer, completing whatever busywork she'd tasked me with—especially once I was old enough to realize how my half-siblings were spending *their* summers, which focused heavily on European vacations and less on 'You have to stay inside so no one suspects you're Robert Underwood's illegitimate child.' But she also spent those summers equipping me to become more than my mother was, and it was because of them that I now know HTML and how to write a grant proposal. It's because of them that I'm even willing to *hope* I can pull this whole thing off.

I'm yawning on only two hours' sleep again Thursday as Molly walks me through the software over the phone. She reminds me that sleep deprivation is negatively correlated with longevity, and that, on the whole, poisoning Jeremy would be a healthier solution. She then mentions that prisons in Norway are like spas, though I'm not sure how that's relevant to my situation. I think she just really wants Jeremy poisoned.

I'm so tired I'm almost numb as I shepherd the twins through the grocery store after school. I barely have the energy to get down the aisles, much less stop them from pulling food off the shelves. When Henry accidentally knocks over a display of gift cards, it takes all my self-control not to burst into tears.

Feigning calm with blood rushing to my face, I kneel on the

ground and start picking up the gift cards while Sophie opens a bag of chips I hadn't planned to buy.

"Ma'am, your children can't block the aisle," says an employee. "And you're going to have to pay for the chips."

My mother wouldn't take this shit. She'd look him dead in the eye as she dropped all the gift cards she'd gathered to the floor. She'd take that bag of chips Sophie's opened, dump them out and say, *"Oops, looks like you've got some cleaning to do."*

I died a million deaths as a kid watching her tell people off, but right now...I get it. Guys like this want someone they can squash easily, someone too weak to fight back, and I very much would like to show him he chose the wrong girl.

After a lifetime of trying to be different from my mother, am I about to become just like her the minute I face some adversity?

"Come on, guys," I say, setting the gift cards on the shelf beside me and heading toward the checkout though we only made it through half the store.

The cashier rings us up while Sophie attempts to sound out the caption on a tabloid. I regret teaching her phonics. "In...cuh. In...cuh...sss. Mommy, what's that word?"

The caption reads *Incest! Shocking Details About America's Favorite TV Dad!*

"Ma'am, your credit card was declined," says the cashier.

I blink. It's got to be a mistake, but there's a line of irritated shoppers behind me and it's faster to use another card than argue.

The second card doesn't work either, though, and a slow, certain dread begins to spin in my stomach. "I'll just use my debit card."

I insert it with heat climbing up my neck while the guy behind me starts groaning in frustration at how long I'm taking.

"It says you have insufficient funds," she announces.

The three grand is gone. Somehow, Jeremy managed to

empty a checking account he wasn't even *on*, which means we have almost nothing—a tiny bit of cash back at the house and not a penny more until I get my first paycheck.

The only surprising thing about this entire situation is my failure to anticipate it.

My mother...she'd have anticipated it.

6

CALEB

Lucie enters the conference room Friday morning in a sleeveless, fitted green silk dress, red lips, her dark hair slicked back in a high ponytail.

She doesn't look like a woman going through a divorce with two little kids to support. She looks like the colleague Hunter's about to make a fool of himself over, based on his wide smile and the way he jumps to his feet the second she struggles with the smart board—she should be able to figure it out on her own at this point.

"Not your fault," he insists. "This is a garbage laptop. We need to get you a new one."

If he keeps flirting with the new hire, I'm going to give her *his* laptop.

"Can we get started?" I ask, my fingers tapping impatiently on the table. "I have places to be."

She and Hunter exchange a quick glance.

He's such a dick, Lucie's gaze says.

I'd never treat you like that, Lucie, his replies.

She starts to review the prizes, and Hunter is watching her, no doubt memorizing every flick of her hand, every smile and sigh—in the rare moments when he's not staring at her rack, that is.

"I'm so impressed," he says. "The prizes and the—"

"Show us how you'll track it," I snap. If Hunter wants to suck up to her, he can do it on his own time. Better yet, he can do it from someone else's company.

Her gaze jerks to mine and it's a visceral thrill, that spark of irritation in her eyes—as if she's just marched across the room and grabbed me by the lapels. I have a sudden, sharp memory of her climbing up the ladder last weekend. I'd be better off if I could forget.

"We've created a software program," she says, her jaw grinding as she progresses to the next slide. "It allows employees to connect their devices and shows their progress in a couple of ways—a graph charting what they've done and one showing where their team stands compared to others."

The software looks like something Apple spent years developing. Something I know she herself didn't create...she can barely figure out how to connect to the Wi-Fi.

"Who authorized you to use a programmer for this?" I demand, though I already know exactly who did it. *Harvard MBA, my ass.* "We're already short-staffed. I can't have someone wasting hours on this shit."

Mark and Debbie are both staring at me when it's *Hunter* they should be appalled by. *I'm* not the one blatantly hitting on a low-level employee. I have the right to know what the actual costs of this are.

"I didn't use one of your programmers," she says between her teeth. "I had a friend help me."

A *friend* did all this for her? Was he treated to a little Lucie-swimming-in-a-tank-top show before he agreed? My eyes catch on the green of her dress, on her bare legs. Something about her leaves me unable to focus and it's really becoming a problem. "We'll let you know," I say, gathering my things and heading for the door.

I need out of the goddamn room so I can think clearly.

No, I need *her* out of my goddamn company. This is not sustainable.

The moment I get to my office, I call the one person who might be able to fix this situation.

"Look who remembered how to use a phone," Harrison says as he picks up. "You finally ready to file for divorce?"

We've been friends for more than half my life, which means I get to ignore half of what he says. It's possible I ignore more than half. "No, I was wondering if you're hiring. I've got a temp employee. She's doing good work, but only here for a few more weeks. I thought you might have an opening. Something in the business office or human resources?"

"Caleb," he says with a laugh, "I'm at a firm of thirty people and you've got a company with what—five hundred? I think if one of us has the flexibility to make a position for someone, it's you. I'm sure as hell not hiring some chick you're desperate to be rid of."

"I'm not desperate to be rid of her," I lie. "She doesn't do anything we need."

"Again, if she doesn't have a single skill you can find a use for at an enormous company, what skill is she going to have that *we* can use? You don't want her and you're trying to pawn her off on me. Unless this is about your hot neighbor."

"*What?*"

He laughs. "We all know. Mark told Liam."

Fuck. The fact that Lucie works at my company is something I really wanted to keep to myself. "Look, she's a hard worker. It's just...uncomfortable."

"Maybe," he says, "uncomfortable is exactly what you need."

I groan after I've hung up. I'm going to have to sign off on her walking program, and at the rate she's going, I'll never be rid of her.

Even I don't understand why I find that prospect so harrowing.

7

LUCIE

I can't believe he called Molly's gorgeous software 'shit.'
I can't believe he's turned out to be such a dick.
I can't believe how badly this day is going.

It's after lunch when the bank manager finally returns my multiple calls, and the first words out of her mouth are, "I'm not sure I can help, since this is between you and your husband."

"Have you asked him to reinstate the funds?" she continues, as if Jeremy took the money by *accident*.

"I'm confused," I reply through clenched teeth. "You're telling me that if someone hacks into my checking account—I didn't give him the password, he just guessed—there's nothing you can do? How is that possibly legal?"

"You created an account with us off your original account, which he's still on," she says. "I'd change my password if I were you."

I have one credit card in my name, acquired in college—if I can even find it. My entire adult life was held in Jeremy's tight fists, and he turned it to dust in the blink of an eye. I'll have to cancel the appointment with the lawyer, and I've got no one to blame but myself. Scorpions sting—that's what they do. I was the moron who thought the scorpion wouldn't sting if his kids were involved.

I hang up and spin around to find Caleb standing there, eating up the entire opening of the cubicle, tugging at the knot of his tie. I don't care how pretty he is, how stressed he looks...I'm not about to forgive him for this morning. *Molly's software was fucking amazing, and he had no right—*

"Let me guess," he says, "you used your children's names and birthdates for your password."

I've been wondering why his wife is still away—maybe she just needed a break from his bad attitude. I've been here five days and I need one myself.

I sigh. "You know, the polite thing to do here isn't to *accurately guess* the stupid thing I did."

"This might come as a shock to you, but *polite* is not a term often used to describe me. Do you, uh, need an advance on your salary?"

I stare at him with my mouth ajar. You don't offer an advance to someone who isn't *staying*. "Why would you offer that when you're desperately hoping to be rid of me?"

He rubs his eyes. "We're approving the software. That's what I came down here to tell you. And I know you won't have results by next Friday, but Mark thought it might be a good idea if you came to the interview, to discuss it." He frowns, hesitating for one long, drawn-out breath. "Lucie, it's not about you, okay? You've been doing a really good job."

My eyes sting. It's been a long time since someone said I'd done anything right. *Do not fucking cry in front of him, Lucie. Do not.*

It must be obvious, despite my efforts. His eyes widen and there's concern there before he turns away. "You've had a rough week," he says as he leaves. "Go home and get some sleep."

That sweetness is still there, under everything, that sweetness from another life.

I wonder why he seems so miserable in this one.

I don't leave early, as he suggested, because if he needs results as soon as possible, I need to get going *now*.

I open the email I'd already drafted explaining the walking program to the entire company. I look it over one last time, and my hand shakes as I hit send. It still seems impossible that anyone trusts *me* to write five-hundred employees at once.

I'd planned to leave soon afterward, but I'm immediately deluged with responses. There's a lot of sniping about the software and whining about the guy on the fourth floor who runs marathons, but there are also compliments and emails simply saying, '*thanks.*'

A woman from HR comes to my cubicle to give me other ideas she has for TSG. People call to clarify the prize structure. Kayleigh even puts down her phone long enough to bitch about Wyatt, the marathoner, as I walk past.

The work day is nearly over by the time I've had a second to breathe and discover new texts from Jeremy waiting.

> JEREMY
>
> Did you manage to drop the twins at school on time for once?
>
> Should I send over some multivitamins? God knows they must need it with the meals you serve.

He's just angry that his little stunt with the checking account didn't provoke a response and lashing out, but I deflate regardless, the way I always have when he criticizes me.

Because he's right. Yes, we've been late to school. Yes, I've made crappy meals. And those things are probably true of every parent, at some point, but I've never had much perspective. He was six years older and already a success when he walked into the restaurant where I was waiting tables. He thought my youth and naïveté were "cute" at first. He loved that

I didn't know how to pronounce "tapas" or use a corkscrew, that I'd never been on an airplane and couldn't ski. But that all that changed once we were married. Suddenly, the things I didn't know or couldn't do well were flaws. He was *eager* to point out the ways I was failing—at home, in public, as a mother, in bed. I was a worthless failure, nothing more, and it was hard to argue when I had no proof to the contrary, when there were no voices around but his.

Today, though, there are. Caleb said I'd done a good job, and people are excited about a program I created. Even if it's temporary, even if I ultimately fail, I deserve better than to live in an echo chamber of Jeremy's criticism. The three of us might not get the fairy tale, but we at least deserve better than we've had.

I haven't cancelled the lawyer yet, and I'm not going to. I'll put what I can on the old credit card and apply for new ones to cover the rest. Whatever it takes to get free of Jeremy...it's worth it.

AFTER LUNCH ON SATURDAY, the twins and I drag the rusted old boat from beneath the deck and row out onto the lake. There have been no signs of life at Caleb's house since yesterday. Not him, and also no lovely wife getting the paper or sipping coffee by the shore. Where the hell is she? If he was away for two weeks and she's been gone since I arrived here...that's a very long time for them to be apart.

The twins toss a net into the water and jostle the boat under the afternoon sun, hunting for pirate treasure. It's the childhood I once envisioned for them, and if I can just get free of Jeremy, perhaps I can give it to them.

"Go that way, Mommy," Sophie commands, pointing at the

section of the lake where branches are sticking out of the water, a warning I failed to heed once upon a time.

"I can't," I reply with a smile. "Remember me telling you about the time I got stuck out here? That's where it happened."

"Where that boy saved you when you were pretending to be Lady Victoria?"

She *loves* that story. "Yep."

"When will you read me the Lady Victoria book?" she asks. "When I'm eleven?" She's completely forgotten about the net now.

I sink the oars into the water and start rowing us back toward the dock. "Not until you're an adult."

"*You* read it when you were eleven," she argues.

I laugh. "I assure you, Sophie, I shouldn't have."

It was on a shelf of books my aunt said were 'not for children' and sneaking it was unusually rebellious for a kid who'd never so much as walked into the backyard over the course of five summers. But my aunt was gone for the night and my feelings were hurt because my mother hadn't shown up as planned. So, I snuck the book, and when I realized I'd gotten away with it, I became even bolder: if Lady Victoria could successfully manage to row a boat onto the lake unchaperoned, why couldn't I? It was dark out. No one would see me.

In a turn of events straight out of Lady Victoria's life, however, the boat got stuck, and it was Caleb who heard me calling for help, Caleb who cut across the water in the moonlight to rescue me.

It was...unbelievably romantic, and my tears dried instantly, watching him approach.

He reached me fast, grasping the side of the boat as he pushed his wet hair back from his forehead. He'd grown a lot more than I'd realized. Lord Devereaux had '*a face chiseled, as if by the Creator Himself, and a mouth made for sin*', but I was pretty sure Caleb's face was more chiseled, his mouth even more sinful, though I wasn't clear what exactly made a mouth sinful in the first place.

"I'm stuck," I whispered. "And I don't know how to swim."

"Hang on. I'll get you out." He grinned at me, flashing a dimple I didn't know he had. "While I'm working, maybe you can explain why you stole Miss Underwood's boat."

I knew I couldn't tell him the truth. I'd spent eleven full years not telling anyone the truth, but I really wished I could.

"I borrowed it." I tucked my feet close as he laid a muddy oar beside them. "But I was going to bring it back."

He went to the far end of the boat, twisting it to and fro until it loosened at last. "You borrowed a boat in your *pajamas* and took it out at night when you don't know how to swim?"

"That was more Lady Victoria Jordan's fault than mine. From my book."

As he began pulling the boat to shore, I told him all about her rebellion, her long white gown, and the wicked charms of Lord Devereaux.

"Why is she so against marriage?" he asked. "And what makes Lord Devereaux's charms *wicked* as opposed to being, you know, charming?"

He'd actually been listening to me, something my mother had never done. My love for him grew tenfold in that moment. "She's fiercely independent. And he's wicked because he doesn't want to settle down."

He raised a brow. "So they want the exact same thing, but it only makes *him* wicked?"

I was about to explain that Lord Devereaux was also a *rake*, which was apparently both the best and the worst thing a man could be during that historical period, but we'd already reached the dock. It had gone too fast, this time with him, and I'd wasted all of it telling him about a *book* when I'd meant to tell him about *me*.

I wanted him to know that I'd won an art contest, that today was my birthday, that my mother was beautiful and if he could just wait a couple of years, I probably would be too. But I didn't know how to get it all out, so I stood in silence while he dragged the boat back under my aunt's deck.

"I'm not going to tell anyone," he said when he returned, "but you've got to promise me you won't go out on the lake again until you've learned to swim."

When I nodded, he gave me one last grin. "In that case, Lady Victoria, I bid you good night."

We'd speak a few more times after that—me sneaking out of the house whenever my aunt was gone and making enough noise for him to hear me—but four years' difference was a big deal back then. I was always a child, and he was always nearly grown.

Everything Ruth had went to me—her way, I think, of apologizing for all those years she spent keeping my father's secret —and in the end that money helped me pay for college, but I wonder what might have happened if Caleb and I had had the chance to get to know each other as teens, as young adults. If Ruth hadn't died and if his mom hadn't sold their house, might something have happened between us? Could we have become the thing I dreamed of as a kid?

Because it still feels like I lost something I was meant to keep.

"Mommy, who's that guy?" Sophie asks, interrupting my reverie. She is pointing at the dock, where that boy I was meant to keep is climbing off a much nicer boat than ours. He's in shorts and a t-shirt today, and I stare against my will at his sharp jaw, his hard calves, those corded biceps bigger than my thighs.

I can't fault the childhood version of me for being tongue-tied the night we met—a whole lot of fully grown women would be tongue-tied faced with *that*.

He sets down the big hunk of metal he's carrying when we

pull up and holds out his hand for the rope to help us dock, though it's clear his assistance is being provided reluctantly.

"Sophie and Henry," I say, lifting them each from the boat, "this is our neighbor, Mr. Lowell."

Henry, normally reticent, steps forward and picks up a piece of the metal thing Caleb laid on the dock.

"Henry, stop," I scold, climbing the ladder after them. He ignores me, grabbing a second piece and fitting it to the first.

"How did you know they went together?" Caleb asks Henry. There's curiosity, not irritation, in his voice, as if he's speaking to another adult.

Henry doesn't answer, but a glimmer of something like a smile passes over his face, and I feel that familiar tightness in my throat, pinching behind my eyes. I want so much for him I could burst with it, and I'm not sure I'll ever be able to give him anything at all.

"Do you have kids?" Sophie demands. I'm sure none of this is countering Caleb's disdain for children.

A muscle flexes in his jaw. "No."

"Do you have a girlfriend?" she barrels on. "My daddy has a girlfriend. Her name is Whitney and she's still in college. That's why we live here now."

Oh, God.

"Who told you that?" I croak, the blood draining from my face.

"Lola," she chirps in reply. "Her mom said it's because you're not the Peach Queen anymore and Daddy wanted a newer model."

Fuck. Fuck. Fuck. I hate that they're already discussing this at school, and that they're discussing it with my kids. On a lesser note, I hate that Sophie's just told my boss.

Caleb's eyes are wide as he looks from her to me, and I see a hint of the boy I once imagined he was—the one capable of concern, of kindness. But it doesn't even matter if that's really who he is, and I've got much bigger shit to deal with right now.

Without a word to him, I grab Sophie by one hand and Henry by the other and march them both straight to the house.

I take a seat on the ottoman across from them once we're inside, hesitating before I speak. "I'm sorry you heard Lola say that," I begin.

Sophie's head tilts. "But it's true, right?"

I bite down on the inside of my cheek. I spent my entire childhood wishing I had a father. I chose the wrong one for them, but...he's still their father and they'll be dealing with him in some capacity for the rest of their lives. They deserve, as much as possible, to have a relationship with him that isn't tainted by what he did to me. "Daddy and I just weren't very happy together."

Henry sits in my lap and rests his head against my chest, while Sophie frowns, deep in thought. "Is Whitney the Peach Queen now?"

"No," I say with a sigh. "She isn't anyone."

It's a struggle not to sound bitter, and I guess I don't quite succeed. Sophie squeezes into my lap beside Henry and places her small hand on my cheek in consolation. "It's okay, Mommy. I still think you're pretty."

8

CALEB

My daddy has a girlfriend.

You're not the Peach Queen anymore and Daddy wanted a newer model.

I wish I could remove that moment from my brain, forget the way Lucie paled as her daughter spoke.

I'm not sure what it is I thought happened between her and her husband, but it wasn't...that. Because who the fuck cheats on *Lucie*? How the hell does anyone get lucky enough to wind up with *her* and choose someone else instead?

I see her later that evening, swinging her feet off the dock's edge. From a distance, she doesn't look all that different from the girl she once was, the skinny kid who'd sneak down to the dock at night, all wide-eyed and uncertain, and whisper her secrets to me as if she couldn't stand to hold onto them a moment longer. I'd only seen her here a few times before she admitted her dad was Robert Underwood—and then it started to make sense, that uncertainty of hers. Because even among tech CEOs like my dad, Underwood was a big deal. And I already knew he was the type of guy who wouldn't hesitate to ruin someone who stood in his way.

"He wanted my mom to get an abortion," she'd said on one of those nights, her slender shoulders hunched over. *"My mom says she would have, if she'd known how cheap he was gonna be."*

It was the kind of shit no kid should ever know about their parents, but especially not at her age. And when her mouth trembled as she tried to force a smile, I felt sick, and helpless. I wish, now, that I'd done something for her, though I still don't know what I could have done.

My feet hit the dock and she turns, unsurprised to see me here, and raises a brow. "Did you wait until nightfall so my daughter wouldn't pepper you with personal questions?"

"Yes, I'll be doing all my boating and sunbathing between midnight and five a.m., henceforth."

That only wins me half a smile.

"I guess nothing about that incident made you decide you like children."

I drop down beside her before swinging my legs over the dock's edge for the first time in a decade. "I don't actively *hate* kids, you know. I just think they're monsters who require an unreasonable amount of care while offering you very little in return."

She leans back on her hands. There's something gentle in her eyes. "They offer you everything in return. But it's...intangible."

"Excellent. You enjoy your intangible benefits. I'll enjoy keeping all my free time and expendable income to myself." This wins me a full smile at last.

"If you need anything," I add haltingly, "money for a lawyer or something, let me know."

"Thank you. I'll be fine. Though it would be amazing if you could stop witnessing my most embarrassing moments."

"You do seem to have quite a few of them, if we're being honest."

It's the joke you'd make to a friend, not an employee, and

even though she laughs, I probably shouldn't have said it. It's dangerous, how familiar she feels. How easy it is around her. "And about the job—"

She waves me off. "It's not your fault. I was told three months at the start. I just thought it was a standard probation thing, not a firm end date."

"I'll keep you on until you find something else."

"You don't have to—" she begins and I cut her off. I know I was a dick last week. I wish I could explain why.

"Lucie, you're doing an amazing job. If TSG's financial situation was different, I'd think you were the hire of the century. So stay as long as you need to, but don't blow all my money on stupid shit."

Her eyes crinkle. "You mean stupid shit that lets your employees know you care?"

"I pay them," I argue. "Why do I need to pretend I care too?"

She grins. "I mean, it would be better if you *actually* cared."

I laugh quietly. "I prefer all my relationships remain transactional, if possible."

She tucks a lock of hair behind her ear. "I look forward, then, to meeting your mail-order bride."

My *bride*. Eventually she's going to ask where the hell Kate is. I should probably just tell her, but...it seems safer not to, somehow. It would have been safer not to walk down here in the first place, actually.

I climb to my feet. "You're settling in okay, aside from my insistence on firing you?"

"I could still use a tour. I'm trying to figure out where I can put a climbing wall."

"I'll make sure you continue to not get a tour, then."

She laughs, and I feel like a kid who's won the hardest game at the fair. Which is exactly what makes Lucie so dangerous: because every time I see her, I want to see her again, and every time she smiles, I want to be the one who put that smile there.

I want to win that game at the fair, when the prize isn't one I'd be able to keep.

9

LUCIE

Kayleigh shows up at my cubicle first thing Monday morning, looking even more displeased than normal, which is truly an accomplishment. "Caleb told me I'm supposed to give you a tour," she says with a heavy sigh. "Where do you want to start?"

I'm on my feet before I really have time to think about it—Kayleigh doesn't strike me as someone who likes to be kept waiting.

I've seen most of the offices at this point, but I must have missed something, because...it's *all* offices. "Maybe the spaces where people relax. Like break rooms?"

"You mean the cafeteria?" she asks.

I'd assume she was joking if she wasn't already back on her phone. I've been to the fluorescent-lit cafeteria in the basement, with its cheap plastic tables and linoleum floors. The one time I went down there to eat, I chose to skip lunch rather than experience a damp sandwich in cellophane or green beans floating in a haze of greasy water.

"No, I meant, like...if you want to chat with a friend here... where do you do that?"

She rolls her eyes. "Nowhere. It's not really that kind of place."

I'm not sure if this is a TSG issue or a *Kayleigh* issue, since she's not exactly friendly. But if she's correct...it's definitely a problem. I sat beside my aunt for enough summers to know that while people stay at a job for the salary and benefits, what keeps them there when the grass looks greener elsewhere is when colleagues feel like friends. Which can only happen if they've actually hung out a bit.

"Is there no other large space? In a building this size, there must be something."

She shrugs. "Yeah, but it's closed now."

"Can you show it to me?"

She glances up, a single brow raised as if I've asked to read her private texts. "I guess. But if anyone asks, you're the one who put me up to it."

I follow her to the elevator, and we ascend to the seventh floor. She's on her phone posting something to Instagram. I'm fairly certain she just took a picture of my heels. My own phone chimes, but I ignore it. It is, undoubtedly, Jeremy and anything he has to say can wait. Forever, preferably.

The first door she attempts to open is locked, but we manage to get in through a side door, where I discover a huge room flooded with sunlight.

"We've got this amazing space up here and we're using the dungeon downstairs for lunch instead? Why?" My head is already spinning with plans Caleb will hate, and the walking program has given me enough confidence to hope I might be able to pull them off.

She doesn't answer until she's done typing. "It was something about cutting costs."

"But there shouldn't be a cost to maintaining a break room," I argue. "The food wasn't free, right?"

She shrugs. "I don't know. It was before my time. I heard

Caleb went through some personal stuff a few years ago and changes were made."

I assumed Caleb lives for his job. Maybe it isn't entirely by choice.

∼

I'm SITTING down by the shore Thursday night with the twins when Caleb appears, still in suit pants and a button-down.

His eyes flicker to my bare legs and remain there a moment before jerking away. "I have a conference call soon," he says, "but do you have a minute to discuss the interview?"

I consider pointing out that I'm *off work*, an entirely foreign concept to him, but he's clearly stressed out, so I remove my phone from the Adirondack chair beside me and gesture for him to sit.

He stretches his long legs in front of him, looking ridiculously out of place. One false move and he's going to ruin those pants.

I hold up a hand to block the dying sun as I meet his eye. "I was just thinking about that raft you and your friends tried to build. Remember that? You'd have been twelve, maybe?"

He frowns. "I can't believe *you* remember that."

"Are you kidding? It was the highlight of my week. You guys spent the whole damn day on it, but some older guy was with you and when he climbed on, it freaking exploded."

"Beck." His smile is a bare thing, nothing like what it was when he was young. "He wasn't older. He'd just hit six feet before the rest of us had even entered puberty. That was a fun day."

The sun is beginning to slip over the horizon. I slide my feet into the sand, burrowing them there for warmth. "They *all* seemed like fun days."

He hitches a shoulder. "I thought so, yeah."

There's something darker hidden there. "You don't sound sure."

He exhales. "It was hard for my mom. She bought this place hoping it would get my father to work less. Instead, he was just relieved we were gone so he could work more."

"Did he ever slow down?"

Caleb rakes a hand through his hair. "Not exactly. TSG was his company, but he got into some financial trouble and died of a stroke right after I left Wharton. I've been trying to sort it out ever since."

"I'm sorry," I tell him. Did he actually *want* to take over at TSG or did he have other plans that got derailed? I'm not sure how to ask, though, or even if I should.

"It was a while ago," Caleb says, shrugging. "Anyway, are you ready for tomorrow?"

"I'm not sure." I narrow my eyes at Sophie, who seems to be threatening Henry with a bucket of mud. "We've still got no results, but also...the reporter's going to ask me how the company has changed, and it hasn't really, right? I mean, be honest—you hate everything about this."

"Look, I just think people should settle for the benefits that were outlined in their employment contracts. Everyone expects a morning massage and Frappuccino waiting on their desk these days, as if they're doing the company a favor by showing up at all. I might be willing to throw money at something if you can prove the potential benefit, but I'm not writing you a blank check so you can blow it all on therapy dogs and incense."

"I was thinking more along the lines of meditation candles and healing crystals."

His mouth twitches. "I'm not at all surprised by that."

Sophie and Henry stop bickering and Sophie runs to me with a bucket of sand. "What flavor do you want?" she demands.

I hold out my hands. "Can I have strawberry?"

She shakes her head. "I-D-H-T."

The code game again. Sophie's now the only child in her class who joins the first graders for reading, which makes Henry's struggles that much more obvious. I feel guilty for introducing it in the first place and guilty that I'd take Sophie's success away from her if I could, to protect Henry. Your children grow and change—the one constant of motherhood is the fucking guilt.

"I don't...have that?" I guess. "Ummm...mint chip?"

"Okay," she says, dumping the wet sand on my hands...and all over my legs. Caleb's gaze lands on my thighs again.

"What's with the initials?" he asks as I brush the sand off.

"Just a phonics game I play with them. It mostly gives Sophie ample ways to express her disapproval."

A wistful thing passes over his face. "It's cute."

There's a small, strange twist in my heart. *Cute* is the last word I'd expect from a guy who called children '*monsters who require an unreasonable amount of care.*'

Henry walks up the beach like Sophie did, but rather than coming to me...he goes to Caleb.

"No, Henry," I say. "Mr. Lowell is in nice clothes."

Caleb's gaze softens as he looks at Henry. "I'll take...peach."

Henry shakes his head *no*, a ghost of pleasure on his face. I swallow hard—sorrow and joy at once.

"What about rum raisin? Do you have that?"

Henry shakes his head again and Caleb laughs.

"I really feel like your business could stand to diversify, but fine. I'll have vanilla. Please tell me you have vanilla."

Henry nods and shovels the wet sand into Caleb's open hands, which promptly seeps straight through to his pants. And to my absolute shock, Caleb laughs. A real laugh—the kind you can feel in your chest, the kind that would make you smile even if you didn't have a clue what it was about.

That dimple of his hits every bit as hard as it did thirteen years ago.

He rises, brushing off his pants. "Just do your best tomorrow," he says abruptly, and he's already walking away before I've thought of a reply.

Who are you, Caleb Lowell? What happened to the boy you once were?

Because it sort of seems like one of us should be trying to find him.

10

LUCIE

The next morning, I don the same green dress I wore for my presentation to the executive committee. It's the most businesslike thing I own, but when I walk into Caleb's office, he frowns, his eyes catching on the dress for a moment too long. I kind of assumed no one would notice I'm repeating an outfit so soon.

I run my sweating palms down my sides. "I wanted to see when we're leaving."

His brow furrows. "For the interview?"

I grin. "No. Coachella."

"Look who's suddenly a smart-ass."

"To be fair," I counter, "I was always kind of a smart-ass. You just didn't listen to me before."

His mouth curves, but his gaze is already back on his laptop. "Still not listening, actually. Eleven thirty, but let's plan to drive separately."

It seems silly to take two cars, but what can I say? *I'm crazy nervous about this interview and I inexplicably find your presence comforting?*

Ninety minutes later, Caleb reaches the front doors just as I do and comes to a sudden stop. "Are you okay?"

"I'm a little nervous," I reply, giving him a tight-lipped smile. "Careful, though. You almost sounded worried about an employee there."

"I figured it was better than saying, 'Don't make us look like assholes today.'"

I give him a weak wave. "I guess I'll see you there."

He regards me, quietly wrestling with something. "Ride with me. I can't have you passing out at the wheel."

"Because I might die or because I might not be able to provide you with some good PR?"

"The PR, obviously," he says. "Your death would save the company money."

I laugh and my nerves begin to dissipate. I follow him to his truck, where he's already opening the passenger door and throwing tools and grout in the back. "Sorry about the mess," he says. "I'm supposedly renovating the lake house, if I ever get the time."

It seems ambitious for a guy who already works way too much and has the money to hire someone. And I can't imagine his wife feels like waiting for a renovation that will take place in Caleb's nonexistent downtime.

Don't ask about his wife, Lucie. Don't—

"Are you hiding her in the attic?" I blurt as he climbs into the car.

The seat belt he's holding is suspended in mid-air. "*What?*"

"Your wife."

His jaw shifts. He clicks the seat belt and turns on the engine. "No. She's just...away for a while."

"That sounds like exactly the kind of shady thing a guy would say if his wife was imprisoned in the attic or buried in the yard."

He raises a brow. "The yard? I work too much. When would I have time to do that much digging?"

I choke on a laugh. "So she must be coming home soon?"

"Yeah," he says, but there's more grim resignation in his voice than anything else. "Maybe. I don't know, to be honest. She's in rehab."

I stare at him, open-jawed. When he said she was *away*, I pictured her fucking around somewhere like the yoga moms at school who take a girls' trip to Cabo together each winter. *Rehab* never occurred to me once. "I'm so sorry. Is she almost done?"

He swallows. "I assume so."

"That's...a very vague answer."

He turns onto the road, then glances at me. "It's something I've tried to keep quiet, but...about a year ago, Kate went on a bender and cleaned out a TSG corporate account—she was out of her mind on cocaine at the time and apparently owed some dealer a ton of money. That's why my name has been scrubbed from the website—so that if I'm implicated in anything else she does, it won't come back on the company. The board agreed not to press charges as long as she went to rehab. So she went, unwillingly."

Wow. There's a lot to process in that statement. But one thing stands out most. "She left a *year* ago? I had no idea people went to rehab that long."

His nostrils flare. "They don't. And it hasn't been a full year. She went in at the end of July, checked herself out in September, and disappeared entirely until a few weeks ago when she checked back in. I haven't even heard from her. I only know because I got the bill."

So she's been gone nearly a year, with no contact, and he's still waiting. No one—not Jeremy, not my own family—has ever really wanted me at my *best,* yet here Caleb is, wanting someone who left at her worst and did terrible things to him while she was at it.

"You must miss her," I say softly.

"It's...complicated," he replies as we pull into the restaurant's parking lot.

Not the response I expected. *It's complicated* means...no, he doesn't miss her. Or perhaps yes, he misses her, but he's not sure she's coming back.

And I have no idea why it feels like the answer matters.

I follow him inside, far more focused on Caleb's personal life than I am the interview, until he curses under his breath.

"Goddammit," he says. "We're screwed."

He's already marching toward a table nearby before I can ask what's wrong. I flash the hostess an apologetic smile and race after him, arriving just as the man sitting at the table rises and extends a hand to Caleb. "David Murphy. I'm taking the story over from Anna."

The way he says it is combative, as if they're two boxers greeting each other before the fight begins.

"I know who you are," Caleb replies, mouth pinched. He gestures to me. "This is Lucie Monroe, our new Director of Employee Programs."

Murphy shakes my hand, but it's Caleb he's focused on...in a clearly hostile way. He hits *record* on his phone before we're fully seated. "TSG was just nominated for the dubious honor of 'state's worst employers,'" he begins. "Do you have any reaction to that?"

I swallow. I had no idea TSG's reputation was *that* bad. But what worries me more is that David Murphy has already gone on the attack. I sat quietly through a hundred interviews at Ruth's house, and none of them began like this. It's as if he isn't here for information at all, but simply wants to bury us, and if Caleb answers with one of his rants about employees wanting Frappuccinos, he'll succeed.

"Obviously, it's not what any company wants to hear," Caleb replies smoothly, "but it's been a wake-up call: employee satisfaction needs to be our first priority. That's why we've hired Lucie. Ultimately, I think the experience will make us stronger."

It's absolute bullshit, but I can at least admire Caleb's willingness to say what he has to for the company's sake.

The waitress takes our drink orders and drops a basket of bread on the table, giving Caleb multiple once-overs despite the ring on his finger.

"Some might say the timing of your change of heart is suspicious," Murphy says when she leaves, "coinciding with the nomination."

Caleb grabs a roll. "Not at all. This has been in the works for some time. We were waiting to find the right candidate."

My stomach sinks before Murphy's even turned to me. I already know what question he'll ask next.

"And is there some way," he says to me, "in which *you* were uniquely qualified to address the problem?"

No. I'm in no way uniquely or even *generically* qualified, and while I could probably shut this guy up by admitting *whose* daughter I am—and that I've watched and read hundreds of my father's interviews and spent many, many weeks of my childhood silently listening to him lead the conference calls Ruth was on as his head of Human Resources—that's not the path I want to take.

"I don't know if I can claim to be uniquely qualified," I reply with my best beauty pageant smile, "but one thing I understand better than most is the importance of belonging, and how vital it is for any company to find ways to make the office feel like an offshoot of home, especially when your employees are young. Because it's easy when you're young to leave a job, but it's harder to leave a family."

It's the exact answer my father would give. He loves talking about the importance of family, an irony that is not lost on me.

I launch into a description of the walking program before Murphy can ask what my actual experience is, and slowly, his aggression turns into curiosity. Sweat is trickling down my back the entire time I'm talking, but my smile holds, and when the conversation finally veers back to Caleb, it's almost civil.

I pick at my lunch while they talk and am spared answering more questions until we're leaving the restaurant. "So what else do you have planned for TSG?" Murphy asks as we step outside.

"I have several expensive ideas, but you've got to let me break the news to my boss here first." I glance at Caleb with a smile that says *I covered for you and you owe me for this* and Caleb, oh so reluctantly, smiles back. That dimple makes an appearance, along with the tiniest laugh lines around his eyes, and my heartbeat changes its rhythm in a way it should not. In the way it used to when I'd watch him from my window.

Taken, I remind myself, as he holds the car door open for me. And he wouldn't be my prince anyway. We don't want the same things from life.

Caleb waits until we're both in the car before he turns, raising a brow. "Well, that was interesting. Given how terrible you are at using a smart board, I would not have expected you to handle that so well."

I laugh. "I spent all those summers with my aunt listening to her conference calls and interviews. Sadly, she didn't have a smart board. I could have used the practice."

His smile fades. "I hate that that happened. I hate that it's still happening—your father should be helping you. Why are you putting up with it?"

"Caleb, it's not like I've turned down his generous offer of assistance out of pride. He doesn't want anything to do with me. He didn't even let me attend my aunt's funeral."

He glances over. "You could go public with it, then. Show the world he isn't the *superdad* he wants everyone to believe he is."

I stare out the window. I've considered all these things before, but I'll never act on them. "My own father knows exactly who I am and still wants nothing to do with me. It's a story I'd rather keep to myself."

"Lucie—" He *croons* my name as if it's his favorite song. "The fact that he's denying you exist has nothing to do with who you are. And, at the very least, force his hand. Tell him he needs to make it worth your while to stay quiet."

I shake my head. My father wants to believe I'm some trashy mistake he made with a stripper. He wants to think he's better than us, than *me*. The moral high ground is really all I've got left. "This is how I tell myself that I can be the product of something ugly without being ugly myself. By being a better person than either of them."

"You don't need to prove it. But anyway...consider yourself a permanent part of TSG. We clearly need you."

"You don't have to say that."

He shakes his head. "I never say or do anything I don't mean. You should know that better than anyone by now."

I guess I do. He says what he means, and as much as I resented that when I started at TSG, I'm starting to appreciate it. He's not the fairy-tale prince I'd have designed as a six-year-old, but he's awfully close to the one I'd design now.

"You're not all bad, Caleb. Aside from believing children are monsters."

"We'll see what you think in twenty years when I've got a private plane and you're paying for Sophie's ninth year as a gender studies major."

I laugh. "I'd still choose them, cheapskate."

He's silent for so long that I've assumed the conversation is over by the time he speaks again. "The kid thing? It's less about the money than it is the responsibility. And the fear. It would be terrifying to care about someone that much."

My eyes fall closed, picturing Henry. Is he happy today? Is he ever going to find a friend? "Yeah," I tell him. "It can be."

JEREMY ARRIVES Sunday to take the kids to lunch, still tan from the 'work' trip he took to Hawaii with Whitney.

Though he's spent the last week calling me every name under the sun and hacking into my bank account, he smiles when I open the door. He's always done that, though—he'll smile at the wrong moment, in the middle of saying or doing something awful, as if he's mistimed the appearance of an emotion he never felt in the first place. I once watched a documentary about serial killers and what struck me most was how much they reminded me of my own husband.

"Aren't you going to invite me in?" he asks.

I don't want him in my home. I don't *trust* him in my home, this man I was sharing a bed with two weeks ago. The fear, the revulsion...it was always there. Sometimes, though, you can't allow yourself to feel the full force of a thing until you've escaped it. Now I wonder how I lasted so long.

I continue to block the entrance. "They're almost ready."

His smile holds but his eye twitches, a tiny flash of annoyance he somehow masters.

"You look good, Lucie." It's a significant change from what he said a mere twenty-four hours ago, which was that my looks were 'already fading' and that my ass would be as big as my mom's any day now.

"Sophie! Henry!" I shout up the stairs. "Daddy's waiting!"

"Can we talk?" he asks. "I feel like we've never talked this through." He stares at the ground. His shoulders sag. He is laughably bad at pretending to be sorry.

"I don't see what there is to talk about."

"Just...there are some things I want to say to you. Important things." His eyes meet mine. "I miss you."

And there it is.

Jeremy doesn't like to lose. It would be one thing if he'd left me, but the fact that *he's* been left is finally starting to rankle. And he really believes that after everything he's done, he can briefly don that face he shows the world—the face he fooled me with when I was a naïve college student—and I'll come trotting right back.

Sophie runs past me without a backward glance, but Henry lingers, pressing his head to my leg and wrapping his little arms around me. I wish he wasn't leaving, and I suspect he wishes it too.

"We'll talk later?" Jeremy asks.

If I argue with him, he'll take it out on Henry, which is how he's kept me in line for most of our marriage. I nod, lips pressed tight, as he grabs Henry's hand and pulls him away.

I stayed with Jeremy as long as I did because I knew he'd make the twins' lives difficult if we left. It was only when he began including Henry in the potshots aimed my way that I knew we had to go. "*Apparently, he's as dumb as you,*" Jeremy said when we got Henry's first school report. Both the twins were sitting across from me at the table, and as I watched the light dimming in Henry's eyes, I knew it was time to do the hard thing, the scary thing.

Except leaving was only half the battle.

As long as he has the power to hurt my children, I'm never going to be free. And neither are they.

11

CALEB

I'm in the garage on Sunday afternoon setting up a sawmill when a BMW swerves into Lucie's driveway at high speed. Henry and Sophie emerge from the back of the car and run to their mother, who wraps herself around them as if they've been gone for a year.

The man who climbs out after them is the exact kind of jackass I hate—the type who spends the weekend dressed for golf, whether he's playing it or not, and smiles like a smug prick at the woman he just cheated on.

I'm about to enter the house, but when he tells the twins to go inside, there's something about Lucie that holds me in place. Her jaw is set hard, but it's not anger I sense in her posture—it's fear. I fight the urge to go out there and ask if she's okay.

"Can we get dinner sometime this week?" he asks. "I'd like to talk things through."

She hugs herself tighter. "There's nothing to talk about."

That fake fucking smile of his falls away even faster than it arrived. "Are our children nothing?" he snaps.

I quietly set the wrench down on the shelf behind me.

"Look," he says, his voice calm by force, "I'll admit it. I cheated. I'm a big enough man to admit when I'm wrong."

This motherfucker. Jesus Christ, Lucie. You married this guy? Why?

"It's big of you to admit it," she says, "now that I have it on film."

His nostrils flare and his eyes narrow, but it's followed by a small, condescending smile. "You aren't blameless either. I made a mistake, but you were always so busy with the kids you stopped making time for me. I wanted to come first with you once in a while, but I should have let you know that instead of trying to find comfort elsewhere."

"*Comfort?*" she asks. "Is that what we're calling our babysitter's vagina now?"

I'm inclined to laugh until he slams his hand against the roof of the BMW. It's not so much the action as it is the look on his face, the rage and loathing.

I'm already heading toward them when he turns to his car. "Fine, Lucie. I tried to give you a chance, but you aren't capable of loving anyone but yourself. Enjoy these last few days with the kids. You're about to lose them for good."

She stands still as a statue with her shoulders back and watches him drive off as if she hasn't heard a word he said. And once he's out of view, her shoulders start to shake and she buries her face in her hands.

As Kate's amply proven, I just make a bad situation worse, but here I am, walking outside to her anyway, though I should not.

She wipes her eyes and forces a smile. "It never fails. You witness every shitty thing that happens."

My hand reaches out and falls uselessly back to my side. She's still an employee, even if I've known her since we were kids. "A lot of shitty things happen because your ex is a fucking asshole. I don't understand how you could have married him in the first place."

She wipes her eyes again. "The fairy tale," she says grimly, her voice slightly hoarse. "That's why I married him."

"What fairy tale?"

She hitches a shoulder. "*The* fairy tale. You know—you meet someone and it just feels meant to be, then the two of you get married and take your carload of children to Disney every summer and live happily ever after."

"Interestingly, your idea of the fairy tale sounds like my idea of hell."

That wins me a laugh.

"You'll let me know if you need anything, right?" I ask.

She grins. "Apparently you'll be right there when it happens, so you'll definitely be the first to know."

I wish to God she'd tell me how I could help. And it would really be better if it was help I could offer from far, far away.

I made excuses to get out of meeting my friends at Beck's bar but decide to go after all. I wait until Liam's walked off and Beck's gone to refill our pitcher before I lean toward Harrison. "Hey, you do some family law, right? Like, you could handle a complicated divorce?"

He sets his glass down. "I thought I'd made that clear during the one million times I tried to get you to file for divorce, but I doubt yours will be that complicated."

"It's not me. It's my neighbor." I look around once more. The less Liam and Beck know about this conversation, the better. "She's got kids and her ex is a dick. You should hear the shit he says to her. Anyway, she's in a bad spot right now, financially. I was thinking you could tell her you were taking the case pro bono and send the bills to me."

His eyes widen. "You like this girl so much you'd pay for her divorce?"

"I don't *like* her. I'm just trying to help her out."

Harrison lifts his glass and drains it. "Caleb, I'll take it for free if it means that much to you. But do me a favor and ask yourself *why* it means so much to you, because what you're doing isn't sustainable."

I regret ever broaching the topic. "And what is it I'm doing?"

"Remaining alone on the off chance Kate returns. It was never going to work, but with this girl living next door and you refusing to admit you're borderline obsessed with her—"

My mouth opens to object and he holds out a hand to silence me.

"Whether it's with her or someone else, you're going to slip up eventually—and no matter what Kate's done, I don't think that's the guy you want to be. File so you've got a clear conscience when it happens."

I roll my eyes, but I think about what he said the whole way home. Am I going to slip? I thought I was fine, until Lucie entered the picture. It can't be with her, but the amount of time I spend fantasizing about it probably indicates that Harrison is right.

I never cheated on Kate, and that's pretty much the only way I *wasn't* a shitty husband. I'd like to hold on to that, if nothing else.

12

LUCIE

I arrive at the lawyer's office fifteen minutes early on Monday morning, fielding texts from Jeremy while I wait for the meeting to begin.

JEREMY

You want me to drop off your old maternity clothes? Based on your current weight, it looks like you're definitely going to need something bigger.

Heard you're putting on a show every morning at school drop-off, by the way. Good luck with that. None of those guys would touch you with a ten-foot pole.

I haven't gained weight. I'm not putting on a show. But, Jesus, I hate the fact that what he says even has me questioning if it's true. I hate that it's so easy for him to make me feel inferior, and it says more about me than him that he succeeds.

An hour later, Darryl Fessman, Esquire, shows up—all smiles and bluster and apologies—and leads me back to his office, where he proceeds to blather about the weather and ask how the kids are handling the divorce before he finally tells me he requires ten grand upfront—because apparently normal people are supposed to just have that much money burning a hole in their pocket. I didn't have it *before* Jeremy emptied my checking account.

The money worries me, but the picture he offers of my future is slightly better than the one I've been envisioning. He insists I'll get enough interim support to live off of and that, as primary caregiver, I'll be given possession of the house for two years. I shudder at the idea of moving back into the McMansion Jeremy's so proud of and shudder more at the idea of *telling* him I'm taking the house, but this isn't the time to start cowering.

I answer his questions, and nothing I say seems to faze him...until he asks for my husband's name.

"Boudreau," he repeats, frowning. "No relation to Enson Boudreau, right?"

"That's his uncle. Is it a problem?"

He winces. "He's the DA and that's a very litigious family, in general. It won't make anything easier, that's for sure."

My pen presses so hard into my notebook that the paper tears. "What won't it make easier? Money? Custody?"

He looks at me. Any enthusiasm he had for taking this case is gone. "It will make everything more difficult," he says, pushing his legal pad away. "If he's at all like his uncle and father, it'll take a lot of money to fight him."

"What if I don't have a lot of money?"

He sets his pen down. "Then you should carefully consider if this is really what you want to do, because it's not likely to go as well as you think."

My stomach twists. Because I didn't expect it to go well in the first place.

~

Is this really what I want?

I've asked myself the question a hundred times since lunch and I continue to ask it as I clean up dinner.

I know I don't want to stay with Jeremy until the twins leave for college—enduring the insults, the threats, the cheating—but maybe what's best for me is no longer relevant. The kids' lives would be so much better in a thousand ways if I went back: a big house, amazing trips, and all the stupid things that matter to teenagers. Most importantly, I'd be able to stay home with them. I could help Henry with his reading and whatever else is coming down the pike.

I just don't know.

My head jerks when the back door closes. The twins know they're not allowed to go to the lake without asking, but sure enough when I look through the kitchen window, Henry's traipsing across the backyard toward the dock, where Caleb's got pieces of an engine spread out on a tarp.

By the time I reach them, Caleb is showing Henry how to sweep a rag inside some metal tubing. My breath holds when he attempts to hand it to Henry, who is apt to simply stare at him or walk away.

He instead takes the tubing and rag from Caleb's hands and begins to do what Caleb asked. There's another of those painful twists in my chest, the ones I feel so often where Henry is concerned.

"This is the anti-ventilation plate," Caleb says, holding a rectangular piece aloft. His voice is gentle and patient—wildly different from the one I hear at work. "Ventilate means *let air out*. You don't want to let the air or gas out near the propellers."

"Because it will make them slow," Henry says, his words so exact and precise that I have to swallow hard to fight the lump in my throat.

Caleb glances at me just as I blink my tears away and points to a toolbox that sits on the back stairs to his deck, holding a screwdriver in the air. "Can you go up and get me the other one?" he asks Henry. "If you bring it back, I'll let you put this together."

Henry nods eagerly and runs across the yard. He looks so normal, like a kid excited to go to a party or say *hi* to his friends. Except Henry's never been excited for those things. This is a first.

I force my gaze away from him and back to Caleb. "Thank you. Henry doesn't...engage with a lot of people. This is different for him."

Caleb glances up at me and back to the engine. It takes a moment for him to speak. "He's extremely bright. A lot like a cousin of mine, actually."

Is he trying to tell me something about Henry, or was it a meaningless aside? I bite down on the questions that follow. *Is your cousin happy? Does he have friends and a family and a good life? Will Henry have those things too?*

I'm not sure I want to know the answers.

Henry runs between us with the screwdriver, and I glance toward the house. I won't ruin this for my son, even if I have to drag Sophie outside by the ankles. "I've got to get Sophie. We'll just be up on the deck?"

Caleb nods at Henry. "I'll send him back to you when we're done. I could use the help."

And there it is, on Henry's face, another ghost of pleasure. It's a small thing, but it's a bridge—the first sign of him reaching out beyond me and Sophie. And it's Caleb, of all people, who made it happen.

From the deck, I watch the two of them standing side by side. Henry reaches up and pulls one part loose from the other, then smiles at Caleb.

He would never do that with Jeremy—he wouldn't approach, he wouldn't try, he wouldn't smile—because he'd know it wasn't safe. He'd know he was more likely to be ridiculed, to be told he's failed, than any other outcome.

The answer I've been seeking floats silently to the surface, though I think it was there all along:

What I owe my children isn't the biggest house or the fanciest trips. What I owe them is simply a place where they feel safe, where they'll be accepted for exactly who and what they are.

And that place will never be with Jeremy.

13

LUCIE

The man hovering near my cubicle Friday morning is blond and attractive—if you put him in a lineup of Hemsworth brothers, he'd fit right in, and he grins with the confidence of a guy who is well aware he looks like a Hemsworth too. "I'm Wyatt Smith. Kayleigh said you were back here."

"You're the marathoner," I reply, forcing myself to return some version of his smile though I can't imagine what he wants from me. "I've heard about you."

He shrugs. "Yep. I'm the troublemaker. That's kind of why I'm here. I figured I should take myself out of the running for the grand prize. I'd rather be the hero than the guy everyone hates."

"That's really nice of you."

His mouth curves on one side. "But I do have an ulterior motive, actually."

I sigh. *Of course you do.* At least, unlike Jeremy, he's admitting it.

"I thought showing you what a super guy I am might convince you to go out with me."

I freeze. I haven't been asked out in years. *Hit on*, sure, usually by married dads at St. Ignatius or Jeremy's gross fraternity brothers. And it's what I want, isn't it—another shot at the fairy tale? He's as good a candidate as any. I don't know why I'm more horrified than pleased.

"I...but you've never seen me before," I stammer.

He laughs. "Everyone in the building has seen you. You're kind of the talk of the fourth floor."

I'm shaking my head *no* before I've even formed a response.

There's nothing wrong with this guy, but something inside me says *no. No, this one isn't your prince.*

"I just...I have kids, and I'm recently separated. I haven't even filed for divorce. So I'm not ready to date."

He smiles, white teeth and smile lines on full display. "So you're saying...maybe. Once you've filed."

Shouldn't I be charmed by his persistence, by his cockiness? Somehow, he leaves me cold.

"I'm sorry. I have no clue when I'll be ready, if ever."

Agreeing when you're not sure is how you wind up with another Prince *Sort of* Charming, and I want the real thing or nothing at all.

"You said *no*?" Molly shouts over a glass of wine on my deck. "Chris Hemsworth asks you out and you say *no*?"

I laugh. "I didn't say he was Chris Hemsworth. And if you keep yelling, you'll wake the twins."

She wrinkles her nose. Her feelings about children are much like Caleb's. "Why the hell didn't you go for it?"

I hug my wine to the center of my chest. "I don't know. I've told you this...I want the fairy tale the next time around."

"You're not being realistic."

"That's rich, coming from a woman who just told me she

was going to disable her car so her boss would give her a ride home."

She sighs. "Anyway, you've got to fuck a few frogs before you kiss your prince there, Cinderella, and you deserve a couple years of no-strings sex because I guarantee Jeremy sucked in bed. I know his type."

Jeremy's the only guy I've ever slept with, so I have no idea if she's right. I've always been under the impression that sex is nowhere near as exciting as people make it out to be, while Jeremy insisted I was simply 'broken.' I wish I knew which of us was correct. Probably him.

"He just wasn't the guy. I don't know why."

"I do. It's because you're obsessed with *Caleb*."

"I'm not obsessed."

"Of course you are. Every time you tell me about a conversation with him, you're so...impressed. Every time he says something to you—not even something nice; simply something that isn't horribly rude—you're like, '*He's such a good guy.*'"

"You're making me sound like I'm twelve. And he's married."

"Yes, he is. And you have a crush on him anyway."

"I don't," I argue. Because even if I do, I'm not admitting to a crush on someone who belongs to someone else. And I'd certainly never act on it.

It sure doesn't help, though, that his wife is never around. If she was here, we'd be friends and we'd laugh together about what a jerk he is at the office and my crush would die a quick death.

"His wife's been gone for nearly a year, though," I say, refilling Molly's glass. "That's got to be hard."

"Yeah," she says, toying with her braid. "But that doesn't make him any less married."

She leaves, and the house is painfully quiet and lonely in her absence. Is that why Caleb works the way he does—to avoid the quiet of that big lonely house? Who was he before the personal stuff Kayleigh referenced led him to close the seventh floor?

I curl up on the couch under an ancient quilt and attempt to watch a movie I used to love, but my mind keeps going back to work. What TSG lacks is a place where employees can relax, unwind. A place where they can at least *imagine* they're valued as human beings. And the seventh floor is the perfect location for it.

I throw off the quilt.

No matter what Caleb's reasons were for shutting it down, if I can prove it won't hurt his bottom line to reopen it...how could he possibly object?

I'm not going to ask for masseuses or saunas or free food. Just...couches. Coffee. Music and a few magazines.

I'll need to prove to him that it won't hurt productivity and that the costs are minimal, perhaps even offset by revenue generated elsewhere—an in-house café or vending machines—but I know I can convince him. I know it.

I work until the wee hours, casually watching the house next door, and his truck never returns.

Maybe I should worry a little less about him being lonely...only one of us, after all, is technically alone.

14

CALEB

I 'm pulling into the driveway when my mother calls. "Are you busy?" she asks. She begins every call this way, because she knows I'm exactly like my father—always working, even when I'm not supposed to be.

I slam the door of my truck closed. "Your timing is perfect. I'm just getting home."

"How's the house?" There's the same forced good cheer I always hear in her voice—it's the sound of a parent trying to pretend she's not scared shitless on her kid's behalf.

I slide my key into the lock. "It's in pretty bad shape. The last owners really let it go, but I'll get to fixing it up eventually."

The sun is slipping over the horizon, painting the sky in streaks of orange and lavender. I'd forgotten how much I liked it at this time of day, growing up. I liked a lot of things back then, though, when the future was simply a highlight reel of everything I wanted and something extra, something magic I knew existed but hadn't yet had myself. When did I fucking lose that optimism, that desire? And how did it take me so long to notice it was gone?

My mother is telling me about the book club she's joined

and how much she misses it here as I shrug off my jacket and move to the back window. Lucie's sitting cross-legged in the grass, her hair twisted high on her head in a messy bun.

"Did anyone buy the place next door?" my mom asks out of nowhere, and I feel like I've been caught at something, as if she somehow knew where my head was. To be fair, though, my head is there a troubling percentage of the day, so the odds were in her favor.

"Yeah. A single mom with twins."

Sophie runs to Lucie with the toy she and Henry were fighting over. Lucie hands it back to her, and even from a distance I can tell Sophie is pissed about it. For some reason it makes me want to laugh.

"Poor thing. That place was falling apart when Ruth was there. I can't imagine what it's like now."

"Her nephew should have fixed it up," I growl, though it's Lucie I'm thinking of more than Ruth. "Or bought her a new house. How the hell could he do so little for her?"

My mother sighs. "Ruth lectured me on self-sufficiency the one time I asked if I could borrow an egg. She wouldn't have accepted help if her life depended on it."

I think of Lucie refusing the advance on her salary when she clearly needed it and insisting later that she didn't need help paying for a lawyer. She may be more like her aunt than she realizes.

"So how are *you*?" my mother asks. "Any news about the merger?"

Lucie is on her hands and knees now, pretending to bury the toy Sophie gave her. Henry isn't smiling, exactly, but he looks amused nonetheless. I kind of want to walk down there, though I've got no excuse for it. "Nothing new. We're on track to have it all happen late summer or early fall."

"You sound...different. In a good way. What's going on?"

She wants to hear that something has changed—that I'm

working less, that I've heard from Kate—though she no longer asks and neither of those things is true. "Nothing's changed," I reply.

Henry runs by Lucie and she turns toward him, laughing as she pulls him into her lap, pressing her lips to the top of his head. And in response, there's a rustling in my chest.

All that optimism I once had, all the things I wanted from life and gave up on...Lucie reminds me they were ever there in the first place.

And that's what's changed: she's making me want those things again.

It's probably for the best that I'm leaving California for good.

15

LUCIE

I'm too excited about the seventh floor to keep my thoughts to myself. I've only waited thirty minutes on Monday morning before I'm standing at his office door with my laptop in hand.

His gaze runs over me like a finger, lingering at points along the way—mouth, hips, legs. "I assume you're here to hit me up for something wildly impractical?"

"Not impractical at all. Your company needs a break area, and that disgusting cafeteria doesn't count."

"I don't suppose you're talking about a *free* break area. Of course you're not. Fine, what ridiculous shit do you want?"

I raise my laptop. "Can I show you?"

He sighs, pointing to the small table in the corner. "If you must."

I take a seat and open the presentation, trying to ignore his heat, his smell, the rough slide of his palm over his pants. "This is what other companies are doing," I begin. "Google has an ice rink. Their employees play—"

"We are not Google," he replies firmly. "And I'm not putting in a rink."

"I know. I figured I'd horrify you before I went to more low-key solutions."

His lips tug upward, a quarter of a smile. "Did Mark give you primers on how to handle me?"

"No. I just know how to deal with men." I didn't intend for it to be a double entendre, but given the way his eyes dip to my mouth, he seems to have taken it as one. My knee brushes against a hard thigh as I cross my legs under the table and there's a flash of something in his face—something hungry—that steals my breath. No matter how boring I've found sex to be in the past...I suspect he'd be different.

"The seventh floor," I reply, swallowing. "It's, uh, sitting empty."

He tenses, the light in his eyes dimming. "We had to cut expenses."

It can't be the whole story. Whatever that space was costing him, it was minor relative to TSG's budget. But my purpose here isn't to quibble over the decisions he made in the past...it's simply to fix them. "The difference in utility costs since you closed the seventh floor are negligible, and this is what it could be." I turn the laptop to show him the rough drawing I created online—ping-pong on one side, a small coffee bar on the other, tables in the center.

He frowns. "That looks like a magnificent place for my employees to fuck around instead of working."

His reaction doesn't surprise me. I'd have died of shock at this point if he hadn't shit all over the idea. "Caleb, people care about work-life balance, whether or not you approve. If you're going to force them to come into the office, you've got to make it palatable."

He groans, leaning his head back against the chair. "I'll consider it. And in the meantime, I'm signing you up to speak about the walking program at this thing. We need to rehabilitate our image a little." He slides a flyer toward me.

The Northern California Technology Consortium. The name, the glossy paper, the pops of royal blue—it all screams *important* and *intimidating*. It makes me want to hide under a desk until it's over.

"Present it? You mean, to *people*?"

A single brow raises. "That's usually how presentations work, yes. It would be very good press for us."

I picture a room full of people far smarter than I am, tearing apart the program, asking questions I can't answer, making me feel stupid. I don't even know what I'd say. Sure, the building feels more lively: there's trash talking in elevators, across divisions, and this week, the call center had the most miles and their office got toilet-papered by another team. It was probably not great for productivity, but people have been laughing about it ever since. I'm not sure I can tell a roomful of executives that one team toilet-papering another is *progress*, however. "Couldn't I just give you the data?"

He tilts his head, observing me. "You've done public stuff before. Weren't you, like, the Papaya Queen or something?"

"Your grasp of our state's produce is surprisingly weak. Yes, I used to do beauty pageants, but that was different."

"How?"

I stare at my hands. "Beauty pageants don't involve having your ideas criticized or being asked questions you can't answer." I got criticized plenty at home, though—my mother laughed when I told her I was entering and said I didn't stand a chance. Proving her wrong only made things worse.

"There's nothing to be scared of. Anyone willing to attend a session on a walking program has already swallowed the Kool-Aid. They want their employees all holding hands and singing 'Kumbaya', same as you."

"Yes, you sound super accepting of what I'm trying to do with my *hand-holding and singing 'Kumbaya.'*"

He grins. "It's a lecture *I'd* avoid like the plague. But that's just it...people only go to a breakout session if they're open to the topic. And I'll go over it with you in advance. You must realize no one there will be a bigger asshole than me." He leans back in his chair with a grin.

Ah, there's that dimple. I'd agree to anything he asked when that dimple appears.

"True," I agree. "No one could possibly be a bigger asshole than you."

He laughs. Somehow, I knew he would.

I take another look at the flyer. "You know what would really make my presentation exciting? If I could tell them about our new break room."

His jaw falls. "Are you actually trying to blackmail me into agreeing to that?"

"I prefer the term *strong-arm*, personally. That way it's not a felony."

The dimple makes another appearance, and it unfurls this small seed inside me—something warm and hopeful that shouldn't be there.

"Fine. Go ahead and pull some costs together and we'll show the executive committee, but I'm not paying any designers or architects or whatever. It's got to be bare bones."

"Violate building codes. Got it. You won't regret this, Premier Stalin."

"I already regret this," he mutters, but I leave with a smile.

I wanted to save TSG. It's starting to feel as if it's saving me too.

FOUR DAYS LATER, I'm in front of the executive committee and once again, I'm struggling with the smart board.

"Sorry," I tell them. "It'll be just a minute. Technology and I are not friends."

Hunter starts to stand, ready to come to my aid.

"I've got it," Caleb says, shooting Hunter an unnecessary scowl as he jumps to his feet.

He nudges me to the side, towering over me though I'm in heels. His fingers move confidently over my laptop—his hands are so fucking *large*. There's something about the sheer size of him that makes me think of being manhandled.

I look away. I have enough issues with the smart board...I need every available brain cell.

"Go to HR when the meeting is done and tell them you need a new laptop," he says as the slides load. "This thing is a piece of shit."

He takes his seat, and I show them the initial idea I had for the room, as well as the anticipated costs.

When I'm done, Debbie turns to Caleb in shock. "*You* approved this?"

He frowns, with a tiny clench in his jaw. "Why wouldn't I? It's a good plan."

"I *know* it's a good plan," she says. "I'm simply stunned that you agreed to spend money without a fight."

I grin. "There was a little fight."

"It's not *much* money," he reminds me with a growl. "Correct, Lucie?"

"Wow," Mark says. "Next you'll convince him to throw a holiday party."

"Actually," I reply, "I think we should start doing staff meetings. There's research that shows—"

"Meetings are a waste of time," Caleb says, cutting me off. "I ask for work to be done, pay a good salary, and the work is completed. What's there to discuss?"

"Use the meeting to tell them they're doing a great job," I suggest. Employees are scared of him and they shouldn't be—he's someone they'd want to work for, if they really knew him.

"Tell them what's next for the company or what they have to look forward to."

His eyes roll. "Why isn't continued employment enough to look forward to?"

I laugh, perching on the edge of the table. "Caleb, if continued employment was enough, you wouldn't have needed me in the first place."

I wait for him to point out that he did not, in fact, need me. His mouth tilts, but he doesn't say it, which is generous of him.

"The cost would be minimal," I continue. "Just bagels and coffee. I'll do all the leg work."

His gaze meets mine and there's still reluctance in his face, a desire to argue, but it...softens. Unexpectedly, quietly. "Fine," he says.

"And you'll be there," I add, sounding uncomfortably like Sophie issuing one of her warnings. It's a *you'll be there or I'll fight you over it.*

His lips move into one of his almost-smiles again, as if he's thinking the same thing. "My schedule is getting packed. If this is really necessary, I can do it two weeks from now, but after that, no promises." He pauses then, a flicker of worry on his face. "Is that okay? Do you have time to pull it together by then?"

I never thought I'd see the day when Caleb Lowell would appear legitimately concerned about whether he was asking too much.

Mark grins, as if he never expected to see it either.

16

CALEB

Lucie is in the green dress today and her hair is down. "Can I show you something?" she asks, holding up her laptop and I know this is the last thing I need right now—her in my office smelling like roses and sunlight, her in that fucking dress and those heels—but I can't think of a reason to say no.

She strides toward me, hips swaying like an invitation.

She comes to my side of the desk and sets her laptop in front of me before opening up a spreadsheet. The numbers blur, though, because her smell is in my nostrils and her ass is an inch from my arm, and if I were to look really hard—I swear to God I'm not going to look—I'd see some cleavage as she leans over.

She shuts the laptop. "You're not even listening," she says. "What are you actually thinking about?"

My expression, I'm certain, is guilty. My head is blank. I say nothing, and she smiles. "Caleb, tell me."

I shake my head. "Nothing."

She steps in front of me and takes a seat on my desk. Her dress is bunched up now, barely covering her ass and when her thighs spread wide, it's covering nothing at all. She reaches between her legs and tugs the tiny black thong she's wearing to the side. "Was it this?" she purrs, her fingers sliding over her center, circling her clit.

I should deny it, but I'm already rising, already ripping off my belt. I can't undress fast enough, as if she's an apparition that will vanish if I close my eyes. She reaches for me, smiling as her mouth lowers, moaning as I hit the back of her throat.

I wake. I'm so close to coming that for a second I wonder if it's going to happen entirely on its own.

I slide my hand into my boxers and grip myself tight, just the way I'd want her to do it before she took me into her mouth.

I spent the entire past week thinking about her and I'll spend next week doing the same. This isn't sustainable. Harrison was right.

I'm going to slip.

17

LUCIE

On Saturday, Jeremy comes to pick up the kids for their first overnight.

He's only watched them for twenty-four consecutive hours once before, and though I try to assure myself they'll be fine, I can't quite take a full breath as he swerves into the driveway.

This time, he doesn't get out of the car. He just lays on the horn while staring right through me as if I'm now invisible to him. I doubt that I am, given he was texting only yesterday to tell me how selfish I am for 'destroying our family.'

I walk the twins to the car, my hand gently resting atop each little head, dropping to my knees when we reach it and pulling them to me. Small lips are pressed to my cheeks and Henry clings, briefly, which makes it so much harder.

Jeremy deigns to climb from the car at last. "Let's go, guys." His voice is hard, edged with threat.

They release me and climb into the back. By the time I rise, he's already walking away.

"Sophie's allergy meds are in her bag," I begin. "I wrote the instructions on a—"

"I know about her allergies," he says, swinging the door open.

He doesn't. I can't think of a time he ever reminded her to take her meds or came to her appointments. I barrel on anyway. "Henry will need the night-light—"

He turns, smirking. "Parenting isn't rocket science, Lucie. If you'd ever done anything significant with your life, you'd understand that."

My stomach sinks as they drive away, knowing he won't remind Henry to pee before he goes to bed or move his milk away when it's too close to the edge of the table. Knowing he'll be enraged when it goes wrong—when the milk spills or Henry has an accident or Sophie's eyelids swell after they've just arrived at the park because he didn't remind her to take her meds.

I've done this to my children, by leaving. How many days and nights of their lives will they spend under his thumb, suffering him because I couldn't stand to keep doing so myself? Will there ever come a day when I'm *certain* it was the right decision?

I work on the plans for the seventh floor all night. Even once I'm in bed, I work, trying to distance myself from the loneliness of this empty house and the fear that it's always going to be this way.

I'm woken in the middle of the night by the ringing phone. The lights are on, the laptop still open beside me, and I nearly fall out of bed trying to grab my cell before it wakes the kids, until I remember that they're not here to be woken.

It's Jeremy. My hands shake as I swipe over the screen to answer.

"Open the door," he demands.

I'm still too panicked and sleep-dazed to ask why. Blearily, I rush downstairs and fling the door open to find him standing on the porch with Henry sound asleep in his arms.

"What happened?" I ask.

Jeremy's gaze goes to my tank top and boy shorts. I guess I should have put on a robe, but it's certainly nothing he hasn't seen before. He was barely interested even when I wore *less*.

"Take him upstairs," he says, thrusting Henry at me. I stand frozen, open-mouthed as he returns to the car to get Sophie. Whitney is sitting in the passenger seat, her face lit by her phone screen, as if none of this is happening around her.

"What are you doing?" I demand when he returns with Sophie. "It's the middle of the night."

"Yes, Lucie," he says, "I'm aware of the time. I have to head out of town, so I'm bringing the kids back."

My eyes are still barely open, but I feel rage rushing through my bloodstream and it's a thousand times more effective than caffeine.

"You *what*?"

He glares at me. "Unless you want them to wake up, keep it down."

Grinding my teeth, I head up the stairs with him at my heels. I tuck Henry in while he deals with Sophie, and then I follow him back outside, the grass damp and sticky against my bare feet. "What could possibly have come up this late at night?"

He's already rolling his eyes, bored with this conversation before it's begun. "We're taking a road trip. Whitney's friends rented a place in the mountains."

I know better than anyone how selfish he is, yet I'm still appalled. It's the first night he's spent with them since we left, and he couldn't even manage that.

"They're going to wake up to discover you just ditched them," I say, my voice low with fury—a fury that threatens to turn into tears if I back away from it for a second. "How's that supposed to make them feel?"

He rolls his eyes once more. "This is so typical. You should be fucking ecstatic. You want them all the time, and now you get them, but you're still bitching."

"Yes, of course I'm bitching! You're running off on a last-minute trip with your teenage girlfriend and you don't give a shit about how that will make the twins feel."

He laughs. "Do you hear how bitter you are? Maybe that's why you're home alone on a Saturday night."

I sink to the front step as Jeremy peels out of the driveway, trying hard not to cry. Part of it is frustration at how little control I have here, that he can hurt my children and there isn't a damn thing I can do about it. But it's also that his words, as always, carry just enough truth to do damage. He was right—I had a free Saturday and I chose to spend it working before falling asleep alone. Maybe I *am* bitter. Maybe I deserved the way he treated me, the way my mother and father treated me too.

Maybe it really is me who's the problem.

"Hey," says a voice. Caleb—hair sleep-tousled and eyes barely open—emerges into the circle of light cast by the lamp on the side of his garage. The sight of him briefly knocks every other thought from my head. He's in nothing but shorts—smooth skin and taut muscles on full display. He runs his hands through his hair and his biceps pop in response, his abs flashing to life, stacked neatly one atop the next like a pack of dinner rolls.

And then he yawns, and reality intrudes. He was asleep and we woke him up with our fighting. Why must every humiliating incident I suffer have an audience, and why is that audience always *him*?

"I'm sorry," I whisper. "I guess we woke you."

He shrugs. "My window was open, and he was being such a dick that I thought you might need some backup. I couldn't find my shorts, so it took me a minute."

I try to ignore the image that comes to my head unbidden—

of him *before* he added the shorts. Was he naked? In *very* fitted briefs? My mind is capable of diving into the gutter at even the worst of moments, it seems.

"I hope you've got a good lawyer," Caleb says.

"I do," I reply, though I'm not sure it's true—Darryl left me a message saying he was *'really busy right now'* and would have his associate, Sharon, take over. She's done absolutely nothing.

"Seriously, Lucie...that guy is unhinged. I don't know how you ever thought *he* was going to provide you your fairy tale."

"I didn't." *I came back here once the house was legally mine, hoping to see you, and met Jeremy instead.* "I went through most of college with my friends telling me I was too picky, so I decided to see if they were right and got pregnant almost immediately by accident."

"Shit. I'm sorry."

"No, *I'm* sorry. You must feel like you're living next to the set of a trashy reality show."

"Believe me, Kate and I have been the *interesting* neighbors more often than I'd like." He sees the sympathy in my gaze and shakes his head. "It wasn't just the drugs, and to be honest, it was pretty entertaining at times. Kate's probably the smartest person I know. I used to enjoy listening to her tell off neighbors whose yard signs offended her."

It shouldn't bother me to hear the admiration in his voice, but it does. "You must really love her to be willing to wait like that."

He pushes a hand through his hair again, and infinite muscles in his stomach ripple in response. "I'm not waiting, actually. I had my friend Harrison—he's a lawyer—file for divorce."

My mouth falls open. "You did? What led to that?"

"He's been on me about it for a while. I realized I was going to—" His eyes are wary as they meet mine. "For all my failures, I've never cheated on anyone. I wanted that to remain true."

In other words, Caleb wants to get laid. The idea of Caleb sexually deprived and eager makes a muscle in my core clamp down so hard it almost hurts. I think of what it would be like, slowly undressing as he watches, and that muscle tightens further.

We're both single, so none of what I'm picturing is impossible, but I'm the opposite of what he wants. If he just escaped a committed relationship—the one that convinced him he didn't ever want to be in one again—he sure isn't interested in a single mom with two kids.

"If you're a free man, shouldn't you be off living out your single bachelor fantasies?"

"I'm not entirely free yet. We have to prove we've tried to reach Kate first, but..." He raises a brow. "*Single bachelor fantasies?*"

I grin. "You look like a threesome-with-supermodels-type, if I had to guess."

That dimple of his flashes in the moonlight, and the muscle low in my belly spasms *again*. "I'm pretty sure every guy is a threesome-with-supermodels-type if he can make that happen."

I wave a dismissive hand at him. "Look at you. Obviously, you can make it happen."

A half-smile tugs at the corner of his mouth. "So you think all I need to do to get a threesome with supermodels is ask for it?"

I groan. "Shut up. You already know you can get pretty much anyone you want."

He regards me quietly. "But not you, because you're holding out for the fairy tale."

He's offered this up as if it's a statement, but I almost sense that it's...a question.

Would I? Sleeping with Caleb wouldn't necessarily rule out waiting on the fairy tale. The two things could, in theory, occur simultaneously. It could happen right here and now, me sitting on this step with my legs spread wide.

Yes, yes I would. I'd do it without question if that was something he was open to.

He huffs out a low laugh. "You have no poker face, Lucie."

I blink out of my reverie. I wonder if he knows I was trying to figure out how we could have sex on my cement front steps. But I'm not what he wants and he's not what I want either, if he's got no interest in a family. Plus he's my boss. It would be a disaster of epic proportions. "I'm definitely still holding out for the fairy tale," I reply. "But I'll stop telling the neighbors you buried your wife in the backyard."

He grins. "Thanks. You've been making it really hard to lure their supermodel daughters over."

I laugh and climb to my feet, only realizing how very little I'm wearing as his gaze slides over me. My pajamas cover more than a bathing suit but feel like less. Especially after the conversation we just had.

"Thanks. For coming to my rescue."

"Any time," he says, keeping his eyes carefully trained above my neck.

18

LUCIE

I'm walking fast toward aftercare when Mrs. Doherty, the head of school, stops me. She's not normally here this late and the way she's jumped in front of me out of nowhere makes this all feel intentional.

"Lucie," she says with a practiced smile. "Do you have a moment?"

No. No, I do not. I'm tired and Henry is undoubtedly sitting at that table staring at the clock...but you don't say *no* to St. Ignatius's head of school, not when there are four hundred families dying to take your child's spot.

I follow her to a spacious office, outfitted for a college dean rather than the head of a school that ends at sixth grade. She offers me a beverage from the small glass-fronted refrigerator full of Topo Chico and Diet Coke. I shake my head, sitting on my hands to keep them from tapping out my impatience.

"I wanted to discuss Henry's progress with you," she says. There's a warning in her fading smile. "Mrs. Kroesinger has mentioned he isn't progressing with his reading the way we'd like."

My stomach knots. "Yes," I reply. "She gave me some

things to work on with him at home." And I was doing so, religiously, until I started working. The realization that we only did the flashcards once this week makes my breath stick in my chest.

"We'd like to get him evaluated before we plan for next year," she says. She hands me a typed list of names. "To see if there are any issues we're unaware of."

"Issues," I repeat. I don't want him to have a reading problem. I don't want to know he's going to struggle for the rest of his life. But what worries me most are those fears I've kept to myself. Because what if it isn't *only* reading? What if it's something more?

She gives me a forced smile. "We just want to make sure we can meet his needs going forward."

Which sounds less like concern for my son...and more like the process of kicking a kid out of St. Ignatius. *We've reviewed the evaluation*, she'll tell me later, *and I'm afraid we aren't equipped to provide what he needs.*

Would this be happening if I'd played the game? If I'd told anyone and everyone that my father is Robert Underwood? I doubt it.

I thank her, the words sticking like glue in my throat, and arrive at aftercare to find Sophie playing while Henry does a puzzle alone.

Why couldn't it all have been easier for him? Why couldn't he have gotten a touch of Sophie's extroversion to help him socially? Or her joy, her grasp of phonics? I just want him to be happy and the fact that I can't guarantee it'll happen breaks my heart.

As soon as I have the twins buckled in, Sophie is asking about dinner, which I haven't even thought about, and demanding time at the beach, and telling me she needs me to find her baby photos for show-and-tell tomorrow and I want to scream at her to stop. It's what my mother did to me, constantly, and for far less. I hate that I'm tempted to emulate her, but I need a second to breathe, to not be in charge.

We climb out of the van just as Caleb exits his garage. His timing could not be worse—I'm not sure I can manage even a brief, neighborly conversation.

He walks over to us with something in his hands. "I was about to—" he begins and then looks at me and falls silent. He hands both Henry and Sophie pieces of metal. "See if you can figure out how these go together. Your mom and I will be right back."

With a hand on my elbow, he leads me around the corner. "What's wrong?"

His quiet concern threatens to break me, and I cover my face with my hands. I'm about to insist that it's nothing, but it's not nothing, and I need to tell one other person. One person who won't insist that it's my fault, the way Jeremy and my mom will.

"The school wants me to get Henry evaluated. They said it was for reading, but I'm worried there will be other things too and—" Saying it aloud makes it so much more daunting. I've known there was something different about Henry's development, about the way he interacts with people. I've known it for years. But Jeremy told me it was that I coddled him too much, and the pediatrician blew me off and oh, God, *why* did I listen to them? Was it because I wanted them to be right? Because I didn't want to know? *What kind of mother just lets it go?* "I've been worried for a while, and I should have pushed harder to figure it all out." My voice breaks at the end and I have to stop.

"Lucie," he whispers, desperation in his voice, his hands on my biceps. "He's a great kid and it's going to be okay. No matter what you find out, he's the same little guy who left the house this morning. All that will change is that you'll have a name for it and can make plans."

God, I hope he's right. And God, I wish I'd married

someone who would tell me things were going to be okay, even when they're not.

"I have to pull myself together," I whisper, forcing myself to step back though I really don't want to, wiping my face with my hands. "If the kids see I'm upset, they'll know something's wrong."

"Go home and get it out of your system. I'll order a pizza and keep them here as long as you need." He turns me toward the house, and I'm too broken to resist.

I stumble home and start calling the specialists on Mrs. Doherty's list. Most of them have a long wait, and while a part of me thinks *yes, yes, let's wait as long as possible*, it's not in Henry's best interest. Every week that slips by without us figuring out what's going on with him is a week he's not learning as well as he could be. I take the first opening I find, months and months from now, and there's nothing left to do... but tell Jeremy.

> The head of school says she wants us to get Henry evaluated for learning disabilities. I can't find anyone to do it until late August.

JEREMY

> Gee, you decide you want to break up the family and work full time and Henry starts having problems. Who could have predicted that?

I'm almost too numb right now for it to bother me. Almost. But if I hadn't left, would Henry be keeping up better than he is? Could this all have flown under the radar?

I rise from the couch to change clothes and splash cold water on my face. Though I'm still spent and want to sleep for a hundred hours, I can hold it together a bit longer. What Caleb said was right: nothing has changed. Who Henry is remains the same. I already suspected he would struggle, that he wouldn't make friends as effortlessly as Sophie and wouldn't have the same life she would. No matter what the tests find, he'll always have me and he'll always have his sister, and he's the same kid who left our home this morning.

I cross the yard and tap lightly on the door before entering Caleb's house for the first time—though it barely qualifies as a home at present. Half the drywall is down, and the other half is water-stained beyond recognition. Why on earth did he take this on? He already works the equivalent of two full-time jobs, and this equals a third.

Then I notice the twins. "Do you have my six-year-olds *stacking drywall*?"

"I'm paying them," he argues. "They love it. Although your daughter talked me into an hourly rate which is, frankly, exorbitant."

The doorbell rings. "That's the pizza," he says. "Do you mind grabbing drinks from the basement?"

I nod and head downstairs, expecting another demolished room. Instead, it's so crammed he couldn't fix it up if he wanted to. Boxes and furniture are stacked high on every wall. And a whole section is labeled *Kate*. Kate-books, Kate-closet, Kate-bathroom. This girl left her whole life behind, and Caleb's spent the better part of a year simply hoping she'd reclaim it.

I move toward the fridge but then stop and look at her belongings again. At the crisp white frame leaning against the wall behind the boxes.

It's a crib. A *new* crib. I step closer and spy a rocking chair beside it and a folded-up changing table just to the left.

He and Kate bought these things. And they're nothing you'd buy unless you were really certain you'd need them.

Kate's drug addiction, the personal stuff Kayleigh alluded to...did it all begin here, with a crib and chair and changing table Caleb now has no intention of using? I grab drinks and climb the stairs slowly, wondering how I can ask. Wondering if he'll tell me the truth.

Upstairs, Caleb's grabbing paper plates and napkins. "I've only got two chairs," he says. "So should we sit outside?"

It's probably for the best: if we were all around his table, it would feel a lot like playing family.

Which is something it seems he might have wanted, once upon a time.

"Sure." My voice is slightly too cheerful, but he doesn't notice.

We get down to the beach and the twins take their paper plates to the shore while Caleb and I sit in the Adirondack chairs. When he's been down here with us before, watching the kids' antics...did it hurt? Have I been rubbing something in his face I didn't even think he *wanted*?

Sophie comes up to him and starts speaking gibberish. "Oooh, blah, blah, la, la, oh lay."

He raises a brow, waiting for her to explain, his mouth softening.

"That was French," she announces.

He grins. "Y.A.I.E."

He's playing the code game with her. I melt, but she frowns at him.

"*That's* too hard," she says, placing her hands on her hips.

"It stood for 'your accent is exquisite.'"

Her mouth curves upward as she returns to her pizza.

All his bullshit about children being a pain in the ass—is it really what he thinks, or is it simply easier than admitting they were something he once wanted but didn't receive?

He reaches for another slice. "You've gotten very quiet."

I force a smile. "It's been a long day."

"I'm sorry," he says. "You shouldn't have to deal with this alone."

"There are worse things. At least I'm not alone while locked in your attic."

"Are you still on that? You know I wouldn't have gotten around to soundproofing the room. You'd have heard her screaming by now."

I laugh and then fall silent. I want to ask him about the crib. I want to know if, once upon a time, he *did* want kids. Except I can't think of a single way to broach these topics without potentially causing him pain.

After another long moment of silence, he sighs heavily. "You saw the crib, didn't you? I forgot all about it until you were halfway down the stairs."

I turn toward him. "I did. It's none of my business. I was just surprised."

He swallows. "Kate and I had a daughter. Hannah. She only lived for a few minutes."

My stomach sinks like a stone. The day they handed me my twins was the happiest of my entire life, the one I'd spent nine months building toward. I can't imagine reaching that point and having them taken from me. I can't.

"I'm so sorry," I finally reply. "What happened?"

"Meconium aspiration," he says. My brow furrows and he reluctantly continues. "Meconium is held in the baby's intestines, but sometimes during labor it gets expelled, and if the baby inhales it ..." He stops talking. His voice is lower and quieter when he continues. "She lost lung function. It happened so fast. Kate was holding her and trying to nurse, and then Hannah started gasping."

"Oh, Caleb," I whisper. "I'm so sorry. That must have been so hard for you both."

"It was hard on Kate," he corrects, excluding himself entirely. "I wasn't even there when it happened...I'd gone to this meeting in San Diego and by the time I got to the hospital, it was too late. She went through the whole goddamn thing alone."

He hasn't said it directly, but there's blame in his voice. He's holding himself responsible for some reason, but then...he's the sort that would. There are men in the world who blame everyone but themselves. He's the opposite.

"It wasn't your fault, Caleb," I reply. "You know that, right?"

"I should have been there. There were signs I might have noticed. And I wasn't there for Kate afterward, either. She completely fell apart. I avoided it because work was easy and she was hard. This whole fucking thing, start to finish, was my fault."

This is why he waited for a woman he hasn't heard from in nearly a year, a woman who stole from his corporate accounts and God knows what else. Because he thinks he's the reason she did it.

"Caleb, you were grieving too. Maybe you couldn't deal with Kate because you were trying to keep yourself afloat."

He shakes his head. "I wasn't grieving, Lucie. I just wanted to work. My dad was exactly the same way. Sometimes it's best to accept your limitations early on."

"So you work too much. People change more significant pieces of themselves than that."

"Except I don't *want* to change," he replies. "I'm responsible for a company and I don't ever want to be responsible for anything or anyone else."

It seems like a really lonely way to go through life. And I also don't believe him. He says he didn't grieve. He says it was hard on Kate. But Caleb cares about things a lot more than he lets on, and there's no way what happened didn't hit him hard.

He's punishing himself with all this enforced isolation, and some ridiculous part of me is already hoping I can change his mind.

19

CALEB

I've never minded traveling. Living in a hotel is simple, easier in many ways than living at home. There's no excess, there are no chores to be done. Your life is stripped bare, and you don't have to feel bad about how empty it all is because you're there to do a job, to save your company, and no one can criticize you for that.

But my hotel room in Austin looks out over a parking lot, and I miss the views at home. I don't wake up excited to see anyone. I miss that too.

For the next three days, as I travel to Houston, then Chicago, then Denver...not a single person makes me laugh. Not a single person has me throwing off my covers in the morning and feeling as if something worthwhile might happen. I'm not going to turn a corner and discover Lucie there in the green dress. I'm not going watch that slow, unwilling smile open wide on her face when I find myself in her path or hear her laughter echoing over the water while I throw a frozen dinner in the microwave.

So what if I miss seeing them? Yes, I thought I wanted

complete privacy, but is it a *crime* that I prefer not being out there alone?

I head to the Denver airport on Friday afternoon. I'm supposed to be in Seattle by seven for drinks with a possible investor.

I open my phone to pull up my boarding pass and then turn around and walk to the ticket counter. "How fast could I get on a flight to San Francisco?" I ask.

This doesn't mean anything. There's nothing wrong with a man just wanting to go the fuck home.

I GET BACK to the lake as the sun's starting to fade. Lucie's car is in the driveway, but there are no lights on in the house and they're not at the beach.

My frustration is made worse by the fact that I know I shouldn't be frustrated, that I shouldn't care at all. I change into shorts and a t-shirt and head for the path that circles the narrow end of the lake to the north. There's a little footbridge that lets you cross from one side to the other and Lucie takes the twins up there on occasion. I start jogging in that direction, hoping it's where she's taken them now and telling myself to anticipate disappointment when I'd have no right to be disappointed anyway.

Nothing can come of it whether I find her or not.

I hear them before I see them. Sophie is chattering away, and I run faster toward the sound until I come round the bend and find them.

Sophie's in the middle of telling a story and Henry's examining a log.

It's exactly what I *don't* want, and yet this thing in my chest soars when Lucie looks up, when her eyes come alive. As if she missed me as much as I missed her.

"Well, hello there, Monroe family," I say, coming to a stop.

"My last name is actually *Boudreau*," corrects Sophie, skipping toward me. "Did you know that if you drop a penny from the top of the Empire State Building, it will kill someone?"

Lucie and I exchange a grin. "I've heard that," I say to Sophie. "I didn't know if it was true."

"It's not," Henry says quietly to Sophie. "The wind resistance slows it. I told you that."

"Not if an alien is riding on it!" she says with a scowl before stomping ahead. "You don't know everything, Henry!"

"How the hell does your *kindergartner* know about wind resistance?" I ask Lucie.

"My friend, Molly," she says with a smile. "She's determined to turn them both into scientists. I think Sophie might be a lost cause."

The twins are arguing loudly about the potential size of an alien. Lucie is still smiling, and it hits me out of nowhere—this wave of longing.

I wish all of this was mine.

20

LUCIE

"**Y**ou said no life jackets."

My daughter has her arms folded, and she's staring me down, as much as someone who is four feet tall can stare down a grown-up.

I groan. "Sophie—"

"You promised."

I'm not sure I actually *promised* they could swim without life jackets today. I think I merely suggested it was *possible*, and now I'd like to suggest it's not. I'm always outnumbered with them. I could save one drowning child—I can't save two. But they both know how to dog paddle, and I guess, at some point, it's sink or swim...literally.

"Okay," I say with a sigh, and she runs out the back door gleefully, screaming, *No life jackets!* at the top of her lungs.

I'm grabbing my beach bag to follow them when my phone chimes.

JEREMY

> Do you ever bother to even take the kids anywhere, now? Or is it just easier to put them in front of the TV all day?

There's a brief *ping* in my gut, as if I should question this text more carefully, because how does he even know we're home? But there isn't time, with my kids running headlong toward the water and toward Caleb, who stands on the dock.

A thrill climbs up my spine at the sight of him, only in part because he's currently shirtless. He has a tattoo high on the back of his shoulder, one I never noticed before. I want to inspect it up close, except if it's for his wife, I'll wish I hadn't. Sophie is talking to him, and when he glances up at me as he replies, I walk a little faster. God only knows what she's told him.

"Mommy!" she shouts. "Caleb says we can go on his boat, which is way better than ours!"

"Full disclosure," he says as I approach, "I never claimed my boat was better. That was her."

He also didn't *suggest* this outing. My hands go to my hips. "Sophie, did you ask Mr. Lowell to take us on his boat? Because we've discussed this."

"*We* call him Caleb," she scolds. "And he said it was fine."

"You do not invite yourself into other people's homes, *or* onto their boats."

Caleb shrugs. "It's okay. I'm not doing anything."

I still don't want to reward Sophie for a behavior we've had several conversations about, but the twins are already scrambling aboard. "Yes, they're monsters who will steal your youth and your disposable income," he adds, "but I doubt your kids can do that from the inside of my boat."

I'm laughing as I concede. He helps me climb up, his hand warm and rough and so much larger than mine. For just a moment, his eyes are on my face and we're standing close and my stomach *tips*, a tiny but thrilling rise and fall.

"Thanks," I whisper, looking away. It would be a lot easier to stop picturing him as Prince Charming if he'd stop fucking acting like him.

I go to the back and Sophie and Henry snuggle up beside me while Caleb unties the boat then jumps in—surprisingly graceful for his size.

He takes the seat up front and backs away from the dock carefully, his tricep popping when he moves the throttle, his bicep bulging as he grabs the wheel.

Jeremy started going soft months after we got married, while there is nothing soft about Caleb. He's long and lean, ridiculously muscular for a guy who does nothing but work. I picture him flat on his back, spread out for me like a banquet, and feel a deep pinch of desire, so sharp it steals my breath.

Sophie leaves me at last and goes to the front of the boat. "Come on, Henry," she says—bossy, parental—and he follows happily. For the next ten minutes, she delivers a nonstop dissertation on pandas to Caleb while he drives, and then he cuts the motor and comes back to sit with me while the twins take turns pretending to steer the boat.

"Thanks for this," I tell him. "Obviously, it's the highlight of Henry's year."

"It's kind of fun to have some company," he says. "I'm happiest surfing, but this is a close second."

I smile to myself. "I remember you guys with all the surfboards in the back of someone's truck."

"You sound like you did nothing but watch my life from the window."

I laugh. "A bunch of hot, teenage surfers staying at the house next door to me? Find me one pre-teen girl who wouldn't have been obsessed."

His grin turns sly. "*Obsessed*, huh? This is getting interesting."

I'm not about to let him know just how obsessed I was. "Why'd you move to the lake instead of the ocean if you'd rather surf?"

He hesitates. "I didn't really buy this place for myself. My mom always pictured renovating and retiring here with my dad, hosting all the grandkids." He gives me a half-hearted smile. "I guess she wanted your fairy-tale thing too. I'm trying to give her the house at least."

"It's not *my* fairy-tale thing. Everyone wants to matter to another person. Everyone wants someone to grow old with. It doesn't have to include kids."

He shakes his head, watching Sophie march toward us. "I don't. Life's a lot easier when you don't matter to anyone at all."

Before more can be said, Sophie appears in front of me.

"Swim time!" she announces.

My arms fold over my chest. Stripping down to a bikini in front of my boss was not part of the plan. "That was before you cajoled your way onto someone's boat."

Caleb laughs. "It's okay. I like it out here."

"Fine," I say to Sophie with a sigh. "But you've got to keep the life jackets on because I'm not going in with you."

"You said we didn't have to!" Sophie cries. "And you put on your suit."

"Go ahead," says Caleb, who probably thinks I'm simply being polite. "Seriously. Just remember this the next time you start crafting some plan that's going to cost me ten grand."

"I'll cancel the poetry center," I reply, turning away from him to shimmy out of my clothes.

The twins jump in, and I follow. The water is freezing, but when my head reemerges to find them waiting for me, small limbs flailing as they propel themselves around, I can't help but smile. Black storm clouds roll behind the mountain, but here on the lake, the sun beats on my face and my children are happy. No matter how many things I've messed up, I've created *them* and we're all okay. Right now, it's enough.

When I glance back at the boat, Caleb's leaning against the rail, his gaze trained on the three of us as if he might have to jump in to save us in a second. I like it. I'd like to have someone watching over us all the time. Even when I was married, I felt like I was alone. I don't want to be alone anymore.

We don't stay out long. Within a few minutes, the twins' lips are pinched and blue, and when I tell them it's time to go, Sophie doesn't even argue, which means she must be on the verge of hypothermia. They splash their way back to the boat and climb the ladder, with Caleb waiting to help them in before wrapping a towel around each of them in turn.

It's another of those moments that make me ache. The twins deserve to have more than just me in their lives. They deserve to have another parent who can care for them when I'm tired, when I'm busy, when I'm still climbing into the boat. If I'm going to find that person, I can't keep waiting for some family-focused version of Caleb to appear. I need, as Molly said, to fuck a few frogs.

I grip the base of the ladder to follow them up, my foot slipping on the final rung. Caleb's hands come under my arms, but when he hoists me in, I stumble, my whole body falling into his before I can right myself. He's so firm, like a fucking statue. His smell—some combination of soap and salt—should be bottled.

And I've been noticing it all instead of pulling myself away like a normal person would. He's staring at me wide-eyed, an animal in a trap. He steps away quickly, but not before I feel the hard press of his erection against my stomach.

A very *sizable* erection.

"We should get back," he says, gruffly, heading for the front of the boat. "It's about to storm."

By the time we reach the dock, it's all behind us. Sophie is telling Caleb about the intelligence of cephalopods—"And that's why I won't eat calamari," she concludes, and he grins at me over her head.

But then he reaches out a hand to help me out of the boat and our gazes lock and....no, it's not entirely behind us. There's something here now, and maybe it was always here, but what-ever it is, I think I'm ready to give into it, if he is.

He ties off the boat while the kids run ahead to the shore. "If this house is for your mom," I ask, "then where will you live once she's here?"

His tongue prods the inside of his cheek, as if he's consid-ering his answer carefully when the question didn't seem all that complicated. "I think I'll be moving to New York," he says quietly.

I stare at him. "New York? *Why?*"

He swallows. "The board knows this but it's not public knowledge yet—there's a much larger company interested in merging with us and putting me in charge of both, as long as I can clean up TSG's shit between now and then. You might have heard of the CEO—Brad Caldwell?" I nod and he continues. "He's planning to retire. If it all works out, he'll hand the reins to me at his place in Maui this summer, and we'd start the tran-sition afterward. I'd be in New York by late fall."

No. It's bizarre how fast my brain puts up a fight for this man who was never really a possibility, but no, I don't want him to leave. I don't want to walk into TSG and report to anyone but him. I don't want to see some other man out on this dock.

No.

I shove my hands into my pockets, staring at the wooden boards beneath my feet, not quite able to meet his eye. "And you...want that?"

"TSG can't grow the way I'd like without an influx of capi-tal, which this other company would provide. And I'm only thirty-one. It would be pretty huge to be a CEO of a company that size at my age."

"Wouldn't it just mean...more work?" More work when he has so little time to himself as it is.

He grins, giving me a flash of that dimple that has never *not* made my heart race, even if it shouldn't. "You've got your fairy tale—I've got mine."

I force a smile in response. I can't escape the thought that what he believes is his fairy tale is actually the opposite. That nothing is less likely to bring him happiness than moving away from the town he loves and all his friends to go somewhere with greater demands.

And I also can't stop thinking that somehow, his fairy tale and mine were meant to be one and the same.

But...he's leaving, and he doesn't want kids.

They definitely are not one and the same.

"I'M SETTING YOU UP," Molly concludes when I tell her about the incident over our lunch break two days later. "The man spent a year waiting on a woman who clearly doesn't want him, and now he's moving to New York? Come on, Lucie. This guy is the ultimate dead end."

I frown. "Okay, but it's actually pretty admirable that he—"

She stabs her salad with unnecessary aggression. "Lucie, did he or did he not tell you point blank that he hates kids?"

"That's not exactly what he said," I mutter. She may have a point, though: there's absolutely no benefit to persisting with a crush I wouldn't act on even if I could. "But I don't know if I want to be set up."

There's guilt in Molly's laugh. "I misspoke earlier when I made it sound like something I was *going* to do. The guy's name is Stuart and he's at a lab in Germany this month, but he's going to call you when he gets back to town."

"Molly," I groan. "No. I'm not ready. And also...his name is Stuart. Name one cool guy named Stuart."

"Look, he's a physicist. None of them have hot names. That's why my son will be named Damien. No one named Damien grows up to be a geek."

"I'm pretty sure if your name is Damien, you grow up focused on ruling hell," I reply. "But anyway, I'm not sure about being set up and—"

"Luce, he's cute. If I didn't already have wedding preparations with Michael O'Connor underway, I'd be all over it."

I choke on the water I'm swallowing. "Yes, you sound very close to a wedding, what with the way you still use his last name when you refer to him."

"You need to get Caleb out of your head, and the way to do that is to put another man there in his place. Hopefully one who also rocks your world in bed."

"Stuart the physicist sounds unlikely to *rock my world* in bed."

She shrugs in agreement, carefully pressing a napkin to her lips—she's the only person I know who can perfectly keep lipstick on throughout a meal. "This is true. But Damien O'Connor would, right?"

"Yes, Molly. Your unborn son, my future sexual partner, will be amazing."

She sighs. "You always have to take it too far."

21

LUCIE

Caleb's been coming to the beach almost every night. Maybe my first weeks at TSG were unusually hectic for him, but he seems to leave the office a bit earlier each day. Sometimes, he's got a little project for Henry. At others, he plays the code game with Sophie—guessing ridiculous words for the letters she's offered him.

G, he suggests, must stand for *garrulous*. *R* for *residuals* or *recividism*. She argues that he's being unfair, but the very next night she's using those new, big words on him.

She's just run back to Henry, after attempting to use the word "homogenous" and botching it, when I turn and gently remind him not to be a dick at the upcoming staff meeting.

"A dick?" he repeats. "You fucking millennials want a meeting and your free coffee and you're getting it, on my dime. How could anyone possibly think I was a dick?"

"Use of the term 'fucking millennials', for starters," I reply.

I spend Wednesday fretting, wandering through the auditorium and worrying that it will be too crowded with the tables for coffee and bagels inside rather than out. I oversee the setup of the sound system I rented, and have just closed the auditorium doors, determined not to worry anymore, when Kayleigh calls to say I've got a delivery.

I frown. I'm picking up the food tomorrow myself. I didn't order anything else. "What is it?"

"You'll probably figure it out when you get it off my fucking desk," she replies, helpful as ever.

I head downstairs and my stomach drops from twenty feet away.

A bouquet of roses so huge it takes up half the reception desk sits there. Stuart and I have been texting and he seemed relatively normal, but sending two dozen roses to a woman you've never met is definitely *not* normal and I can't imagine who else would have sent them.

I swallow as I reach for the card attached to the bouquet.

> *I miss you. Dinner tomorrow? I'll get a sitter.*
> *All my love,*
> *Jeremy*

He was always this way—the cycles of punishment and excess. He'd fail to come home for a weekend or strand me and the twins at a party somewhere, and then return a day or more later with a wide smile and a piece of jewelry, as if that's all he had to do to make up for it.

And these flowers—they're the jewelry. They're *sorry I stole your money and cheated and implied I'd take your kids from you* flowers. I can't believe he thinks they'd work.

"You don't seem excited," says Kayleigh. "Even if you don't like the guy, flowers are flowers."

Except these are so much more than flowers. These are a gift given with expectation and when that expectation is not met, he's going to punish me for it.

I take them back to my office. I'd rather not see them, but it's better than having everyone entering the reception area ask Kayleigh who they're for.

My stomach is heavy with dread as I dial Jeremy's number. He's never hit me, but his words can carve up my brain and make me doubt everything. I simply don't need it right now.

"Hey, babe," he says, his voice warm and confident. "I guess you got the flowers."

"I did. Thank you. But..."

"I was passing this flower shop and I saw the roses in the window and thought 'Those would make Lucie happy,'" he says. "I know how much you love roses."

I *don't* love roses. I told him my favorite flower a hundred times—the same one in my wedding bouquet—and he never remembered once.

It didn't surprise me. I'm just a story Jeremy tells—yesterday, I was the bitch wife not giving him enough time with his kids. Today, I'm the generic female who loves roses. Nothing he's saying or doing is about me. Even his desire to win me back isn't really about me. Jeremy only knows winning and losing, and this is a tactic. Tomorrow there will be a new one.

"So, about dinner," he continues. "We can maybe head down to Santa Cruz? Stacy next door said she'd watch the kids."

He's got it all planned out. He really thinks that after everything he did and said, I'm going to let him buy me dinner then give him one of those blow jobs he demanded, then criticized, in turn.

"We're getting a divorce," I say, my voice as firm as I can make it. "I appreciate the flowers, but they don't change anything."

"Lucie," he says, "give me a chance. I know I fucked up. I know I didn't appreciate what I had. Sometimes it takes losing everything to make you love your old life."

"I—"

"It's what I want, it's what the kids want, and I think underneath it all, it's what you want. We had a nice life together and now you're slumming it out at that cabin, working long hours. And what about the kids? I know it must kill you to send them to aftercare. It must. And how are you going to help Henry if you're working full time?"

My shoulders sag. Nothing he said mattered until he brought up the kids. And he's right. I'm so tired when I get home from work that I can barely stay awake when I'm reading to them at night. How am I going to summon the energy when they get real homework next year, or if Henry needs extra help? I thought the hardships would be balanced out by Jeremy's absence from our lives, but he isn't disappearing the way I hoped.

Give in now, even a little, and you are lost.

"I'm sorry, but I don't want that," I say, still trying to soften my words, still trying to placate him in the futile hope he won't turn vicious as a result. My stomach twists already, anticipating his response. "And I don't want to go to dinner."

There's silence then, and I regret being so blunt. I do believe that somewhere, deep in Jeremy's very fucked-up head and heart, there is a molecule of legitimate regret. And perhaps if I loved him, or believed he loved me, that would be enough. But that's just it—I don't love him. I thought I could and maybe did when we first met, because I was young and stupid and woefully inexperienced. But it wasn't love at all—it was simply relief that someone, anyone at all, wanted me and claimed he was willing to have my back.

"You're going to regret this," he says, and he ends the call.

I press my palms to my face, wishing I'd somehow handled it better.

He's going to make me pay.

22

LUCIE

The next morning, I'm running frantically through the house, buttoning my skirt while I try to find Henry's missing shoe. In an effort to keep costs down, I said I'd pick the bagels up rather than getting them delivered, which means I somehow need to get the kids to school, pick up bagels for five hundred people, and have it all done by nine a.m. It already bordered on impossible, and then Sophie opened a yogurt and got it all over the front of her uniform, the floor, and me. By the time I've got her changed and myself cleaned up, we are five minutes behind schedule on a day when we can't be behind schedule at all.

"Come on, you guys. Come on!" I shout, grabbing my bag and phone as I hustle them out the door.

"Mommy," says Henry. "Where's the car?"

I exhale heavily, fumbling for the keys in my purse. "Henry, I don't have time for games, okay?" It's at times like this that I can almost understand why my mother lost her shit with me so often. Because I want to have a tantrum, and children are so easy to rage against. It's not like they can talk back, or at least they couldn't in my mother's household—Sophie seems to manage it just fine in mine.

I find the keys and sling the bag over my shoulder as I walk outside. Henry and Sophie are standing on the walkway, staring at me.

I look beyond them to the driveway and blink repeatedly at the empty space where the car should be. The alarm would have triggered if someone had tried to steal it. It takes me another long second to realize it must have been removed by someone with a key—a key only one other person has.

"Did somebody steal our car, Mommy?" asks Sophie tearfully.

I am not going to fall apart. I am not going to fall apart. I am not going to fall apart.

"No. Nobody stole our car." My voice trembles with both sadness and rage. "I think Daddy might have borrowed it."

Why did Jeremy have to do this now? It's like he knew how important today was, but he couldn't have. He just happened to choose to fuck me over at a time when I really needed everything to go perfectly.

And what the hell am I going to do? I still need to get the kids to school, pick up the food, and set up the smart board and mic. I could ask Molly, but she's got a big project of her own today and isn't anywhere near us.

I can really only think of one other person to ask.

"I'll be back in a minute, guys." I grab my phone from my bag and hit dial as I step into the house. "I need some help," I tell Caleb, struggling to get my voice under control. He's already at work, of course, and has probably been there for hours.

"What's going on?" There's something so certain and assured about him, and that makes the desire to cry even worse. Caleb's like a blanket I want to wrap myself in, except...he isn't *my* blanket.

"Jeremy took my car," I whisper. "I'm going to call Uber so I can get the kids to school, but I was supposed to pick up all the bagels for the meeting. They're already paid for—" That last word cracks and I swallow once more. "I don't know what to do. I'm not going to be able to get them in time."

"What do you mean, he *took your car*?"

"He's punishing me for something. He had the keys and the car is in his name, so I don't think I can even call the police—" My voice breaks again. It's not sadness so much as it is frustration.

Jeremy can get away with anything he wants, and I have no recourse—ever. Is it always going to be like this? The twins are only six. I'm not sure I can deal with a decade or more spent waiting for him to lash out at me, of being unable to get away from him and his endless rage.

There's a moment of tense silence. Caleb is, undoubtedly, regretting everything: not firing me, agreeing to this meeting, the fact that my baggage has suddenly become his.

"Where are the bagels," he asks, the words clipped, "and what do you need done to the room?"

I start giving him a list, and he stops me. "Send it to me as a text. And don't call Uber. I'm coming to get you."

TEN MINUTES LATER, he swerves into the driveway, and I usher the kids into the back of his truck.

"You don't have car seats," Sophie announces.

Caleb glances at me. "Do they still *need* car seats?"

"Until our eighth birthday or when we are over sixty pounds," replies Sophie primly.

"Booster seats," I tell him. "It'll be fine. Just try not to wreck."

"I generally try not to wreck."

I laugh, despite the situation. "They go to St. Ignatius, over in Elmdale. I'm really sorry about this."

"It's fine." He glances over his shoulder. "But once we're done at the school, we need to have a little talk. And what were you thinking, planning to pick up all the shit for the staff meeting yourself?"

"I was trying to keep costs down," I protest.

He sighs. "Lucie, never do that again. I'm cheap, but I'm not that cheap."

We near the school, but the carpool line at this late hour stretches around the block. "Holy shit," he says. "Do you go through this every morning?"

"You said shit," says Sophie. "You said it twice."

"Now you said shit," Henry tells her.

"Shit. Now everyone in the car has said it," I announce. "Guys, hop out and I'll run you up to the front."

"You don't have to do that," says Caleb. "We've got time."

"It's okay." We definitely *don't* have time, and the last thing I need is someone seeing the twins in here without booster seats, or me pulling up to the school with a strange man. I'm sure the rumor mill is running at full speed about me and Jeremy as it is.

I climb from the car and walk the twins to the front as fast as I can in heels and a pencil skirt, giving them each a quick hug.

"You said *shit*, Mommy," Sophie says with wide eyes. "You never say bad words."

"I'm full of surprises, sweets," I reply, brushing my mouth over the top of her head.

They walk away just as my name is called by someone behind me.

"Lucie Boudreau," says the voice. "Looking good."

I turn, forcing a weak smile.

Tom DuPlantis is one of the gross dads I attempt to avoid

most of the time, a big-time lawyer with an ego to match, somehow under the impression that I'd be interested in him. "Hi, Tom." I start to step past him and his hand wraps around my elbow.

"Hey, don't rush off," he says. "We need to talk. I heard a rumor that a certain mom I know is back on the market."

I pull away, a small, stumbling step. "Sorry, I'm late for work."

He moves toward me. "I'll call you, yeah?"

Heads are turning. The other moms' eyes go sharp, and I can imagine exactly what they're thinking: that I'm single and desperate and making a play for someone else's spouse. Now that I'm a divorcee, running around in this utterly seductive knee-length skirt and low heels, everyone will say I was encouraging him.

Did you see Lucie hitting on Tom, with her kids right there? And the outfit—who wears heels to drop-off?

"Things are pretty hectic," I call over my shoulder. "I'm sure I'll see you around."

Caleb is only two cars back now, for better or worse. I swing the door open and slide in before Tom catches up. "Sorry," I say breathlessly.

His jaw flexes as he steers past the parked cars and onto the road. "Who was that guy?"

I raise a shoulder. "One of the dads in the twins' class."

"One of the dads who's hitting on you, you mean."

"He hits on everyone," I say, opening up my notes for the meeting. "So, I think today if you could thank everyone for their hard work, it would go a long way. You intimidate people."

Caleb doesn't appear to have even heard me. "That guy? Tell him to fuck off the next time he does it."

I raise a brow. I'm not sure why he's so fixated on Tom, of all people. Dealing with the Toms of the world is just a part of being female. Tom can do what he's always done—make comments, let his hand brush my ass 'accidentally,' hug me at parties for a little too long, and sidle up to me during every school event—but if I say a single word, I'll be seen as dramatic and attention-seeking.

"It really wasn't a big deal."

"He can't go around grabbing you like that," Caleb insists. "If you punched him once, like a square hit right in the face, I bet he'd never do it again. But remember not to tuck your thumb. Chicks always make a fist the wrong way. And speaking of people who need a fist to the face, you need to call your lawyer about the car. This is complete bullshit."

My laugh is short and miserable. "He's not going to do anything. He pawned me off on some junior associate once he heard that Jeremy's uncle is the DA, and she's the worst." During my one and only phone call with Sharon, she told me that she and Jeremy's attorney had found some apartments I could move into because Jeremy thought I was too far from the school. I'm not sure whose interest she's trying to serve, but it doesn't seem to be mine.

"Then you need a new attorney."

I know. I know. I need a new everything. Mostly I need a new way to get through life because every path I take winds up making things worse. I force a smile, and once again, I'm trying not to cry. "Let me get through today, all right?"

BY THE TIME we arrive at work, the instructions I sent Caleb have been executed perfectly. The food is set out and there's a buzz of excitement in the air. It's bizarre how much people love free food.

Caleb enters through the side door just before nine, frowning, his brow furrowed as he searches the room—until his gaze falls on me. And then his eyes soften and he smiles.

I smile back.

I wish...I wish...

I wish for so many things.

Mark gets up and makes a small presentation about productivity, and then someone else discusses the software that's about to be launched.

When it's finally Caleb's turn to speak, I can't look away. He stands there, imposing and beautiful in a suit that does nothing to hide the sheer power of him—the size of his shoulders, his chest, his broad hands. I'm not the only female here watching him with something that exceeds professional interest.

Kayleigh, the most obvious of them.

He thanks us for our hard work and our commitment to the company, just like I suggested. He discusses the plans for the team-building retreats I'm organizing and reminds everyone there's only a month left to get miles in for the walking program.

"And let's have a round of applause for Lucie Monroe," he says at the end, "for making all this happen."

Our eyes meet, and I feel no different than I did as a small child, certain he was the one I was meant for.

"Pretty impressive, Lucie," Wyatt says, slinging an arm around my shoulders.

I force a smile. "Nothing's happened yet."

He grins. "I have faith in you."

I glance back at Caleb. He's no longer smiling.

He's glaring at that arm around my shoulders like it's everything he hates in the entire world.

~

ONE HOUR LATER, Caleb appears at my desk. His eyes land on the bouquet—I set it by my trash can last night and the cleaning people placed it back on my desk instead of throwing it away.

"Do you have time to run a quick errand with me over lunch?" he asks. His eyes revert to the bouquet.

"Sure," I reply, grabbing my purse. "What kind of errand?"

He turns stiffly. "You'll see."

"Based on how cranky you are, I assume someone else has nominated us worst employer in the state?"

His gaze flickers to the roses as he rubs the back of his neck. "Sorry, if I was abrupt. I just thought you, uh, might have plans."

He almost seems...jealous.

"Nope, no plans," I reply, following him down the hall. He frowns, dissatisfied by my answer.

We get into his car, and he heads toward the other side of the lake, away from his cabin and mine and closer to the suburb where Jeremy and I once lived.

"So are you going to tell me what this secret mission is?" I ask. "Have you also consulted with Jeremy's lawyer and decided I should move?"

He gives a short laugh. "No. We're getting your car back."

I stiffen. He clearly believes my ex is far more reasonable than he actually is. If I take the car, Jeremy will call the cops and have me arrested. Knowing Jeremy, he's hoping I do it.

"Caleb, *no*. I can't. It'll make everything worse."

He shakes his head. "Your ex is a ruthless asshole, Lucie— do you really think he's just going to *stop* without forcing you to give up things that matter?"

No, probably not. I've been hoping he'd tire of this whole thing, that he'd fall madly in love with Whitney and forget about us, but I'm not sure Jeremy is capable of loving anything more than he loves *winning*. He isn't going to be happy until I've begged him to take me back or am destroyed completely.

"I appreciate what you're doing, but fighting with Jeremy

always makes things worse. I'll lose something much bigger than my car in the end."

"I'm not suggesting we *steal* the car. My friend Harrison is an attorney. Hear him out. I promise he won't steer you wrong."

He pulls up to Beck's Bar and Grill, which I've passed a hundred times without entering—something that can be said of most bars, as I was married and pregnant shortly after my twenty-first birthday.

The hostess puts us out on the deck, leaning over Caleb unnecessarily to suggest that if he needs anything, he should come find her.

I frown as she departs. "I didn't know women actually batted their eyelashes outside of bad movies about the south."

"That's because you don't have to resort to batting your lashes. You just flash a smile and men do anything you ask."

I feel a flush climbing up my neck. "I thought men cared about other things a lot more than smiles."

"I'm pretty sure they care about lots of things." His gaze drops to my chest and he scrubs a hand over his face. "You're not lacking any of them."

The chair next to Caleb's slides out and a handsome guy in a suit drops into it and extends a hand to me. "I'm Harrison," he says. "If Caleb's told you about his friends, I'm the good-looking one."

"If I told her about my friends," Caleb replies, "you'd be the arrogant one. Or the argumentative one."

"I have many good qualities," Harrison agrees, settling into the seat next to Caleb's. "What I don't have is time, so let's get to it. Lucie, your ex is a dick."

I laugh. "Yes, I've been piecing that together."

"Caleb says he was cheating?"

I sink a bit in my seat. "Yeah. He was on a work trip to Hawaii and took our nineteen-year-old babysitter with him. I had him followed."

Harrison raises a brow. "You must have already suspected he was cheating then?"

"Yeah, but it took me a while to act. I knew he'd make things hard if I left and that it might go poorly...and it has. I hired Darryl Fessman, this big-shot lawyer and he pawned me off on someone named Sharon, who's letting Jeremy dictate her legal strategy."

Harrison nods. "Fessman is scared to piss off your former uncle-in-law, so he pawned you off on Sharon Davies, who's worthless. I'm not saying that because I want the work—I'm not planning to charge you—but simply because it's the truth. However, it's probably going to be ugly, so I need to know you've got the stomach for it."

I look from him to Caleb. "I really appreciate it, but I can't accept that. It's too much, and I suspect it's going to drag out."

"Look, you need to stop trying to do this on your own," Harrison says. "Don't worry about me. I'll force him to pay legal fees, and every time he does something frivolous to drag it out, I'll sue him for more legal fees. By the second or third time it happens, we'll get some traction, I promise you. At least let me get your car back."

I meet his eye. "Can you?"

He gives me the widest, cockiest smile ever, yet it's still sweet somehow. "Of course I can. I'm the best lawyer in this city. And I always get my way."

While Caleb crosses the bar to greet a friend, Harrison details our next steps...which include having my car back by morning and the petition for divorce ready for my signature the following afternoon.

"Thank you so much," I tell him. "Between this and Caleb saving me this morning, I'm just speechless."

Harrison's gaze on me sharpens. "How did Caleb *save* you?"

"Oh, he, uh—" I glance to the side. *Is it supposed to be a secret?* For all I know, Harrison's wife is Kate's best friend. "He, uh, drove my twins to school and had someone deal with all the meeting details."

His eyes lighten. "That's good. It's nice to see him reentering the world again."

"I'm glad you persuaded him to file for divorce."

A smile plays at the corner of his mouth as he looks over at Caleb, who's heading back to the table. "*I'm* not the one who persuaded him, Lucie," he says.

I replay those words, looking for some other way to interpret his meaning.

There is none.

Harrison thinks Caleb did it...because of me.

23

CALEB

"So that's her, huh?" Beck asks, looking across the room to where Lucie and Harrison are deep in conversation.

"Don't start," I reply. "We're friends."

Beck grins. "Really? If you're only friends, then why are the rest of us forbidden from talking to her?"

"I never forbid anyone from talking to her."

He raises a brow. "Sweet," he says, sliding under the bar. "I must have misunderstood. I'm gonna go introduce myself."

I step in front of him, and he laughs, swinging a rag over his shoulder.

"I wasn't going over there. I just thought I'd prove conclusively that she's not merely your *friend*."

I give him the finger and head back to where Lucie and Harrison are finishing up. The three of us walk out of the bar together and Harrison shakes Lucie's hand. "Congratulations," he says, "you're about to be a free woman."

"I can't thank you enough," she tells him, while I blink at them like I've taken a bullet to the chest.

Of course she's about to be free...That's why we met with him.

But I didn't think it would be so soon. I've gotten used to having her and the kids next door, to seeing them out on the beach. I've been cutting out of work early in the hopes of finding them there, and while I knew it would end one day, I suppose I thought that day would be off in the future, some distant point after I was gone.

She's quiet on the way back to work. Is she planning how she'll move forward once Jeremy's in the rearview mirror?

"So I guess you're about to be single again," I finally say.

She shrugs. "I guess. I'm not sure a divorcee with young kids is a hot commodity these days."

My teeth grind. Lucie could be raising an entire busload of orphans and she'd still have a line down the street of men who want to be near her. Wyatt, Hunter, that asshole who grabbed her this morning...If I already know of three men who'd cut off a limb to take her out, how many more must there be? "I'm sure you'll do fine." The words are bitten off, angry. I sound jealous when I meant to sound ambivalent. "You should be getting out there," I add, just in case she heard the jealousy too.

My eyes are on the road, but I feel the way she stiffens beside me.

"I do have a date, actually," she says. "It's not for another few weeks because he's traveling."

Is it Hunter or some other asshole at TSG? And, whoever this guy is, does he have any chance of being her fairy-tale prince? "What does he do?" I ask. It sounds more like a demand.

She shrugs. "He's a physicist in Molly's lab. I don't know much about him, but she says he's sweet."

I'm angry and relieved at once and I can't explain either of those emotions to myself. "That won't work for you," I say too quickly.

"Just out of curiosity, how are you so sure that a man you've never met won't work for me based *solely* on his occupation and the fact that he seems nice?"

Because you don't want candlelight and rose petals, though you clearly think you do.

You want someone so fucking eager to be inside you that he can't wait long enough to take you home, to light those candles or scatter rose petals.

You want someone who's going to devour you, who's going to sink to his knees and eat you out with your skirt bunched around your waist, who'll have you soaked before he finally bends you over a desk and pushes inside you.

You want someone who'll defend you with his life, but demand everything of you when you're alone.

And Jesus Christ, I want that person to be me—except I'd fail her. Anyone she winds up with will fail her occasionally. But me? I'd fail her all the time.

"Educated guess," I mutter. "Where's he taking you?"

She frowns at me. "He suggested Nobu. I guess there's something wrong with that too?"

"He's probably going to expect something, you know. You don't take a woman to Nobu and end it with a kiss on the cheek."

"Who's to say *I* won't want more than a kiss on the cheek?" she counters. "I've been single for months now and was unhappily married for the six years before it."

That angry thing in my chest tightens until it's hard to get a full breath. Is she really going to sleep with this douchebag just because it's been a few months? *Try going for a year without it, Lucie.* "You're the one insisting on the fairy tale. Sleeping with a guy on the first date hardly sounds like *that.*"

"And your point?" she asks, her arms folding.

I'm starting to piss her off and I *want* to piss her off. I want everyone in the fucking world to feel as angry as I do, though it's still not clear what I'm angry about. But I need to stop. I'm acting like a jealous ex rather than her friend/neighbor/boss, and it's time to rein it in.

"The kid who was all obsessed with Lord Devereaux probably wouldn't approve."

Her irritation gives way to a reluctant grin. "I can't believe you remember that."

I sigh, running a hand through my hair. "I don't forget much."

Which isn't true. I forget everything. But suddenly I've become photographic where she's concerned. I'm cataloging every laugh, every smile, every shared glance. Maybe because these are fleeting things, things that won't remain mine forever...and I'm really starting to wish they would.

24

LUCIE

Only a few hours after the lunch with Harrison, my car is unceremoniously left in my driveway and by the following Monday, Harrison has filed the paperwork for my divorce and begun negotiating an interim agreement so I'll finally get child support.

Fessman's office says they can't return my retainer—and that I've somehow already spent most of it. One phone call with Harrison has them agreeing to refund the entire thing. I have no idea what he said; I'm just happy things have turned around.

Work, too, is going well. The staff meeting was deemed a success and we're getting closer to that break room I want for the seventh floor. Using an online design program, I've created several potential layouts, which I assumed I'd just show to Caleb at the lake, but he's been missing in action ever since the day he introduced me to Harrison.

After nearly a week of silence on his end, I'm forced to schedule a meeting to show him the drawings. Somehow it makes the discussion seem more formal and intimidating, so I ask Molly to look them over first—she excels at finding the flaws in a plan as long as she's not its architect.

"Hello, my nearly divorced friend!" Molly cries as I walk up. We've met over lunch in the mall's very crowded food court, and every head nearby swivels at this announcement. "Let's celebrate by getting you some lingerie."

I laugh. "Let's celebrate by having you look at my break room layouts as discussed."

"Let's just *peek*," she says, continuing to pull me *away* from the food. "I guarantee you own nothing but Hanes for Women, and once you stop lusting after your boss and agree to sleep with Stuart, you'll realize what truly mattered today."

"I'm not lusting after my boss." My crush on him is so wrong and pointless that it *should* be true, if nothing else. "If you want to shop, that's fine, but be fast because I'm starving, and I *do* need you to look at my layouts."

"I'll look at them afterward. But seriously—only you could work with a million single dudes and pick the married one."

"I thought we agreed I was going to hold out for your future son Damien to rock my world. Did I misunderstand?"

She narrows her eyes. "I'm going to have a hard time naming you as his godmother if you keep making that joke."

We arrive in the lingerie department, where—surrounded by satin and lace and bras too sheer to be functional—I'm completely out of my depth. I was too young for lingerie when I met Jeremy, too innocent, and I was too busy for lingerie soon after that, with newborn twins taking up every free second.

Molly shoves a black lace thing at me that appears to be more straps than fabric. "Go try that on," she demands.

I roll my eyes before I spin to the mirror and hold it up against me. "I don't even know what this thing *is*. What's with all the straps?"

"Oh my God, it's like you're still thirteen years old," she says, looking at a teddy. "It's called a merry widow and those are garter straps. It's how you hold up your stockings. How do you not know this?"

"Maybe because people stopped needing to have their stockings held up just after World War Two," I reply, turning back toward her. "I don't wear—" My words die off mid-sentence. Because not ten feet from Molly is Caleb, looking every bit as wide-eyed as I am. "Caleb," I gasp. I clutch the merry widow more tightly against me, as if that will somehow make it disappear.

"That's some interesting shopping you're doing." His voice has dropped an octave, and his gaze falls to my chest.

Heat climbs up my neck and I press a hand to my cheek to stop it. His eyes follow, grazing over my skin in a way I swear I can feel. "It's not...my friend was—" I frantically glance around me, but Molly is nowhere to be found.

Goddammit, Molly.

"What are you doing in here?" he asks.

I raise a brow. "I'm a female in a store's lingerie section. I'm not the outlier. What are *you* doing here? And if you don't have a plausible explanation, I'll just assume it's your sex doll's birthday."

His mouth twitches. "Kimberly's birthday isn't until January. I'm getting something for my mom."

"What an interesting relationship you two must have." I turn to the rack of lingerie. "What's her size?"

He slaps a hand over his face. "She wants a *robe*, but thanks for putting that seriously uncomfortable image in my head." His eyes revert back to the black thing I'm still holding. "Shopping for the big date? If you're wearing that, he's not going to settle for second base."

I sigh. "If I'm wearing this, *I'm* the one who won't be settling for second base."

He runs a thumb over his lower lip, his nostrils flaring as if he's scented prey, his eyes liquid under the store's fluorescent lights. "So what exactly *are* you after when that's on?"

There's a trickle of delight in my chest. I don't wear lingerie like this, and I don't have the money for it even if I did, but suddenly I'm seeing myself through Caleb's eyes: as a woman who might wear a merry widow on a date. As a woman who might go in with some demands of her own. I grin. "Use your imagination."

He winces. "I am. That's the problem." There's a rasp in the words, something low and dark and tinged with yearning.

He walks away, broad-shouldered and glorious in that perfectly tailored suit, his words on replay in my head.

I am. That's the problem.

Those words—the rasp as he uttered them—pulse brightly inside me, deep in my core, so sharp it's almost painful.

Molly reappears, looking at his retreating form in the distance and then me with pure glee. "Oh my God. I take back everything I ever said about him being a creepy weirdo who's obsessed with his ex. Seduce him immediately. I want you to walk straight into his office, bend over his desk, and beg."

I roll my eyes. "It's interesting, the way you can suggest the boldest possible plan while failing to pursue your own boss in any manner whatsoever."

She glances off to where Caleb disappeared. "The difference is that *he* was two seconds from kissing you in the middle of the store. I'm serious, Lucie. Be bold. Give him the smallest encouragement and he'll fold like a deck of cards. The two of you were so hot."

I laugh. "That wasn't *heat*. That was the intense awkwardness of having your boss discover you with kinky, role-play shit during your lunch break."

"Believe me," says Molly with a small smile, "if I'm reading him correctly, he's going to be imagining you in that thing for a good, long time. With his dick in his hand."

~

THE NEXT DAY, I ask Caleb to meet me in the future break room so he can better visualize the plans as I show them to him. Molly found nothing objectionable, though she did offer several suggestions about surfaces upon which Caleb and I could have sex, leading me to conclude that once she wins over Michael, I'm never eating in her home again.

I'm in the room, waiting for Caleb, when she texts.

MOLLY
Go for it.

Go for what?

YOU KNOW WHAT I'M REFERRING TO. My God, he must be DYING after a year of celibacy too.

I swear I'm going to ignore what she's said, but when he walks up behind me just as I'm leaning over the table, trying to get the plans to lie flat...I'm thinking about it.

He's so tall. He's not even touching me, but I can feel him along my spine, my tailbone, the back of my thighs. I picture him wrapping one large hand around my hip, the brush of his breath against my ear as he tells me to stay bent over, just like I am.

"I've got it," he says gruffly, pinning the left corner of the plans down with my laptop.

I slide away, my face too hot, my breathing uneven.

"I'll try not to take up too much of your time," I begin. "I'd planned to just show you these at the lake, but we haven't seen you around."

He rubs his jaw, looking at the plans rather than me, though I suspect he's not really looking at *them* either. "It's been pretty busy," he says. "I found a little engine for Henry to take apart, though. I'll try to drop it off at some point."

It's kind of him, but I don't want him dropping things off. I want him hanging out with us, the way he was. He seemed to enjoy it.

"Thank you," I say quietly. "School gets out in early July—he'll need a project."

"He should learn to surf once school's done. He's the right age for it."

I glance up. I'm not sure if that was an offer or an offhand suggestion. "I've never surfed. I wouldn't have the first clue how to teach him."

He tugs at his collar. "I might be able to, if a little time opens up."

"You know Sophie will insist on coming too. There's no way she'd allow you to only teach Henry."

His smile is wistful, as if he misses her, misses *us*. "Well, if I can find time to teach one, I can probably teach two." He looks away, his face stern again. "No promises, though. Let's see these plans."

I move the layouts closer. "You can tell me you hate them. Not that you've ever been reticent about ripping someone's hard work to shreds."

"Why would I be?" he asks, leaning back in his seat. "It's one of the few perks of my position."

This is good. We're back to playing *grumpy asshole boss and reasonable employee*. It's normal and non-sexy and...well, it's still sexy, I guess, because I find Caleb-as-grumpy-asshole unbelievably hot, but at least it's familiar.

I rise, leaning over to indicate the upper lefthand wall of the room. "So, in the first option, we'd put a coffee bar here. And yes, they'll be paying for the coffee, and yes, I know we're not Google. It should completely cover its own costs."

I start to sit and then stop myself. "Oh, I almost forgot. Over here"—I lean over once more—"we'll have ping-pong and foosball."

"Cool," he says distractedly, but when I turn, his gaze isn't on the plans at all. It's on my ass. Molly would have any number of suggestions for things I should say right now. I'm just worried I sat on something, however.

"What's wrong?" I ask, running a hand over the back of my skirt.

He pulls at his tie as if it's strangling him. "I was wondering if you were wearing stockings. I noticed the garter thing yesterday and…Jesus, never mind. This isn't anything we need to discuss."

This is the opening I thought wouldn't occur. This is where I say *'maybe you should check,'* but I can't quite summon the courage.

"So you wondered if I was wearing it?" I ask.

"Like I said, this is nothing we need to discuss."

I could tell him the truth, which is that I wouldn't have the first clue how to hook up garters. But I sort of like the idea of him considering it. I lean over once more to pin down the corner of the plan. "Use your imagination," I reply.

"If you're so insistent on your fairy tale," he says between his teeth, "consider not bending over in front of me while suggesting I *use my imagination*."

For a second, I don't move a single muscle while I try to process what he just said. Until I realize there's only one conclusion to be drawn:

He wants me.

This isn't in my head. This isn't because I stumbled into him in a bikini. This isn't me persuading myself of something that isn't there. And I should straighten and make a joke, play it off.

But.

But.

I don't straighten. I don't move an inch. "Or *what*, Caleb?" I whisper. "What will you do if I keep bending over?"

I'm breathless, waiting to see what he does.

His chair scrapes the floor as he rises, and then his hand lands on my ass.

Not a brush of his fingers, not an accident. His whole, hot palm is on my ass, fingers spread wide as if desperate to cover as much ground as possible. His swallow is audible.

He's barely *touched* me, but there's already an ache between my thighs that borders on unbearable. I press into his hand, silently willing him to take more, do more, and suddenly he's gripping my hips, pulling me tight so that all I can feel is the very long, thick press of him against my ass.

"Lucie," he says, his voice a low growl, "be very careful with what you say to me. I have a lot less self-control than you think."

And then he walks away, and the door has slammed shut before I manage to collapse in a chair.

How did that happen?

How did Caleb—so single-mindedly focused on the company and his career—wind up letting go like that, and how did I wind up urging him to do it? I *need* this job. I need our working relationship to remain uncomplicated and friendly.

I guess that means we need to discuss what happened, but I have no idea what I'd say. If this was a movie starring Sandra Bullock or Reese Witherspoon, I'd confess that I've had a crush on him since I was six, that I came back to the lake once I turned twenty-one only to see him—unaware they'd moved—and met Jeremy instead.

But what good would that do? He's moving away and doesn't want kids or a relationship. Molly was right when she said he was a dead end.

I'll apologize.

It wasn't entirely my fault, but I'll apologize simply to set things right. I'll say, *'I'm sorry, I don't know what that was about, but I really value our friendship...can we pretend it didn't happen?'*

I put it off for the rest of the afternoon, and it's not until I'm leaving to pick up the twins that I veer toward his office.

"He left town," Kayleigh snarls at my back. I turn. Her face is as impassive as ever, but there's a small gleam in her eyes. I get the feeling she likes delivering disappointing news. "I'm surprised you didn't know."

I'm sick of Kayleigh's attitude and too disappointed about Caleb's absence to hide it. "Why *would* I know?"

Her mouth presses flat. "You're down here a lot."

"I've been in Caleb's office maybe five times since I started, which hardly seems excessive."

She shrugs. "If you say so."

Has my crush on Caleb been that obvious? Or has she simply picked up on something I'm only just realizing myself:

He wants me too.

25

LUCIE

One week later, I once again put on the green silk dress, the one that inexplicably seems to irritate Caleb, drop the kids at school, and head straight to San Francisco for the conference. My presentation isn't until noon, but Mark assumed I'd want to be here at ten for Caleb's opening panel and there was no subtle way to suggest that seeing Caleb before my presentation might do more harm than good. In the days that have passed since that afternoon in the break room, the incident has taken on a life of its own, looming larger in my head with every minute that passes. God, I wish we'd cleared the air before he left.

I valet park my car and head to the hotel lobby, clutching my bag and the new laptop that was delivered to my desk a week ago. The scene is far more chaotic than I anticipated: there are news crews and police, conference attendees and people who don't appear to be here for the conference at all but who are murmuring, their phones poised.

Caleb is standing with Mark, his gaze already on me, his brow furrowed. He sends Mark off and walks toward me, that worry never leaving his face. I expected him to finesse this, to act as if nothing's wrong. Instead, he's looking at me like I'm someone Mark was supposed to fire but did not.

God, is he going to fire me *here*?

He reaches me and places a hand on my elbow, moving me off to the side and out of earshot of people walking by.

He pinches the bridge of his nose before he speaks. "Your father is on his way," he says, his hand tightening around my arm as if I might need support. "He didn't announce it until this morning. He's going to be on my panel."

My brow furrows. It's so different from what I expected him to say that I can't quite make sense of the words. "Who?"

He moves to my side to shield me from the mob. "Your father. I have no idea what's going on...someone like your dad usually books these kinds of appearances months in advance. I just found out myself or I'd have warned you. You don't need to be here if you don't want to be."

My shoulders sag in relief. "Jesus, Caleb, you looked so worried. I thought you were going to fire me. I couldn't care less where he is."

"*Fire* you?" he repeats, jaw open. "Why the hell would I fire you?"

I shrug, ignoring the heat rushing to my cheeks. "You know."

He sighs. "Lucie, God. Of course I'm not firing you." He runs a hand over his face. "I'm sorry. This is so fucked up. I would never...I can move your supervision to Mark if that would make you more—"

I shake my head. "No. It's fine."

"We clearly need to talk, but...you're sure you're going to be okay?"

"As long as he doesn't come to my presentation, I don't care what he does."

He frowns. "I was wondering if maybe that's the reason he's here. Your presentation. Maybe he wants to see how you do."

A noise comes out of my throat, some combination of a laugh and a gasp. "He's had his entire life to see me. And as disastrous as my presentation is already going to be, I think I'd implode under the pressure if he came to this one."

"I don't think you need to worry," he says softly. "Just watching you attempt to set up a smart board is enough to make someone fall hard and fast."

I stare at him. Mark's walking toward us and I'm probably reading too much into it, again, but I'd really like him to elaborate.

"Caleb, you've got to go," Mark says, walking up beside me. "Lucie, we've got seats saved, but we'd better get in there. It's going to be standing room only."

Caleb hesitates, glancing at me once more before he leaves, and Mark leads me in the other direction, through a throng of people fighting to get into the auditorium.

"This is insane," he mutters, as people push past. "All because of Robert Underwood."

Inside, they're already lining the walls, sitting cross-legged in aisles, quietly gossiping about my half-siblings and their mother. And here I am, about to see my father in person for the first time in my life, and all I can think about is Caleb, the boy I might have grown up beside if I'd been allowed to leave the house.

Just watching you attempt to set up a smart board is enough to make someone fall hard and fast.

If my father hadn't denied my existence, maybe Caleb and I would have known each other well enough for him to say some version of that as a teenager or in college. In a world before there was a Kate, a Jeremy, he might have told me he was falling hard and fast, and I'd have said, *'I've loved you since I was six, so it's about time.'*

Most people go through their entire lives wondering where

their other half is. I'll go through the rest of mine knowing I found him but could never claim him as my own.

Caleb and my father enter the room along with the other panelists and the room quiets. My father gives Caleb a polite tip of the head. Caleb's eyes narrow in response and then he turns away, seeking me out in the crowd, making sure I'm okay.

The moderator leans toward his mic and poses a question about work-from-home, a concept Caleb loathes. I already know he'll be the only one up there who says, *'I'm not paying someone a full-time salary to play Call of Duty for six hours and answer a few calls",* just like I know my father will try to please both sides and wind up saying nothing worthwhile.

I used to watch my father's interviews and think he was this paragon of wisdom, with his perfect answers that made everyone feel heard, but today, all I can think as I listen is how *meaningless* his words are. How he doesn't say a single thing that reflects what he truly believes but is always selling you something...and selling it a little poorly, if you ask me. He's not as smart and suave as he thinks he is, and reminds me, uncomfortably enough, of my ex-husband. I don't want to look at that too closely.

By contrast, there's something blunt and forceful in the way Caleb answers a question—he sounds as if he'd rather not be there at all—and it has me squeezing my thighs together beneath the notepad in my lap. Caleb-as-grumpy-asshole could be its own fetish category, and I'd pay money just to watch him in action.

Toward the end, they're asked about work-life balance. *Robert* weighs in immediately because that's his whole schtick. *Family is everything. Values matter. Always make the responsible choice.* He manages to say it so convincingly that I sometimes wonder if he's just forgotten what he did.

"It's vital," he begins, and I roll my eyes. "My family is what's kept me grounded all these years and gives me the reason I do what I do. Fortunately, I'm quite lucky to have both my children doing it with me now."

I've heard him reference '*both*' his kids so many times that it no longer makes a dent, but Caleb's jaw is clenched. My phone, resting on my thigh, vibrates.

> CALEB
>
> I can set the record straight for everyone in this room. Just say the word.

I love that Caleb is willing to do that for me, consequences be damned, but I glance up and shake my head. I'd rather have people not realize my father has three kids than know he's so ashamed of one he wants to forget her existence.

When the panel concludes, the moderator steps up to the podium. "Before everyone leaves, please note that there's been a change to the schedule. 'Employee Fitness and Community Building,' in Ballroom A, has been cancelled. DeeDee Murray of Underwood Enterprises will discuss 'Empowering Women to Take Leadership Roles' in its place."

I stare at him, confused. *Employee Fitness* was *my* presentation. I look at Caleb...who appears just as dumbfounded as me.

"What the hell?" Mark asks. "They didn't tell you, did they? Because they sure didn't tell me."

"No," I whisper, relieved and disappointed at once. I didn't actually *want* to do the presentation, but it would have looked good on my resume, and I spent a lot of time getting ready for it.

We walk to the stage, where Caleb is talking to one of the conference planners. "That's not an answer," he snaps. "I want to know why the fuck it was cancelled and why she wasn't given any advance notice. This is absolutely unacceptable."

She looks toward me and then murmurs something to him, her eyes flickering toward me as she says it.

Caleb stiffens...and marches back toward the curtain my father disappeared behind seconds earlier.

"I have no idea what's happening," says Mark.

I nod in agreement, though I'm starting to put it together.

Because my session was mysteriously cancelled and replaced with a presentation by an *Underwood* employee, and Caleb just took off after Robert as if he's going to kick his ass.

My *father* told them to cancel me. It wasn't enough to erase my presence as a child. He's doing it here, in a professional setting. Maybe he was worried I'd mention him if given a public forum—does he not realize just how much more *public* this could get? My mother signed an NDA. *I* haven't signed shit. And sabotaging me professionally is *not* the way to keep me silent.

I run up the stage steps and push back the curtain just as Caleb's fist slams into Robert's face. The only thing keeping my father upright are the guys in suits behind him. I'm standing by Caleb's side when he finally looks back at us, and there's recognition in his eyes—which I guess makes sense given how much I resemble my mom.

This is a moment I've pictured a thousand times: the way he'd suddenly realize everything he gave up and the wave of remorse that would hit him afterward. But those were dreams I had as a kid, as a teen. I know they're not going to come true now, and more importantly...I no longer *care*. This asshole let me shuffle from apartments to trailer homes my entire fucking childhood, let me scrape around for scholarships and financial aid to get my degree, and today he cancelled my presentation.

Caleb was right. I didn't need to prove myself—I entered the world a better human than this man could ever be, and there's not an apology in the world that could induce me to forgive him now.

"I hope you have a good lawyer," my father says to Caleb

while he wipes blood from his face with his sleeve, "because I'm going to sue you until you've got nothing left."

That's when I laugh, the sound a surprise even to me. He's far stupider than I thought if he doesn't realize how very, very easily I could destroy his precious *"family is everything"* reputation with a few choice words. "The *responsible thing*," I snap, "would be to walk away as if this never happened. You wouldn't want us all putting out *our* version of events, would you?"

"I won't be bullied," he sneers.

"Oh, it's *you* who's been bullied?" I ask. "Are you sure? We'll see what the press thinks."

His mouth opens, ready to spout off another threat...and I stare him down. *I will tell the whole fucking world who I am and thus, who you are. And we both know you don't want that.*

Two tense, silent seconds pass before my father looks away. "He's not worth it," he says to the group with him. "Let's go."

"If there's any fallout from this," I add to his back, "any fallout whatsoever, we'll be providing our own *very detailed* account."

He stiffens, then continues walking. It's only when I turn to Caleb and see the frown on his face that I realize I'm shaking. I feel like I might pass out.

He places a firm hand on my hip. "I'm not attending the luncheon," he tells Mark, guiding me away.

"Caleb, you're getting an award," Mark calls from behind us.

"They should have thought about that before they cancelled Lucie's session," Caleb replies, leading me to the elevator doors.

"Where are we going?"

"Away from the crowd," he says. "You look like you're going to be sick."

We squeeze into the crowded elevator, and I stare at our reflections in the gold-plated doors—Caleb, tall and handsome and certain; me in front of him, small and safe with my back to his chest, his hand resting gently on my hip to make sure no one bumps me.

Jeremy used to promise he'd do anything for me, but they were mere words—he never defended me once—while Caleb not only defended me today but put everything at risk to do it. If word gets out that he hit Robert Underwood, it could definitely mess up the merger.

He says he doesn't want a commitment, that he doesn't want the responsibility...but he behaves like a man who already has them. And the longer I stare at the two of us in the elevator doors, the less it matters to me that he refuses to be the prince in my fairy tale, that we want different things. Because this is already more than I've had with anyone else, more than I will *ever* have with anyone else.

The bell for the fourteenth floor pings and he leads me off, using his keycard to open a spacious suite. "I'm so sorry, Lucie," he says, running a hand through his hair. "I'm sorry about what happened at work. I *am* going to make Mark your supervisor because I'm clearly in way over my—"

I grab his lapels, go onto my toes, and press my lips to his.

He's stiff, shocked, frozen.

It's the world's least romantic, most mortifying kiss. I let him go, an apology ready. "I'm—"

The next words die on my lips as his hands wrap around my waist.

"Fuck," he says quietly. "I always knew this dress would do me in." And then he kisses me, *hard*. With intent. As if he's waited a very, very long time to do exactly this. As if he's waited most of his life, the way I have.

There is so much of him and not enough all at the same time. His tongue is in my mouth, his scruff rough on my skin, his erection digging into my stomach. *More, more, more.* My arms circle his neck, clinging for support, making sure he stays close. His tongue moves over my neck as his thumb slides over my rib cage, climbing higher. I gasp as the tip of his index finger brushes the underside of my breast.

"If you're going to stop me," he growls, "do it now."

As if I could. There's no version of me strong enough to tell Caleb to stop at this point. "I'm not."

Beneath his palm, my nipple draws tight and he grunts low in his throat. "You're sure?"

I reach for his belt. "Very."

I always imagined this as some slow, romantic unfolding; our clothes removed one by one. Now I see how ridiculous that was. I don't want to watch him slowly undress. I want to grab a pair of scissors and cut his clothes away to make them disappear faster. I want my bare skin glued to his, to have him so embedded in me we can't be drawn apart.

I want it to happen as fast as we can possibly get there.

He pulls me to the bed. His weight presses me into the mattress. My dress is around my hips and I'm arching against him seeking friction, making him groan in my mouth as his hands slide beneath me to grab my ass. He lost the jacket and tie at some point and my fingers tug at the buttons of his oxford, unable to move fast enough.

He reaches to the neck and pulls it and the undershirt overhead, losing a button in the process and not appearing to care as he throws it behind him.

I place my hands on his chest and twenty years of past Lucies are just as amazed as the present one that this is happening. It's even better than the past me fantasized about—his skin is smoother, his stomach harder, his nostrils flaring as if his self-restraint has already been pushed too far.

"I've thought about fucking you in this goddamn dress more times than I can count," he growls, pushing it farther up my hips, looking me over like a feast he's about to devour, "and now I just want it off."

He undoes the zipper, his fingers trailing over my spine as

he pulls the dress down past my hips and lower, tossing it behind him to join his shirt somewhere on the floor. His mouth covers the lace of my bra, sucking hard until it draws into a tight point, while his hand slips beneath my panties. "God, you're so wet already."

"It's been a while." I tug at the button of his pants and reach inside. When my palm moves over his tented boxers, air hisses between his teeth.

"I guarantee it's been longer for me," he grunts. "You'd better not...This will be over in seconds if you do that."

Let it be over in seconds and then we'll do it again. Let it be over in seconds that time too. I don't want to sleep. I don't want to do anything but this, again and again.

He unhooks my bra. I instinctively start to cross my arms— another insecurity Jeremy left behind—and he stops me.

"Don't," he demands. "My God. Don't cover anything. You're perfect."

His lips lower to pull on one nipple while he tugs the panties off, and then he slips a finger inside me. "So tight," he mutters, more to himself than me. "Jesus. I'm not going to survive this."

He starts to slide down the bed, and as he pushes my legs apart, I place a hand on his shoulder. "Not that," I whisper. "Come back up."

"Lucie, I've been dreaming about this for months," he says, his breath hot against my swollen clit. "Let me."

There's a part of me that wants him to, a part of me that's dying to feel the flick of his tongue, the press of his lips. But it's soured by the memory of Jeremy, again. Jeremy and his complaints. Jeremy suggesting I get a breast reduction every time he saw me naked, saying my C-section scar was gross. Jeremy telling me *'most women'* come in a minute or two and that he didn't understand why it took me so long. Jeremy saying he wasn't going to waste his time going down on me if it wasn't going to work anyway.

"I'm not gonna—" I stammer. "I don't finish that way. Just come up."

He slowly moves north, his mouth touching every inch he passes. "What do you like, then?"

Is there anything less exciting than a woman who says, *'I almost never finish—don't worry about me'*? I doubt it. I bet Kate doesn't say that.

I hitch a shoulder. "Do what you were doing before," I reply.

His fingers move over my clit and slip inside me.

The pleasure is so intense that my eyes fall closed, my hips arching upward.

"That's it," he says softly. "Show me what you like."

"That," I inhale. "Just like that."

I reach into his boxers again and this time he doesn't stop me. "God, yes," he grunts.

My palm slides over him once, and again. My thumb circles around the head of his cock, leaking for me already.

Dust motes dance in the sunlight and I'm inhaling the smell of him, huge lungfuls of it, and at the same time my body is tightening and unspooling at once, noticing less. Time seems to be moving faster and faster, until there is nothing left but his fingers inside me and his mouth on my neck and the feel of his cock beneath my palm.

His breath stutters as I continue. "I—" he begins, flinching. "Oh fuck, Lucie. Slow down. I'm—"

He's close. He's already close. The desperation in his voice...That's what sends me hurtling right over the edge. I cry out, releasing him entirely as I ride his hand, nothing but liquid, blinding heat.

When my eyes open, he's watching me, nostrils flaring. He

wraps a hand around his cock and gives it a hard squeeze as if he's in pain.

"Tell me what you want," I demand. It barely sounds like my voice. It's low and raspy, certain.

"Mouth," he groans. "Use your mouth. I'm not going to last."

I push him to his back and crawl down his chest. He inhales sharply as I take him between my lips.

He's big. It's almost uncomfortable, but the anticipation of what he'd feel like inside me already has me clenching on air. My tongue swirls over the swollen head and he gasps, his body rigid, his fingers pressing to my scalp. I slide him all the way back to my throat and let him feel the way I struggle to maneuver. I swallow, and he feels that too. "Fuck," he hisses, so I do it again.

"I'm gonna come," he grunts in warning, trying to lift me off of him. I tighten my grip, sucking in my cheeks. "Oh God, Lucie. Fuck." He explodes down my throat with a low groan, his fingers tangled in my hair.

I swallow, and swallow, waiting until the tension finally leaves his thighs and his hand falls to his side before I release him.

"Holy shit," he gasps, placing a palm over his face. "Jesus, Lucie. Everything I own is yours if you promise to do that again."

I laugh, climbing up and pressing my lips to his neck. "I'm no expert, but I think you're supposed to offer a financial incentive *before* the girl blows you, not after."

He grins. "I would have. I just didn't expect that level of motor control, having watched you struggle with the smart board so many times."

I elbow him. "Two seconds after you've blown your load and you're already criticizing my job performance."

His hand tightens on my hip and he raises a brow. "That

was surprisingly filthy from your G-rated little mouth." He releases me and starts sliding down the bed. He pushes at the inside of my thighs. "Open."

"Caleb—"

"I'm not doing this because I want you to come," he says, as his tongue flicks against my clit. "I'm doing it because it's going to get me rock-hard in about ten seconds."

His tongue flicks again, a sharp, sudden movement that has me jolting in surprise. He moans against my skin, sucking hard and then pulling back. "Jesus, I think I could come from this alone. Make that noise again."

His tongue resumes and it's...good. It's really good. It's not *I'm-just-putting-up-with-this-until-you-move-on* good. It's *I-know-it's-selfish-but-do-that-for-one-more-minute* good.

He slides two fingers inside me, hitting something I didn't know was there, but if it was possible, I'd like to keep his fingers where they are forever—and then he pulls out and does it again. All while his tongue flickers and he makes those noises, as if it's my tongue on *him*, and if he were a robot or a device—something incapable of boredom—I'd let him keep going. "Are you ready?" I plead. "I want you inside me."

That's all it takes for him to move, lightning quick, above me. "Do I need—" he begins.

"No," I say, breathless in my haste. "I've been tested. Pill."

"Thank God, since I don't have anything." He guides himself to my entrance and, with tortuous care, slowly pushes in, no more than an inch. "Jesus, Lucie," he gasps, "you're so fucking tight."

He stops. Swallows. Begins again.

My knees drop open, wanting more even when I know he's going slowly on my behalf, even when the pleasure is accompanied by an edge of discomfort. "More," I plead.

"Oh, God," he says, his jaw clenched. "Don't beg. It'll be over before it's started."

But he gives in at last with a single hard thrust, groaning quietly as he finally bottoms out.

I'm so full, stretched to the point of pain, and I can already tell that I'm going to come again and that when it happens, it'll be beyond anything I've ever experienced. *I wasn't broken*, some stunned voice in my head whispers. *I was never broken. It was just never like this.*

"Am I hurting you?" he asks. He's sweating, though the room is cool. He looks like *he's* the one in pain. "I...it was as slow as I could go."

"No," I whisper, my head falling back, my whole body straining to spread, to take more. "It was a good gasp."

"Oh, God." His hand runs over me, beginning at my neck, running past my breast. "Look at you like this. It's so perfect."

He drags out slowly and pushes back in. His palm grasps my breast, and he leans over to take my nipple between his teeth. "It's so good with you," he murmurs. "I fucking knew it would be."

My muscles begin to clench and clamp down on him against my will. His fingers press into my skin, his tendons strain. A drop of sweat lands on my breast and he licks it off.

"More," I whisper, and he groans.

"It's been too long, Lucie. I'm gonna come if I go any faster." He pulls almost all the way out, then thrusts back in, hard and fast, only twice.

"Do it anyway." My voice is pleading—not my own. My heels dig into his ass, forcing him to move.

He curses as he gives in, rutting into me. I clench around him, overtaken again by that blinding liquid heat and I cling to him through one wave after another as if I'm drowning.

When my eyes finally open, he's looking at me through heavy lids, as if drugged. "Lucie," he says, and his lids fall shut again. He's still hard, still inside me. He pulses softly in and out. "I don't ever want to stop doing this."

I hold out my arms. "Come here," I command, and he does, letting his weight rest atop mine briefly before he falls to my side and pulls me to his chest.

I breathe in, wishing there was some way to preserve this moment—his smell, his arm wrapped around me.

I love you. I have always loved you.

I silence the thought before it can escape. Nothing could ruin this faster than saying *that* to a guy you aren't even dating —a guy who has no clue that you've adored him since you were small. A guy who's moving away.

"Conferences are a lot more fun than I expected," I tell him instead.

"I've got to say this isn't what I pictured." He laughs. "Okay, that's not true. I pictured this outcome repeatedly. I just didn't think it would actually occur."

"The fact that you got a hotel room leads me to wonder if you were at least a *little* optimistic it would occur."

He turns me, pulling my back to his chest. "I'm leaving for Tokyo in the morning. There was no reason to drive back to Elliott Springs."

I grow still. He's gone as often as he's home, and it's one of the reasons he will never want the things I do: because he's decided his career and a family are incompatible.

"I'm sorry," he says, moving my hair away from my neck so he can press his mouth to my skin. "I wish—"

He lets the thought trail off, but he didn't need to complete it. He wishes it was different. He wishes we wanted the same things.

"It's okay," I reply. "You don't need to apologize. It answered some questions."

"Questions?" His lips graze the shoulder I raise.

"I wanted to know what it would be like to sleep with someone other than Jeremy. He used to imply that there was something wrong with me. Because I didn't finish." I laugh. "It's pretty clear that the problem wasn't *me*."

"Ah," he says, his voice playful and unhappy at the same time. "So now you can go out in the world, free to pursue your orgasm-heavy fairy tale."

The words twist around my heart and give it a tight squeeze. "Precisely."

The room falls silent, and this is all so new to me that I'm not sure what happens next. I've never had a one-night stand *or* a one-afternoon stand. I've never gone to someone's hotel room. *Am I supposed to leave, now? He probably needs to get back to the—*

"Lucie?" he asks, his voice quiet against my ear, his cock—hardening again—pressed to my ass.

Ah, thank God. He doesn't want me to leave.

I push backward, a silent *'yes, by all means,'* and he slips a hand between my legs, fingering me until I'm begging him to get inside me. He does, at last, and my eyes fall closed as I give in to the pleasure.

It's slower this time, leisurely, but the consistent pace is already pushing me reliably toward yet another orgasm.

His hand slides over my ribs to grasp a breast, then down to circle my clit. I reach behind me, wrapping a hand around his neck, wanting him to stay near. He continues to thrust and circle, and just as I'm about to tell him to slow down, I realize it's too late.

"I'm close," I gasp. "Fuck. I'm too close."

His groan is against my ear, his breathing labored. His finger circles faster; his teeth sink into my shoulder. I come apart and so does he, pressing me tight to him as his chest rises and falls too fast.

I had no idea that sex could be...this. That I could come so easily and want to do it all over again the instant I'm done, that it could make me feel closer to someone than I already did.

I'm sure it's not as much of a revelation for him, but it's hard to imagine this isn't special. Surely sex this good isn't the norm for everyone all the time?

His breathing grows even, and I start to drift off. God, what I'd give to just stay here and fall asleep beside him.

"I should go," I say groggily. "I need to be out of town before rush hour."

I start to sit up and he pulls me back to him, kissing me hard, with his hand on my jaw. If I didn't have my kids, I'd stay here forever. I'd spend the rest of my life in this commitment-free no-mans-land, hoping I could change his mind.

He releases me and our eyes lock. I want to say something, but the words are all caught in my throat and I'm worried that if I start to say them, I'll burst into tears. Because this was the best afternoon of my life, but it's hard to say that aloud knowing it's over and will never happen again.

26

CALEB

My scotch is down to ice. The airline attendant gives me a refill without raising a brow at the fact that it's my second one. I wouldn't be so generous in her shoes, given we're only in the first hour of an eleven-hour flight.

HARRISON

Mark said you and Lucie went to your hotel room yesterday in the middle of the conference.

She was upset. She needed a break. That's all.

It's fascinating how different companies operate. I don't think I've ever suggested an employee take a break in MY hotel room.

If you and Lucie are going to continue taking a "break," make sure you don't text about it. I bet her husband's watching her phone somehow, and we still don't even know that Kate's gotten the papers, which could bite you in the ass.

I groan. Fuck. Fuck me and my fucked-up decision-making. Fuck me and my insane lack of self-control.

I knew it was a mistake with Lucie, but it was like throwing the first punch in a fight—I did it because I no longer cared about the consequences. Because even if it caused more problems than it solved, in that moment, nothing mattered more than kissing her, than ending the torment of wanting her day in and day out for fucking months.

As if it was ever going to end the torment.

Lucie isn't a meal you eat because you're hungry. She's exotically wrapped candy that leaves you hungrier than you started. It's been less than a day since she was in my bed and I'm already fucking ravenous.

I need weeks, months of her to get full. I need a year of her clenching around me as I drive inside her. I need a decade of that stunned inhale as I bury my head between her legs, a century of her looking up under long lashes as she takes my cock in her mouth.

It's midnight back home when we land, early evening in Tokyo. I should simply be relieved there was no fall-out from the incident with Robert Underwood, but instead I'm thinking about Lucie, just like I did last night, as I laid awake for hours, trying to make an impossible situation possible.

My host drives me to Nobu for dinner. Fucking Nobu—the exact fucking restaurant that guy plans to take Lucie to. You can't get out of here for less than a hundred and fifty a person, yet they are going on a first date.

If it doesn't work out with him, I'm sure Wyatt will offer her the moon in his place. God knows he probably *could* offer her the moon with as much as I pay him.

I glance at my watch. California is seventeen hours behind. She's sound asleep by now, and while *I'm* asleep, she'll be heading into the office, where another guy has a clear path in my absence.

God, what the hell was I thinking, leaving her there to be wooed by some asshole who'll tell her anything she wants to hear: *I love kids, Lucie. I can't wait to take mine to Disney. I'd love to take yours to Disney. When can I meet them?*

I pick up my phone, ready to text. *Don't go out with Wyatt, Lucie,* I'll say. *He's a dick.*

Except...who's worse? Wyatt, the guy who could potentially give her all the things she wants from life or me, the guy who can't offer her a single fucking thing, but would gladly take from her until there was nothing left?

I put the phone down. I'm not texting her. I'm not going back early. I'm staying here to do my fucking job and praying that sometime between now and the flight home on Friday, I get my shit straight.

I MAKE IT TO THURSDAY. It's been nearly a week since I've seen her.

A week since she begged for more when I was doing my level best not to come; a week since she deep-throated me as if she was hungry for it, as if there was nothing she wanted more than my cock in her mouth.

Jesus, I've heard her say '*more*' a thousand times in my head now. I've relived all of it a thousand times: pushing her dress around her hips, sliding my fingers under the elastic of her panties to discover she was absolutely *soaked* and...

Fuck.

A week away hasn't done a goddamn thing. I want her just as much as I did.

I give up and cancel every meeting. To return to a girl I can't keep for myself.

27

LUCIE

I t was hard to breathe when I left Caleb's room, and a week later—waiting on my lunch at the deli down the street from the office—it's still hard to breathe.

I knew what I was signing on for when I slept with him, but it's as if I've lost something, and the ache from it is nearly palpable. It's as if I've lost *everything*, and now the normal bullshit I deal with every day feels as if it's simply too much. Jeremy's texts are too much. The downstairs toilet flooding is too much. The twins' hopeful little faces as they glance toward Caleb's house are way, *way* too much.

Molly's on the other line while I wait for my order, spelling out her latest Michael-focused plan, one she prefaced with *"It's perfect. I just need someone to kidnap me."*

"Molly, don't you think he'd call the cops if he thought you were locked in a shipping container?" I ask when she concludes.

"Not if time was of the essence. But where am I going to find a kidnapper?"

"Dark web?" I suggest. "That was a joke. For the love of God, do not go on the dark web if that's something you know how to do."

"Of course I know how. I've got a hundred and sixty IQ, which you would not guess based on my driving ability. I knocked the side-view mirror off my car in the garage this morning, by the way, so can you drive tonight? And wear something sexy. Something that shows a lot of cleavage."

Molly has insisted that I need to 'get back out there' while the twins are celebrating their grandfather's birthday tonight. I guess it's better than staying home alone, reliving that afternoon in a hotel room, an afternoon against which nothing could ever compare, but I was sort of hoping she'd cancel.

"Fine, but *you'd* better be wearing something that shows a lot of—"

There's a tap on my shoulder and I discover Wyatt standing behind me and not appearing to care that I'm on the phone, which doesn't win him any points. "Let me call you back," I tell her.

"It's cool. I'll just be over here on the dark web looking up mercenaries."

I laugh as I drop the phone in my purse and turn to Wyatt.

"I've been hoping I'd run into you down here," he says, "but you never eat lunch out."

"I don't, but my kids got in the way this morning, so I couldn't pack anything. How are you?"

"That depends," he says with another unmuted grin. "Are you ready to go out with me yet?"

I cancelled on Stuart already because of Caleb, and Wyatt appeals even less. I probably need to move on, but I'm not ready.

He grins. "What if we don't call it a date? What if it's, like, the prologue to a date?"

I grab my to-go container as it appears in the window. "That still sounds like a date."

"Here's why you should go on a prologue to a date with me," he says, holding the door. "A. I'm fun. B. I'm very hot. C. I have superior bedroom skills."

I raise a brow. "Would that matter on a *prologue* to a date?"

"Just thought I'd try to slide it in there," he replies, as the building comes into view. "But I promise if you go on the date prologue, I won't try to *slide in* anything else."

I groan. He's a nice guy, I guess, but even his friendly over-tures are a little pushy. I can't imagine what he'd be like on a date. "I appreciate the reassurance. I'm not sure I'm ready."

"Then hang out with me as friends," he says. "We can...*shit*."

I follow his gaze. Caleb is just ahead of us, exiting his truck. My stomach drops to my feet. He's so lovely, even when he's scowling at me like he is now.

"We've poked the bear," Wyatt says under his breath.

I glance at him. "What do you mean?"

He shrugs. "I get the sense that Caleb is pretty protective of you. After that staff meeting, when I put my arm around your shoulders? I had to watch a video on sexual harassment."

My mouth falls open. "You've got to be kidding me."

He gives a short, unhappy laugh. "I wish I was. A hundred bucks says I have to watch a video about fraternization next."

"Is there a rule against fraternization?"

He glances at Caleb, who's marching toward the office as if he's about to lay siege to it. "If there's not, I bet there's about to be. I'm so done with this job. Caleb's had a screw loose ever since his wife left."

I shouldn't ask. I shouldn't ask. There's nothing I'm going to learn that will make me feel better. "Did you ever meet her?"

Oops.

"Oh yeah," he says. "Hard to forget Kate. No idea what she was doing with Caleb."

The admiration in his voice is like a hard pinch. I should

change the subject, because anything I learn will only make me feel worse. "Oh? She was pretty?"

He laughs. "Kate's a knockout. The guy's probably a million-aire so that part isn't surprising, but she's also fun and fucking brilliant. She could have had anyone, so why him?"

I can think of a thousand reasons why she'd have chosen him, personally.

I return to my cubicle and have just opened my to-go container when I get a call from Mark, who informed me earlier in the week that he's now my supervisor, though he didn't appear to be clear on *why*. "Can you come down to my office?" he asks. "We're talking about a policy change, and I wanted your opinion."

I close the container and head to the executive office suite. Mark's door is ajar, and Caleb is sitting on the couch, legs spread wide, jaw clenched.

God. Even the way he *sits* makes me hot and loose-limbed. I want to kick Mark out of his own office and climb in Caleb's lap, knees planted on either side of his hips.

"What's up?" I ask, addressing the question to Mark.

Step one of getting over Caleb probably involves not looking at Caleb like he's the reason I wake in the morning.

"We were hoping to get some input from you," Mark says, though it's evident from the scoffing sound Caleb makes that *we* does not include him. "Caleb's brought forth a proposed change to our company policies that we are not in agreement on. I thought you, as the person in charge of company morale, might want to weigh in."

"That won't be necessary," says Caleb, his voice a low rumble. "I'm sure Lucie has better things to do."

I stiffen. "What policies?"

"Caleb's proposing we institute some new rules regarding fraternization."

What the fuck? Because he saw me *walking through the parking lot* with Wyatt? The timing cannot be coincidental.

"Fraternization," I repeat flatly.

"Workplace dating," Mark amends.

"I know what it means." I level Caleb with a look. "But I'm not familiar with the company's policy."

"Currently, we don't have any regulations about it," Mark says, "aside from requiring employees to disclose relationships. But Caleb is proposing that we just forbid it entirely."

I'm still staring at Caleb. I can't *believe* he's taken it this far. I want to punch him in his smug, lovely face.

"That seems pretty draconian," I reply. "And in terms of employee morale, that's hardly the direction you want to go in."

"I want my employees focused on their jobs," Caleb says, nostrils flaring. "Not trying to get the hot girl down the hall in bed."

I stare. He is very clearly talking about Wyatt and me. He's not even trying to pretend he isn't. What a fucking hypocrite.

Mark rises. "Okay, this is getting a little more heated than I intended it to. Caleb, you haven't slept in two days. Let's give everyone the weekend to think before we make any decisions."

Caleb walks out, and I follow him straight into his office. "May I speak to you for a moment?" I ask between my teeth.

His jaw sets hard as he turns toward me. "About what?"

"For God's sake, Caleb—this isn't some generic worry about fraternization. You've been at this company for seven years, but suddenly, after seeing me with Wyatt, you're trying to change the policy so people can't date? There's not a chance in hell you just happened to—"

His hands go to my hips and suddenly my back is against the wall and he's standing so close that his exhale brushes my forehead, his chest rising and falling more quickly than normal.

His eyes are on my mouth. "I. Shouldn't. Have. To. Fucking. Watch. It. Happen."

Before I can reply, before I can even process it...he's gone, walking out the front doors of his own building to escape me.

~

"Maybe I should have said *yes* to Wyatt," I tell Molly, draining the last of my wine.

It's been seven hours since Caleb pushed me to the wall, and I'm just as mad now as I was then.

No, actually, I'm angrier. If he doesn't want me, that's fine. If he wants me but refuses to go for it, that's okay too. But it's not okay for him to stand in my way simply because it *bothers* him.

"Of course you should have said yes," Molly says, signaling to the waiter for our check.

I reach for my credit card. "That's funny because I don't see you saying *yes* to anyone. Those guys who offered to buy us a round, for instance."

She flicks a hand in the air, dismissing the idea. "I'm offended by the suggestion that I need a man to buy my drinks. I make more money than either of those assholes. But anyway, Caleb, as ridiculously hot as he is, is a dead end. And when you reach a dead end, it won't do you any good to just sit there, honking your horn."

I smile. "Is that what you're doing with Michael? Sitting there honking your horn? Because it seems to me you're simply idling one street away, hidden from view."

She narrows her eyes at me. "I'm still working out how *best* to honk my horn, and Michael is not a dead end. He's simply a superhot multimillionaire who doesn't yet realize he's meant to settle down with me."

"I can't believe you've been there for two years and I've never even seen this guy."

"Picture Christian Grey, but smarter and better looking."

I bite my lip. "Guys like Christian Grey only settle down in books, Molly. Real-life Christian Greys marry a model and cheat on her until they're ready to marry a new model."

"I believe you're describing your father," she says, "and Michael isn't like that."

I worry that he's just a story she tells herself because it's easier than risking something in real life, but there's not much I can say. Especially when Caleb may just be a story I'm telling myself too.

We leave the bar in our sexy dresses without having said much to anyone but our waiter.

It's pouring rain outside, lightning flashing through the sky so close that we both scream as we run to the car.

"This was stupid," Molly says, cranking the heat once we're inside.

"Going out in this weather?"

She shakes her head. "Going out at all. You're in as deep as I am. Neither of us wanted to meet anyone."

Yeah. And I'm not sure how we move past it.

I navigate around broken tree limbs the whole way to Molly's condo and wait until she's safely inside before I turn back toward the lake—where every light in the neighborhood is out. I want a hot shower in the worst way, but I'm not taking one by candlelight in an otherwise empty house.

I run inside, using my phone's flashlight to make my way to the kitchen. I've just located a candle and matches when a knock on the door makes me jump.

That knock is so much creepier with the power out than it would be otherwise.

I struggle to get the candle lit and the knocking starts up again, louder and more impatient.

When I reach the door and look through the peephole, I discover Caleb standing in the pouring rain with his arms folded across his chest. He isn't forgiven, but I'm also not going to leave him out there getting soaked. I open the door and move aside to let him in.

"I saw your car pull up," he says, pushing his hair off his forehead. His eyes fall to my dress. "I was just checking to make sure you guys didn't need anything."

It was sweet of him to check. I'm already softening against my will.

"The kids are gone," I reply.

His eyes go back to the dress. "Were you on a date?"

Scratch that. I am no longer softening.

"Instead of asking about dates, you should be apologizing for this afternoon."

His eyes narrow. "Apologizing? Why the fuck would I apologize? I'm doing my best to let you go after your fairy tale and you're...throwing it in my face."

I let my head fall to the wall behind me. "I was walking back from the deli, for God's sake. How is *that* throwing anything in your face?"

His jaw locks. His eyes drift over me again. "Was it a date or not? Based on the dress, I assume you've got the garter thing on under there."

"Don't you wish you knew?" I ask bitterly.

"Yeah," he says, stepping close. "I do."

He's so near that all I can see without craning my neck is the uneven rise and fall of his chest. I want—more than I've ever wanted anything—to simply ignore how fucked up and pointless this is. I want to pull him upstairs and pretend that it will somehow be okay. But it won't. I've been miserable, barely hanging on, and I've got two children who need all of me and not some sad shell feigning happiness.

"Caleb, I can't do this," I whisper. "It's too hard to get over you and I don't want to start back where I was a week ago."

"I don't want you to get over me." He moves closer, until his body is pressed to mine, his breath rustling my hair. His skin is damp from the rain, but he is warm and solid and the smell of his soap makes it hard to focus. "Because I already know I can't get over you. Believe me—I've tried."

I swallow hard and shake my head. "I—"

"I want this. I want it too much not to ask you to give me a chance. I don't know that I'll ever be what you guys need, but...please let me fucking try."

Offering to *try* wouldn't be good enough, except...I've seen him with the twins. He cares about them more than he wants to admit and maybe he just needs to see firsthand that those commitments he doesn't want to make aren't so daunting. That he had a very bad break once upon a time, but it doesn't have to ruin the rest of his life.

And I *can't* walk away without discovering what we could become. I can't.

I raise my chin toward him, and he takes it for the permission it is. His mouth lands on my mine, his five-o-clock shadow rough against my skin.

My hands go to his waistband, and his small intake of breath—eager, *masculine*—banishes the last whispers of worry. His fear of commitment, his imminent move...those are problems for another day.

He tugs me tight against him, his cock hard and jutting against my stomach, lips pressed to my neck, and I am suddenly burning alive. I need out of this dress; I need him out of the t-shirt and sweats. I'm dying to feel his bare skin on mine. "God, Caleb...can we go upstairs? Like...*now*?"

In a second flat, he's got me in the air with my legs wrapped around his waist, carrying me toward the staircase with one hand and grabbing the candle with the other.

He reaches the top of the stairs and turns, heading straight to my room.

"How did you know where to go?" I ask as he kicks my door open.

He sets the candle on the dresser and tosses me on the mattress, climbing on the bed after me.

"You think I don't know which room is yours?" he asks, leaning down until our noses are a millimeter apart. "My day doesn't end until I see your bedroom light go out."

I smile. Caleb's been watching my house just as carefully as I've been watching his.

He kisses me again—soft lower lip, unshaved jaw—and his hands move to the hem of my dress.

"I'm not wearing the garter thing," I gasp.

"Good," he says, his palm running up the back of my thigh. "God, that would have pissed me off if you'd worn it for someone else."

He pulls me firmly to that bulge straining between us, and then he leans back on his knees, his mouth wet and open as he looks me over.

"Jesus Christ, this dress pissed me off when I walked in." He gives me a sheepish grin. "I actually *was* going to apologize until I saw the fucking dress."

I laugh. "Maybe you should remove it then."

He gives me a half-smile, tugging his t-shirt overhead before he pushes the dress around my hips. "Now that I know you weren't wearing it for someone else, I sort of want you to keep it on."

He pulls my panties down and sweeps his tongue between my legs.

"Ah," I gasp, arching. "You don't have—"

He laughs against my skin. "Yes, Lucie. *I don't have to. You're not going to come.* I'm not doing any of this for you, I promise."

I almost believe him, and it's freeing. Without the pressure to perform, to do this right, all I have to do is experience it. I've got little basis for comparison, but I'd be willing to stake my life on the fact that no other man alive has Caleb's mastery of this —the pressure of his fingers pushing inside me, the tip of his tongue flicking along my swollen clit then breaking to sweep over me in long, lathing strokes.

I might even be able to come this way, if it went on long enough. But if I let him keep going, he'll get his hopes up about it and then it wouldn't work and he'd be disappointed. He's got to be getting tired of it anyway. "Come up here," I plead.

He takes one last taste and then slides up, thrusting inside me without warning.

"God," he groans. "I'm—already close. Don't move."

"It's okay," I urge. "Just...please."

"Hearing you beg is not helping the situation," he hisses. But he starts to push in and out, his jaw locked tight as he reins himself in. He tugs the dress and bra down to bare my breasts, looking me over with smug satisfaction on his face, thrusting harder and harder as my eyes fall closed, as I start to arch and gasp and plead. And when I finally go over the edge, he follows, groaning into my neck.

"Lucie," he whispers, my name slurred with fatigue. "Haven't slept yet. Too worried."

I wrap my arms around him, and within seconds his weight settles, his mouth still on my neck. He's already asleep. And he's smiling.

The spring breeze blows through the curtains while I marvel at the way this evening worked out, the way my *life* is working out. I've never considered myself especially lucky, but is that true? I think, perhaps, it's not.

Caleb lands on the pillow beside me and reaches for me without opening his eyes once. I'm lulled to sleep by his even breathing, his warm chest, and my dreams are so vivid that they seem entirely real.

I dream Caleb and I are in his office building that crib I saw, that we're both in my aunt's boat when a woman starts swimming alongside us, a woman I somehow know is Kate.

And then I dream about Caleb pushing my legs apart. I dream of his tongue, the tiny, electric flickers of pleasure he elicits with it, his fingers inside me, the wet sounds of my pleasure. I would normally tell him to stop at this point— *It's not going to work, you're wasting your time*—but I'm dreaming, so what does it matter? I can let him go as long as I want. The pressure grows and I want a few more seconds, and a few more after that. I slide my hand into his hair and pull, demanding more.

"Fuck yes," he hisses. I wake—I'm not dreaming after all.

"Caleb—" I whisper.

He pushes his fingers inside me again, more forcefully this time, and I mean to repeat my normal warnings except...I'm strung so tight that I no longer have the air to speak. He does it again, his tongue still flickering, and there's a sharp pulse in my belly, the muscles contracting hard. I cry out, and even as some distant part of my brain still wants to insist to him that I won't finish...I am.

The world goes black and explodes while his tongue and fingers move faster, harder, never letting up until my body goes slack beneath him.

"Oh my God." I'm breathless and really can't come up with any other words. My eyes open to stare at him in astonishment. "Oh my God."

I expect him to laugh, to say *I told you so*, but he does not. He climbs up, looms over me, his face feral and desperate. "Are you ready for me?" he growls, and when I nod, he guides himself in, one hand pressed to the bed beside me, his groan drowning out my own.

∿

He leaves at daybreak for the office, and the next time I wake, the world has never been more beautiful. The lake has never shimmered as much as it is, the breeze through the window has never been more pleasant, life has never seemed this hopeful.

The twins arrive, and as my arms wrap around them, I'd swear nothing can dim my joy—until Jeremy's shadow looms over us.

"What did you do last night?" he demands.

I feel...conspicuous. My lips are still kiss-swollen, my entire body deliciously well-used. *Does some trace of Caleb remain?* I have to resist the urge to wipe my mouth, to check my neck for bruises.

I climb to my feet. "*What?*"

"Did I stutter?" he asks. "What. Did. You. Do. Last. Night?"

I place my hands on the twins' heads. "Guys, run inside while I talk to your dad."

I wait until I've seen them go inside before I reply.

"If you have something you want to address with me," I tell him, "don't do it in front of the twins."

"Or what? You'll run and cry to your lawyer? Good luck with that."

"They shouldn't have to witness us arguing. I'm asking this on their behalf, not mine."

"And I'm asking their mother not to look like a fucking whore when I drop the kids off to her in the morning. Also on their behalf."

I turn away, ending the conversation, but the rage in his eyes has my heart beating hard.

He seems to know something, and I'm not sure what it is, but the more important question is how he'd know it. He's never been inside the house, so I doubt he's placed a camera somewhere. Harrison warned me a week ago to be careful what I said via text in case Jeremy was monitoring my phone, but it's not as if Caleb or I knew last night would unfold the way it did, much less text about it.

I wish I could call Caleb and ask him, but…I'm still not sure what we are, exactly. He said he would *try*. Does that make him my boyfriend or simply a guy who's open to the possibility? Does that mean it's okay for me to text him when he's at work, or is that a step too far? All relationships are ill-defined at the start, but the fact that he's moving this fall makes it a little harder than it would have been.

The day passes in silence. The kids are already in bed and I'm shutting off the lights when there's a tap on the back door. I turn the knob and find myself pressed against Caleb, my nose to the soft fabric of his t-shirt, breathing in his soap. It's hard to worry about anything when he's wrapped around me, as if I'm all he's thought of since he left. It's hard to worry that he's moving when he's here right now—and already hard.

My spine settles as he twines his fingers through mine as he pulls me to the double chaise. We sit beside each other, closer than we should with the twins upstairs. His arm wraps around my shoulders, and I let my head rest on his chest.

"I think my productivity was cut in half today," he says with a quiet laugh. "I thought about last night at least once a minute."

I smile. "It was pretty spectacular. Your tongue is magical."

He grins. "Not magical. *Gifted*, perhaps." He runs a hand through my hair. "You do realize it had very little to do with me, right? All I did was catch you when you weren't in your own head, worrying about shit."

"So, what I hear you saying is that any man could have made me come like that. Any man in the world."

"No," he growls, pulling me into his lap. "You're right. It was entirely because of me. I'll prove it right here."

My lips brush over his. "I'm not sure how we'd explain that to the twins if they come downstairs."

He laughs. "There's no story we could make up that Sophie would believe anyway."

I kiss him again, relishing the warmth of his hands, his end-of-day scruff grazing my skin. I lose myself in it. I allow it to turn sloppy and desperate, with his fingers digging into my ass, his cock rigid between my legs.

"God, I wish I wasn't traveling again," he says against my lips. "Give me the cottage phone number so I can at least *call* you."

"When do you leave?" I ask, as his palm slides into my shirt.

"Tomorrow, right after the board meeting. When are you kid-free again?"

"Saturday." I gasp as he pinches a nipple hard through my bra. "Will you be home?"

He laughs and groans at once. "Now I will be."

28

LUCIE

W hen I enter the conference room the next morning, most of the board members are here in person and nearly every seat is taken. Caleb's already at the other end of the table, discussing something with the guy beside him, but when his gaze lands on me, it lingers far longer than it should.

My phone chimes just as the meeting is called to order.

CALEB

Here's the code you need to open the report: YLBT

It's the code game I play with Sophie. I burst into a ridiculous, inappropriate smile, though I have no idea what he said.

Y obviously stands for *you* or *your*.

L could stand for *like*, or *love*, or *let* or *lips*. *You like*...B. You-like-banana-toast. You-like-big-televisions.

I continue trying to work this out, coming up with increasingly ridiculous possibilities, until Caleb steps to the front of the room. He's so drool-worthy in that suit, so imposing, so stern, that all I can think about is Saturday night. His eyes, dark and heavy-lidded as he asked if I was ready for him.

I never dreamed that I could get this wet listening to someone discuss *due diligence.*

The conversation then moves onto licenses and retraining and all the other things that will be issues as they merge the companies. Even when every topic has been addressed repeatedly, the board members are still dragging the meeting out, chatting about nonsense, when Caleb's reminded them twice that he has a flight to catch.

CALEB

Did the code work?

No, not yet.

Try this one: IRNTBIYA

I read...
I remember...
I wait until the meeting's done before I reply to his text.

Sorry. That code didn't work either.

CALEB

Meet me in conference room A as soon as we're done here.

He rises. "I'm sorry to cut this off, but like I said...I've got a flight leaving."

He walks out abruptly and after quickly introducing myself to board members, I walk down to the other conference room as he's instructed—and find myself tugged behind the door, in the room's only hidden corner.

His lips brush over mine. I pull him by the collar when he tries to move away and deepen the kiss.

He groans. "I really do have to leave for the airport. I just wanted to see you first."

I glance between us at the erection he's trying to adjust. "It appears you wanted to do more than simply *see* me. What were the codes?"

"You look beautiful today was the first one."

My cheeks flush. "And the second?"

His hand slides over my ass, and he laughs, almost to himself. "You'll need to figure that one out on your own, but it involves a place I really need to be again." He kisses me one last time and walks out of the room. I reach for my phone to examine the still-undeciphered letters: IRNTBIYA

This time it only takes me a few seconds:

I really need to be inside you again.

∼

CALEB CALLS me on the landline the next night after the twins are in bed, and we talk for hours. It feels like the part of my youth I missed—the part where you are so giddily infatuated with someone that you laugh for no reason at all, that you can almost taste your happily-ever-after. I am Cinderella, discovering the glass slipper fits or Belle kissing the Beast at last. I stop just short of picturing a wedding the entire village turns out for, assisted with my dress by magical mice and bluebirds... but barely. When he's talking to me, hinting at all the things we'll do when he gets back, it seems as if nothing could ever go wrong.

"How much time do we have on Saturday?" I ask.

"Not much," he says with a sigh. "I've got to fly out again Sunday morning. But can we plan a weekend away this summer? The kids are staying with Jeremy's mom Fourth of July weekend, right?"

I grin. "Yes, but...are you actually going to take a long

weekend off? Is that something you've *ever* done in your adult life?"

He releases a quiet laugh. "It might be a first. I must kind of like you."

"I kind of like you, too." It's the world's greatest understatement, but he's only had a few months of this infatuation while I've had twenty years. I need to give him some time to catch up.

He's back at the office Wednesday for only two hours before he leaves again, and when his meetings in Denver run over, he asks me to meet him in San Francisco because he has to fly out first thing in the morning.

I opt *not* to show up wearing only a trench coat as Molly suggested, a decision I'm grateful for when I'm at the front desk of the Ritz asking for the room key Caleb left for me—a situation which gives rich-guy-paying-for-sex vibes even *without* the trench coat.

I ascend to the twenty-third floor and open the door to find him pacing with the phone to his ear. He waves me in and mouths, *"Sorry,"* while continuing to bicker with someone about licenses.

I kick off my heels and stretch out on the bed, and his eyes grow hazy.

"Look, I shouldn't have to spell this out for you," he barks into the phone, his gaze still on me.

I'd intended to be patient, but watching Caleb lose focus is more tempting than I anticipated. I slide the skirt up, up, up, until he could just make out my panties if he tilted his head to the side.

He tilts his head to the side.

"We'll have to continue this in the morning," he announces into the phone, hanging up without so much as a *goodbye* and prowling toward me.

I smile. "You could have finished your call."

He kneels between my legs and pushes the skirt up to my waist. "I have better things to worry about right now."

I tug on his tie and pull him to me for a kiss. "Oh, really? What *things* do you have to worry about?"

"Where to start?" he muses, running a hand up my thigh before he rises again and crosses the room. "Actually, I thought we could do some reading."

"*Reading?*"

The book he withdraws from his bag has a woman in a blue ballgown being ravaged by a barechested man in riding breeches.

I choke on a laugh. It's *The Desire of a Lady*—the book about Lady Victoria. I take it from his hands, laughing out loud. "I can't believe you even figured out the title."

He grins as he climbs over me again. "It was surprisingly difficult. Devereaux is apparently a super common name among the British upper classes, based on the number of times it appears in historical romance."

He takes the book from me and starts flipping through it. "No pointers yet," he says, lowering it with a frown to glance at me. "So far, it's a lot of Lady Victoria being told she's impertinent and...ah, here we go. '*His wicked mouth moved over her nipples—*'"

He pulls my tank down until my bra is exposed and then he tugs at a nipple through my bra. "Like this, you think?"

My breath releases in a quiet gasp. "Maybe, or maybe it was...more? She probably wasn't wearing a bra."

Caleb's wicked mouth turns up at one corner. "Ah, good point." His fingers graze the lace he just wetted with his lips and pinch the nipple tight. I squirm beneath him, wanting more.

His head lowers as he drags the bra down and grasps my bare nipple in his teeth.

I inhale, sharp and surprised, and he hands me the book. "Here. You read. I keep losing my place."

I glance at the page and pretend to read. "*He tore off her clothes, then fucked her really hard, several times in a row*."

He raises a brow. "Lucie, that's not what it says."

I groan. "Fine. '*His fingers slid beneath her skirts, to the—*'"

His hands are already moving up my thigh. "Why'd you stop? I have absolutely no idea what I'm supposed to do next."

"It says he *parts her spiral curls*. It's just...kind of a gross image. I'm picturing a vagina with long, flowing hair."

"That makes this way less hot suddenly." He leans over me, sliding his fingers beneath the edge of my panties. "Ah, but look how wet you are. It's hot again. What next?"

"'*His fingers speared her—*'"

His fingers, three at once, push inside me. I'm so deliciously full that it's hard to breathe.

"'*And then he grasped his staff.*'"

Caleb stills. "His *staff*? You mean, like, some kind of walking stick?"

In spite of his fingers still inside me, in spite of his erection pressing into my thigh, I laugh. "No, I think they're referring to his genitalia."

"I thought it was about to get really kinky."

"You seriously thought he was about to use a walking stick on her somehow?"

His eyes gleam. "I can see a few ways we might use one. You have other holes."

I swat him with the book. "You're ruining this. Lord Devereaux never would refer to '*other holes.*'"

He moves lower on the bed and his tongue slides over me, slick and hot and eager. "So I'm ruining this, you say?"

"No," I gasp. The book falls to the floor. "I think you're turning it around."

～

LATER, when the lights are off and I'm tucked tight to his chest, we talk about those times I snuck out to the dock to see him as a preteen, and he claims to have no clue that I ever had a crush, which I find difficult to believe.

He asks me how I wound up going to Ruth's house in the first place, and I tell him things I never shared with Jeremy—the way my mother would claim she had 'work issues' each summer and dump me with my aunt when she was actually going on a trip with whatever man was around at the time. How she'd go to Disney or Yosemite or Mexico and promise me a souvenir if I kept it all a secret—a Belle dress from Disney, Hermione's wand from Universal Studios—and then later claim it was stolen or that I hadn't earned it, so she'd given it away.

He asks why I kept lying for her. I guess it's a reasonable question. I only hesitate because that's a worse story—I lied because I eventually grew as desperate to be away from her as she was me. I lied because once I hit my teens, she began to resent my youth and my appearance, and every time one of her boyfriends hit on me, she'd find a way to make it my fault.

I'm embarrassed, once it's out—by how much I shared, by how gross it all is when laid bare. "It probably sounds pretty trashy compared to all your past relationships."

He shakes his head. "It's weirdly similar to my past relation-ships. At least the last one." He pulls the blankets around my shoulders as the air conditioning kicks on. "Kate didn't really know either of her parents. Her mom overdosed when she was little and she had no clue who her dad was. She grew up in foster care."

"She grew up in foster care but got into *Stanford*?"

"She's crazy smart. Probably to her detriment, since it allowed her to hide a lot of shit from me and from her employer for way too long."

I'm not sure it'll do me any favors to learn more about his

smart, beautiful wife who went to Stanford and was super fun. But there's a lot more here, a lot more he doesn't discuss about the baby and how it affected him, and he might need to tell *someone*. I suspect he never has. "How did you meet?"

"We both went to Stanford undergrad and Wharton for grad school," he says. "We were never in the same class, but we met at an alumni event in San Francisco. I don't even remember which school it was for."

There's another internal pinch—she went to Stanford and grad school. I barely finished undergrad at a school no one's heard of.

"And she moved out to the middle of nowhere for you?"

He stiffens again. "Not really. She moved because she was pregnant. It wasn't planned, but..." He shrugs.

Was there ever a time when he was excited about the pregnancy? I'm not sure how to ask, and before I can try, he rolls me on my back.

"Why are we talking about this when we've got a bed and some privacy?" he asks, his mouth on my neck, his hand running over my hip.

I'm not about to argue, but it also feels a little intentional, the way he closed the conversation when he did.

WE SEPARATE EARLY in the morning—me back home and him to the airport—and I am still deliciously bruised and battered and swollen-lipped when Jeremy finally brings the twins home, hours later than they were due.

Sophie and Henry launch themselves at me as I walk out the door and I pull them against me, pressing my nose to their heads simply to breathe them in.

Jeremy drops their backpacks on the ground. "I figured

you'd be doing a whole lot of nothing with them, so it didn't matter when they came home."

He wants me to be angry. He wants to feed on my anger like it's a banquet and he's starving. I won't give him the satisfaction. I tell the twins to go inside. "That's a violation of our interim agreement," I reply calmly, once they're out of earshot. "I wouldn't advise doing it again."

"Where were you last night?" he demands.

"What makes you think I was anywhere?"

He blinks. Only once. It's his version of a long pause. "Sophie needed something. I called the cabin, and you didn't answer."

"I go lots of places when you've got the kids, Jeremy," I reply. "I could have been anywhere."

His nostrils flare. I can practically hear the way his teeth are grinding. "Don't make a mistake you can't fix."

There's an unmistakable warning in those words. He knows I was somewhere he didn't want me to be, and the only reason he's not outright accusing me of it is because he acquired that knowledge in a way he shouldn't have. God, I should have been more careful. The separation agreement is in place, so technically I've done nothing wrong, but Jeremy isn't one to let the truth get in his way.

"I have no idea what you're talking about."

"I think you do," he says. "And if your behavior is reflecting poorly on the kids, I'll have to intervene on their behalf. I don't want to do that to you, Lucie, but I will if you force my hand."

"Again, what makes you so certain that I went anywhere? Maybe I just wasn't inside when you called."

"If you weren't making such a spectacle of yourself in public, I might believe you."

He's found one of my infinite cracks, those tiny spaces in my armor where he can slither in and make me doubt myself. Already I'm asking where I wore something inappropriate or said something stupid, because it seems entirely possible that my heels are too high or my smile is too wide or that I look like a fucking idiot every time I walk into the school or a store. Some piece of me will always be the kid no one wanted around, the kid certain there was something wrong with her. But there's a new piece too. The woman Caleb likes, the one who's actually good at her job and, mostly, pulling off single parenthood.

I turn and head toward the house with my shoulders back.

"Don't fucking walk away," he warns. "I'm not done talking to you."

If I don't placate him, the situation will just get worse, but the more time I spend with Caleb, the less willing I am to let Jeremy push me around, even if it's only going to make my life harder in the end.

I keep right on walking, and he follows. The sound of the door slamming in his face is unbelievably satisfying.

29

LUCIE

CALEB

Flight just landed. Be at office in an hour.

I squirm in my seat. It's only been three days since I left him in San Francisco, but I'm already desperate to see him again. And I'm desperate for this to begin, for it to feel like a normal relationship—one in which our texts don't have to be sent in code, one that actually occurs in person.

Except an hour later, the text that arrives isn't from Caleb... it's from Harrison, asking me to swing by Caleb's office.

I've never seen him here before, and though he's both my attorney and Caleb's, it's a little odd to meet with us at the same time.

I tap on the door and walk in. A smile plays around the corners of Caleb's mouth—the kind of smile that shouldn't really be there when he's greeting an *employee*.

"Hey," he says. His voice is both rougher and softer than normal. "Harrison wants to, uh, discuss things."

"*Things*," I repeat.

"Under normal circumstances, there's a process if two

employees are dating," Harrison says, smirking at Caleb. "You guys would just sign an agreement, since neither of you supervises the other, but I'd prefer you waited, because it could be used against you in court."

"In court?" I ask. "How?"

"In your case, I think Jeremy will simply be harder to deal with. In Caleb's, the process server's having a hard time locating Kate, and until she's gotten the paperwork or we can prove we've made a sufficient effort to inform her, she could still accuse him of adultery."

"Kate would never do that," Caleb says with quiet, unerring conviction and there's a soft thud in my chest, as if someone's tapped me there slightly too hard. Is a guy leaving his wife supposed to be so adamant in her defense?

Harrison's gaze flickers to me before it returns to Caleb. "You have no idea what she'd do until she's done it. Divorce can bring out a whole new side in people. Anyway, my point is that it doesn't benefit either of you to make this public knowledge right now, especially in a county where we could easily be facing a judge who played golf with Jeremy's uncle the day before. So, whatever you two are doing, do it in private. Don't send non-work texts, and if you're out in public, make sure it's a group setting."

I nod, and when Harrison rises, Caleb fights a smile, eager to have him out of the room.

Harrison groans. "You two might also want to cut it out with all the secretive looks. I'm going to leave and shut the door behind me, but please don't use that as an opportunity to work anything out of your system."

The moment the door closes, Caleb rises and walks to my side of the desk, pulling me to my feet. I smile against his lips as he lifts me, his hands wrapped around my waist, and sets me on his desk. "I thought we weren't supposed to work anything out of our systems."

"Harrison is overcautious," he answers, stepping between my legs and kissing me again. And again. Opening my mouth, stealing my breath. He does not push, he just kisses me until I find it's me who wants more, who wants contact, who needs his hands on my skin.

We jump at the knock on the door. I rise, smoothing my skirt. Caleb returns to the other side of the desk to hide the fact that he's got an erection. "Come in," he barks.

Kayleigh enters, raising a brow as if she knows exactly what was going on and does not approve—I'm surprised she's put her phone down long enough to notice anything. "The accountant is here," she says, lips pursed.

"Send him back," Caleb replies, looking only at me.

She hesitates, as if she's waiting to see me leave.

"I'll talk to you later," I tell him.

He nods, his mouth hitching a centimeter to the right.

I'm just passing Kayleigh's desk when she speaks up from behind me. "He's very busy. You need to stop wasting his time."

My tongue prods my cheek. Kayleigh is terrible at her job, so I seriously doubt she's saying this out of professional concern.

"He asked me to come down to his office, Kayleigh. And I'm not sure why you think his interactions with employees are *your* concern."

"Fine, keep making a fool of yourself. A guy like Caleb is never going to be interested in someone like you."

"Like I said, I was only here because he asked me to come to his office," I repeat between my teeth. "But I'm very curious what you mean by '*someone like you.*'"

"Lots of things," she says with a disdainful once-over. "Like, his wife has an MBA from *Wharton*. Where's your master's degree from?"

"Where's *your* master's degree from, Kayleigh?" I snap back as I walk away, pretending that there wasn't another small *plink* in my chest when her target struck its goal.

I PLAY with the twins that afternoon on the beach, excited for Caleb to get home, excited to watch the kids' faces light up as he walks down the hill. Harrison wasn't wrong—Jeremy will definitely make my life harder if he discovers this—but I wish we could just jump six months into the future and arrive at the point where we don't have to hide a thing.

It's dusk when Caleb steps onto his back deck, still in work clothes...and freezes as his gaze lands on the twins. He gives me an awkward, unsmiling wave and turns to go back inside.

What the hell was that? He was clearly on his way down here until...what? *He remembered I had twins?*

If he hadn't met them yet, indifference or uncertainty would make sense. But he's spent lots of time with them...he's seen nearly as much of them as he has me over these past months. So why is it only now that he's acting like he wishes they weren't around?

The twins and I go inside and move through the rest of our night with no sign of him. It's only once I'm back downstairs in the kitchen, unloading the dishwasher, that there's a tap on the back door.

His smile is wide. He pulls me toward him and presses his lips to the top of my head. "At last," he says, and he *sounds* like a man who is happy to see me.

I pull away. "What happened this afternoon? You kind of weirded out on us."

His teeth sink into his lower lip. "I handled it poorly. I'm trying to make sure I don't cross a line."

I swallow. He said he would try...Did he not understand that me and the kids are a package deal? "Caleb, you've been sitting with us on the beach for months now. We've had dinner with you, we've gone on your boat—how would coming down to say *hi* be crossing a line?"

He scrubs a hand over his face. "I just don't...I want to make sure I'm not something they start to count on."

Ouch.

I step outside and sink into the chaise, arms wrapped around myself. "When we started this, you said you wanted to try. I assumed that included them."

He sits beside me. "It did. It does. I don't know what happened today. I saw them and I..." He shrugs. "Can I ease into it?"

I want this for myself. I want this for the twins. I want it for him too, because I think he's still messed up by what happened to his daughter and Kate, and he just needs to realize it's not always that hard, but maybe it can't happen overnight. "Of course."

It's new. I don't have to worry about what I'll do this early, do I?

No. But I'll have to worry about it eventually.

HE JOINS us the next evening at the beach, but it's not the way it was before. He talks to the twins—he even briefly plays the ice cream game—but there's something wary in his posture, as if he's sure we're about to ask him for too much.

I allude to teaching Henry to surf and he looks at me as if he's hearing it for the first time when it was *his* idea.

It's as if, in order to move our relationship forward a few paces, he had to move his relationship with *them* back to the start. And I suspect I know why.

"Your daughter," I begin, as the twins run down to the water. "Did you ever see her?"

He seems unwilling to even answer this one small question. "Yes," he says, his jaw grinding. "Kate was still holding her. She wouldn't...I was the only person who could convince her to let go."

My heart squeezes tight. How can he possibly believe that didn't affect him?

"Who did she look like?" I ask.

He runs a hand through his hair and exhales heavily. "Why the fuck are we discussing this?"

Because it was harder on you than you're willing to admit. Because you need to discuss it with someone and you won't, and I think it's just going to fester. Because I'm scared we'll never become what we could be, what we were meant to be, until you come to terms with it.

"Sorry," I tell him, giving his hand a quick squeeze.

He's quiet for a long moment before he sighs. "She looked like me."

30

LUCIE

He's gone a day later. I try to let him take the space he needs, and when he calls, I don't tell him about the cute thing Sophie said or the way I heard Henry laughing in his sleep. I don't tell him that Henry stared at his house tonight, looking for signs of life, or that I was watching Henry do it and wondering if I'm setting my kids up to be rejected by all the adult men in their lives like I was.

He talks about work, about his trip, about the boat—as he should, because these are things he cares about. But I don't love the fact that it now feels as if I *can't* talk about the thing I care about the most.

The next afternoon I take the twins to the toy store—a rare indulgence. It's less about offering them a moment of joy than it is offering one to myself. It was always hard, having Caleb take off for some distant city or continent, even before we were together. But it's a lot harder now.

Sophie vigorously debates the merits of Legos versus a board game with me, but Henry wanders off. I find him standing in the science section, staring intently at all the models and projects for much older children.

"I want this," he says quietly, holding one of them to his chest.

I squat down to examine the box, which holds some kind of robotic arm you build yourself. He won't even be able to read the directions. "Honey, this is for adults."

"I want to build it with Caleb. For the show."

My heart sinks. He's referring to the kindergarten's end-of-year program, which all the parents attend. Most of the kids plan to do something for it—Sophie is hell-bent on performing a fairly inappropriate pop song—but I assumed Henry would refuse to participate, and here he is, willing—*asking* to do it.

I blow out a breath. "I'll check with Caleb, okay?"

"He'll say yes," Henry says with utter faith.

I wish I believed that as much as Henry does.

Caleb calls me on the house phone from Boston after the twins are in bed. "I'm in my hotel room without a single nude photo of you," he says. "It's troubling."

"I'm not a detective, but if Jeremy is monitoring my texts, sending you nude photos might provide him a *subtle* clue that you are not merely my boss."

"You could have taken a photo with *my* phone as a surprise. The more I think about it, the more it hurts my feelings that you didn't."

I wind the phone cord around my hand. "I'll do my best to mend your *hurt feelings* when you get home."

"Why," he says, his voice guttural with longing, "does every word out of your mouth sound filthy to me now?"

I hop onto the counter. "I'm currently researching ways to spend more of your company's money. How filthy does that sound?"

He laughs weakly. "The filthiest. Do I even want to know?"

"Nap pods. Just like Google has."

"Are we hiring toddlers? What grown fucking adult needs a nap during work hours?"

"Grown fucking adults who work really long hours and need to recharge. You want employees who feel as if they're there by choice, not as some form of indentured servitude."

He groans. "I pay way too much for anyone to call it indentured servitude."

I miss that crabbiness of his that never quite extends to me. "When are you home?" I ask softly.

"Not til Tuesday. *Someone* scheduled a grand opening for the break room on Wednesday that I theoretically have to get back for."

"Maybe *someone* will make it up to you."

"Yes," he says, his tone deliciously bossy, "she absolutely fucking will."

I want to stay in this space where we are both focused only on how I'll make it up to him. Unfortunately, I can't.

I take a deep breath. "I have a favor to ask."

"Will I have phone sex with you? Absolutely. To be honest, I'm already halfway there."

I laugh. "It's a favor for one of my kids."

"That's less sexy." He sighs. "I guess I'll leave my pants on."

He's still joking, but his voice is stiffer, less friendly. If it were only about me, I'd drop the subject, but it's not. There's nothing I won't do for Henry, and if it means alienating Caleb...I'll do that too. "Henry wants to build this robotic arm with you for a show at school." *And it's so unlike him, being willing to branch out. It could change everything if he had this one success.*

"You can't build it with him?"

I take a quick breath. It's unreasonable to expect him to care about my kids the way I do, but I can't help but wish he did anyway. "I looked at the directions and it's beyond me."

He's very quiet. "I don't know, Lucie," he finally says. "It's just...this is a busy time for me."

Every bone in my body wants to let the conversation drop.

Because he did tell me he wouldn't have a lot of time, that he wanted to ease in. *I'm* the one trying to change things. But I can already picture Henry, showing off this amazing project, learning the world can love him as much as I do if he lets them in.

"I'm not asking for anything you weren't already doing before," I say quietly. "Why is it suddenly a problem?"

He's quiet. I brace myself for what's coming. If something this *small* would lead him to end things, it's probably for the best that we quit while we're ahead...but my stomach drops anyway.

"Because you'll expect it, and they'll expect it," he finally says. "And I'll fucking disappoint all of you."

"Okay," I reply, my stomach churning.

I understand his reluctance. I understand not wanting to promise things to a kid and at this stage in our relationship, he probably wouldn't even have *met* my kids yet, under normal circumstances. The problem isn't that he's hesitant to be a part of our lives—it's that he's more hesitant than he was before.

When I was with Jeremy, there were a thousand times I asked for things on behalf of the twins—*please come to their play, please come home on Halloween, please make it back in time for their birthday party*—and when he ignored me, what choice did I have? Leaving him wouldn't solve the problem. It would just create a series of new ones.

This time, I have a choice. And if Caleb continues to not be what we need, I'm going to have to make that choice—no matter how much it hurts.

~

ON MONDAY NIGHT, Jeremy texts me to confirm the twins' homework has been done. I can't imagine why he's suddenly interested, but the demanding way he asks—as if I'm some lowly employee—irritates me. The question *alone* irritates me, given how little involvement he's had. When I don't answer immediately, he calls Sophie's iPad and proceeds to grill her about projects and what they're learning...and then he asks to speak to me.

"Why didn't you read them the horse book Sophie got from the library yesterday?" he demands. "She was supposed to discuss it today."

I'm tempted to hang up. He didn't care for six years, but he suddenly cares now? "Because she never told me I was supposed to read it to her," I snap. "I'm not psychic, Jeremy. If they don't tell me and the school doesn't either, I don't know."

"You were also late on May third and didn't send them in with the posterboard they needed last week."

My jaw falls and my hands start to shake—with anger, with shock. Jeremy is compiling a list of every minor failing to make me look like a bad parent and the school is helping him do it.

"Are you fucking kidding me?" I hiss, glancing over my shoulder to make sure the kids are out of hearing distance. "I'm essentially a single parent, Jeremy. Shit's gonna fall through the cracks occasionally. You'd realize that if you'd ever lifted a fucking finger."

"Why are you so angry, Lucie?" he asks. "You don't sound like yourself."

I slap a hand to my forehead. "Because..." And then I stop. This is ridiculous. The twins need me to help them with their history posters and they still need baths and I'm just not doing this with Jeremy tonight. "I don't have time for this shit," I tell him, hanging up the phone.

Within a minute, there's a text from Molly.

MOLLY
Are you okay?

Of course. Why?

> I just got this weird call from Jeremy. He said you were drunk or possibly had taken something and he wasn't sure the kids were safe.

I stare at the words. Is this his next move? To tell enough people that I'm an unfit mother and create a paper trail to support it? I haven't even replied before my mother calls.

"Hi, Mom," I say with a heavy sigh. "I've got to do something with the twins, so this isn't a great time."

"Are you drunk?" she asks. "Jeremy said you were drunk."

I press a hand over my face to hold in a scream.

I'VE HAD VERY little sleep when I get up in the morning. I was awake for hours last night, considering what I will say to the school. Legally, I assume they've done nothing wrong. Except these are such minor points, they shouldn't have merited so much as a mention.

I normally drop the twins off in front to let the patrols walk them in, but today we park. I still haven't come up with what I'll say to Mrs. Kroesinger when I find her, but I am definitely saying something, and it'll probably just make things worse.

Henry's hand slips into mine. "Are you staying?" he asks, and that tiny hopeful note in his voice breaks my heart. I wish I could stay. I wish I could spend the whole day making sure he had someone to play with and was getting the help he needed. If I'd known how powerless it could feel to be a parent, I might have been too terrified to undertake it and Caleb's *only* experience of being a parent is the heartbreak, the powerlessness, the guilt. No wonder he's scared.

"Not today, sugar. I need to talk to your teacher for a second."

I grab Sophie with my other hand, and we walk up to the

school, past the yoga moms, whose conversation comes to a halt as we pass, their gazes sweeping over my dress and heels. It's probably one of them who told her husband I'm *putting on a show* and perhaps she'll come home with another story tonight.

We've just stepped into the lobby when Jeremy emerges from the school's office with the principal and Mrs. Kroesinger, whose eyes go wide and guilty at the sight of us before her jaw sets and her face hardens.

My mouth is open, but no words emerge.

They just had a meeting without me, about my children.

"Did I miss an email?" I ask, my voice shaking and barely civil, my palms sweaty against the twins'. "I didn't realize there was a meeting."

Jeremy and Mrs. Kroesinger exchange a smug, knowing glance. "No meeting," says Jeremy. "I wanted to address some concerns."

What do I even say? These three people have just met, probably to discuss what a terrible parent I am, so do I throw a fit in front of my children to prove I'm the *better* parent? Do I make threats I'm not sure I can back up?

The principal gives me a firm, chilly smile. "I need to get going. Good to see you, Jeremy. Mrs. Kroesinger, perhaps the twins can walk back to class with you?"

Everyone disperses and Jeremy looks me up and down. "I assume you're the most lowly employee at TSG, based on the outfit."

It barely makes a dent. I'm still stuck on the earlier statement. "What *concerns*?" I finally ask.

"I simply wanted them to understand that our households operate differently, and that the twins may be struggling more when they're staying with *you*."

"What *households*?" I ask. "They always stay with me."

He allows himself a small chuckle. "That's going to have to change too, since you appear not to be up to the job."

He walks away, stopping to talk to the yoga moms on his way to the car. They greet him with smiles and stare me down as I walk past.

My mother would have told them off, and I'd have been absolutely horrified, but now I sort of get it.

It's tiresome, being the designated punching bag every fucking day. You start wanting to show them you can hit back.

CALEB'S TRUCK is at the office by the time I arrive, and I want to see him, but I'm too upset to offer him much of a reunion. I go to my desk instead and call Harrison, who is gratifyingly enraged and says he'll call Jeremy's lawyer and put a stop to all of it.

When I hang up, I discover Caleb standing behind me, his brow furrowed.

"Hey," he says, perching on the edge of my desk, "I thought you'd come find me once you got in."

I swallow. "Sorry. I'm having some issues with Jeremy and the school and I just—" I shrug in lieu of saying the rest aloud: *you don't want to be a part of our lives that way, but the kids are my priority and I'm not willing to pretend otherwise right now.*

He hesitates. "You can talk to me about that stuff, you know."

My nails dig into my palms. "You've made it pretty clear that you'd rather...keep it all separate."

"And that's okay with you?"

I swallow as I meet his eye. "Obviously, it isn't a situation that will work long term for my kids. We'll just see what happens."

He leans forward, staring at his clasped hands. His jaw clenches. "What's that supposed to mean?"

Normally, I'd try to finesse this, but I'm too numb. I bury my face in my hands. "Caleb, my kids come first. That isn't going to change. If what I'm doing isn't in their best interest, I'll stop doing it, no matter how much I don't want to."

His eyes fall closed briefly before he stands. "Okay. We'll talk later."

I nod mutely as he walks away. It sure doesn't seem like this talk will involve any kind of change on his part. So what happens to us when he admits it?

~

I GET the twins a little earlier than normal and we do all the things there's not usually time for in the afternoon: we stop by the park, I help Henry with Snap Circuits and play diner with Sophie (I'm the customer, she's the waitress. She informs me that everything I try to order is 'not very healthy' and suggests a different option instead. I don't see a lot of work in the service industry in her future.)

And the whole time, my stomach is a boiling cauldron of worry. Are Caleb and I done? I regret being as blunt as I was, but that doesn't mean what I said wasn't true.

Over dinner, there's a knock on the door and all three of us startle. Jeremy's the only person who ever comes here when the kids are awake. Sophie races ahead of me. By the time I come around the corner, the door's been flung open wide.

Caleb's eyes meet mine. "I was thinking of taking my boat out. I wondered if you guys might want to come." His uncertain half-smile breaks my heart.

He isn't ending things. He's *trying*.

"You're still in your suit."

He laughs. "Yeah...I was gonna change. I just thought I'd ask first."

"Yes, we want to go," Sophie says in her most polite voice. She glances up at me. "Thank you for extending the invitation."

I have no idea where she got that from, but I think I'd better make sure my aunt's books are hidden away.

"Yes," I say with a smile. "Thank you for extending the invitation."

Caleb turns to Henry. "I understand you've got something you want to build?"

My heart flutters as Henry nods, serious but hopeful.

"Should we start on it tomorrow?"

Henry nods again. A shadow of a smile graces the corners of his mouth. I'm pretty sure my heart is going to burst.

31

LUCIE

The next evening, Henry and Caleb start to build the robotic arm. I didn't think it was possible for Caleb to become more attractive to me, but watching him work with my son so patiently is an unbelievable aphrodisiac.

"If you keep looking at me like that," he says quietly, when the kids run down to the water, "I'm going to yank you off that chair and turn this into an uncomfortable evening for everyone."

I laugh, pressing my palms to my suddenly warm face.

He gives a low groan. "Don't blush either. You have no idea what it does to me when you blush like that."

"I'm not sure I can control the blushing."

"For the love of God," he begs, "*try*." The desperation and command in his voice has me clenching my thighs togeth-er...and wishing we didn't have to wait for the weekend to be alone. I want to put the kids to bed tonight and pull him into my room seconds later. I want to wake up with him. I want everything, and I've wanted everything from him...since we began, but it's too early to say it aloud. He hasn't spent two decades daydreaming about me the way I have him. He's barely had two months.

He and Henry make good progress on the arm, and Henry starts putting the unfinished sections back in the box.

"Can you come to my show?" he asks Caleb.

I swallow a lump in my throat. I can't think of another time in my life when I've heard Henry ask someone other than me and Sophie for *anything*. He refuses to speak up when he's hungry, when he's thirsty, when another kid cuts in line.

But now, with Caleb, he's asking.

Caleb bites his lip as he looks at me. "When is it?"

"June twenty-second." *Please don't say no to this, Caleb*, I plead silently. *Please. You can't imagine how much it matters.*

He nods, but his smile is slightly forced. "I'll put it on the calendar."

He still doesn't want us to count on him, but maybe these are just growing pains. Maybe this is how he'll learn it's not as hard as it seems to balance work and family.

I really, really hope that's what it is.

OVER MY LUNCH BREAK, I meet Molly at the BMW dealership, where she's left her car to get the mirror fixed. I've somehow refrained from pointing out this was the perfect chance to ask her boss for a ride.

"We need to make a pit stop on the way to my office," she says. "This lingerie store has a going-out-of-business sale. I need something for my first date with Michael."

She has enough lingerie for the entire state to go on a first date with Michael at this point.

"You've got to make this fast," I say, turning toward the store she pointed out. "Unlike you, I'm not such a valued member of my organization that I can leave for as long as I want."

"Unlike me, however, you *are* fucking your boss. I bet that gives you all the long lunches you want."

I laugh. Yeah, I suppose.

"So if you're buying lingerie for your first date, that must mean your plan to have him save you from an intruder actually worked out?"

She sighs, holding the store's door open behind her. "You ruined it with all your logic. And I guess it *would* suck to have the police show up instead, especially if I was standing there naked. Anyway, I've got a much better plan."

I guarantee it doesn't involve anything rational, like perhaps telling him how she feels.

She shoves a thong and bra at me. "Get these. It'll make Caleb forget all about how tardy you've been."

I take a look at the price tag and hand them back to her. "It probably would, but I'm not really in the market for a hundred-and-ten-dollar thong at present, plus that bra offers no support whatsoever."

"Everything is half off," she argues. "And a bra like this isn't supposed to offer support. Your aim should only be its removal."

I picture Caleb seeing me in it and I'm tempted, but this isn't the time to splash out on things I don't need. "I'm broke and I don't know when Caleb and I will be alone again. The twins are home next weekend and I can't count on Jeremy even when he's *supposed* to take them."

"Let me watch the twins. I need some parenting practice before little Damien arrives anyway." She pats her stomach as if his arrival is imminent and starts telling me about her latest plan to woo Michael. "Okay, so hear me out. When you and Caleb get married—"

"*Married?*" I laugh. "Molly, we just started dating."

"I told you to hear me out. When you and Caleb get married, I'll ask Michael to be my fake date and he'll grow surprisingly protective of me when my ex, who happens to be there, either professes his love or behaves aggressively."

There are so many things wrong with this plan I'm not sure where to begin, but—

"You're okay if there's a fistfight over me on the dance floor, yes?" she continues, walking to the register. "It won't be during the first dance, obviously. Just later when everyone's drunk."

"Wasn't your last boyfriend in grad school? Why would he be invited to my wedding?"

"You're ruining this with logic again, Lucie. Doesn't Caleb have a friend who'll pretend to be in love with me?"

I raise a brow. "And get *punched* while he's at it?"

"I think men have a higher pain tolerance. He'd barely notice."

"Sure, Molly. At my wedding to a guy *I just started seeing* and who's still married to someone else, I'll make sure he has a friend willing to get punched on behalf of a stranger."

She hands me a bag. "I bought you the bra and thong, by the way. Go have all the sex I'm not having with them on. Plus a vibrator for when he's gone."

I stare at the contents. "Oh, Molly, you shouldn't have."

"It just gets me that much closer to the fight at your wedding you've agreed to help me orchestrate," she replies, "so we both benefit."

I unlock the car and we climb in. "I'm not even sure his wife knows about the divorce yet. You might be waiting a long time."

She pauses in the middle of fastening her seat belt. "What happens if she gets those divorce papers and comes running back home to talk him out of it? Are you sure he'll still go through with everything?"

This entire time, I've pictured it occurring at a distance—his wife in another state, Caleb here. I never pictured them coming face-to-face again.

"Of course I'm sure," I reply.

She winces. We've both heard the truth in my voice, if not my words: I'm not sure about that. I'm not sure at all.

ON FRIDAY, Molly comes over for dinner, and once the twins are in their pajamas and settled in front of a movie, I get dressed, with the new lingerie on underneath. "Don't feel like you need to come home," Molly says as she walks me to the door. "Your kids, like, make their own breakfast and shit, right?"

"I think maybe I'll plan on coming home."

"Oh, and text me as soon as he's seen the bra. If I had your rack, I'd be in Michael's office this minute doing jumping jacks. Maybe I'll try that anyway. I bet he's still at work."

I fumble for my keys. "You're babysitting, so you can't just leave."

Molly waves a dismissive hand in the kids' direction. "They're six. In pioneer days, they'd be married off and starting families of their own by now. They'll be fine for an hour."

I laugh as I head to the car, thinking she's more likely to create an elaborate *plan* in which Michael discovers her doing jumping jacks—probably while kidnapped—than go to the office.

I drive to the bar where I met Harrison for the first time, a bar which is apparently owned by Caleb's friend Beck.

Harrison warned us not to do anything that might make us appear to be a couple, but that doesn't stop Caleb from running a hand over my hip when I walk up to him at the bar and giving me a longer look than he should, head to toe. "We don't have to stay," he says, doing a double take when he glimpses my bra strap. "Red?"

"Early birthday gift from Molly."

His eyes darken, and he gives the biggest, fakest yawn I've ever seen. "I'm exhausted. It's time to go."

"Really subtle, you two," says Harrison, who I hadn't even noticed. "Hey, Beck, come over here and stare into my eyes for a while. You know, the way *friends* do."

The tiny, elegant woman beside Harrison waves. "I'm Audrey, Harrison's wife."

She's not at all what I expected, with her glossy black bob and pedicure to match, her Fendi bag and enough diamonds on her wrist and ears to support a starving village.

I wonder if Kate was pulled together like this too. If she had perfect hair and couldn't *imagine* biting her nails the way I do.

Caleb leans close to my ear. "What do you want to drink? Choose something strong because we're leaving the second it's done."

"Surprise me," I reply, grinning at the filthy look that flashes over his face.

While he turns to the bar, Harrison introduces me to Liam and Beck, both of whom I recognize from childhood—Liam because he has the same wide smile and Beck because he remains the massive hulk of a man he was at age twelve, standing at least four inches taller than Caleb, who's six-two, and at least six inches wider.

"The infamous Lucie," he says, raising a brow. "I figured we'd meet you eventually. Caleb's been talking about you incessantly since you moved in."

"I wouldn't say it was *incessant*," Caleb argues over his shoulder, still waiting on my drink.

Beck and Harrison exchange a look and laugh.

"It was incessant," Harrison confirms.

"I was mostly complaining about how you were spending all my money," Caleb says, handing me a neon-blue drink garnished with about seventeen pieces of fruit on top. "Here you go. It seemed like a fitting drink for the Pineapple Princess."

"You truly have no understanding of our area's vegetation and produce."

We look at each other and smile, prompting another groan from Harrison. "For fuck's sake. Stop that."

We do our insufficient best, but it's not much of an effort. The guys start talking about some fight they got in with a rival football team in high school, and through it all, Caleb's gaze keeps reverting to mine—a knowing little look I like way too much. I can't wait to show him the lingerie.

The football discussion turns into an argument over whose fault the fight was. Caleb gives me an apologetic smile as he crosses the bar with the guys to ask a classmate to settle it, and Audrey moves into the seat he vacated. "He's so different with you," she muses.

I'd somehow forgotten that all these people knew Kate. They probably knew her *well*. Were they at their wedding? Were they at the hospital when Hannah was born? Are they thinking that I'm simply a weak stand-in for the girl Caleb lost?

I hesitate, my certainty that I should not pry conflicting with a strong desire to do exactly that. "Different?"

She glances around to make sure no one's listening. "I can only speak to the last few years. I didn't live here before...But, anyway, it was a pretty miserable situation for everyone, from what I saw."

I bite my lip. "They must have been happy at some point. I mean, they dated for a while before she got pregnant."

"I've always gotten the impression that it was more of a"—she flinches—"primal thing."

I stiffen. "What do you mean?"

Audrey winces. "Kate was...Kate. You'd have to meet her to get it. She's like this black hole, and she sucks men in. Ugh. Ignore me. Suffice it to say that whatever appeal she held, he's much happier with you."

My heart sinks anyway. If Kate *does* come back, how could I possibly compare to a sexual black hole? I can't.

Caleb returns and moves beside me. Beneath the counter, his hands link with mine. Our eyes lock, and everything he feels is written so plainly on his face: that he likes me. That he wants this. I was ridiculous to worry before.

"For fuck's sake," Harrison growls. "I can tell you're holding hands. Cut it out."

"Leave him alone," Liam chides. "Maybe he's broken the curse."

I glance between them. "Curse?"

The guys look uncomfortable while Audrey rolls her eyes. "They had this friend, Danny, who died at Harrison's dad's place under mysterious circumstances and now they all think they're cursed."

Harrison tenses beside her. "Danny didn't die under *mysterious circumstances*. He jumped off a cliff."

"Right," she replies, her voice heavy with sarcasm. "No one has a clue why Danny jumped, but his fiancée was fooling around with Luke, this other guy on the trip who has no alibi whatsoever, and they found Luke's surfboard smashed at the base of the cliff. Nothing mysterious *there*."

"Luke had nothing to do with it," hisses Harrison, and the two of them glare at each other while the rest of us look away awkwardly. It's that ugly sort of public tension I remember in my own marriage, but I never expected to see it in Harrison's.

The guys go back to discussing high school and football as if nothing was ever said, as if arguments between Harrison and Audrey are par for the course. And the feel of Caleb beside me, his hand brushing mine, his breath grazing my hair, has me forgetting too.

God, I wish we were alone right now. I'm already looking forward to our weekend alone the way a kid looks forward to Christmas. I'm not going to let him out of bed once.

Liam starts talking about some building he wants to turn into a hotel. Hidden from view, Caleb's pinky links with mine.

"Tell me about the lingerie," he says against my ear.

I bite my lip. "I think I'd rather show—"

A hand slams down beside me, cutting me off mid-sentence, and I jump in my seat.

Jeremy is there, eyes blazing. "May I speak to you for a moment?" he asks.

"No, you can't, Jeremy," growls Caleb. "Fuck off."

Jeremy's eye twitches. "No one's talking to you, asshole." He turns to me. "Are we gonna talk, or do I need to make a scene?"

Caleb is already pushing away from the bar, and anything he does will make the situation worse. I rest a hand on his arm. "It'll just take a minute."

"It'll just take a minute if I deal with him too," says Caleb between his teeth.

"Please." My voice is quiet, but my fingers press into his skin. Jeremy's incapable of backing down from a fight, and if he's given a reason to feel jealous, he'll only want the fight that much more.

Caleb's jaw shifts with the desire to argue, but he finally gives me a tiny nod and I follow Jeremy to the other side of the bar.

He doesn't appear to be here with anyone, as if he came here solely to talk to me. Which begs the question: how did he know I'd be here at all? Of the three times I've gone out, Jeremy's known about all of them. I assumed I'd been seen by a mutual acquaintance...but *three* times is a little too coincidental.

"Who's watching the kids?" he demands.

I don't owe him an explanation when he's barely seen the kids since we split, but answering is the fastest way to get him out of here. "Molly."

His eyes narrow. "I don't want my kids with your idiotic friend."

If I ever needed proof that what he says to me isn't based in reality, it's this. You can call Molly many things, but *idiotic* isn't one of them. It's just another of those tiny little poison darts he shoots, hoping one of them will sink far enough to sting, and I'm done allowing him to dictate anything I feel, good or bad. "She's got a PhD and is smarter than the two of us put together."

But Jeremy's already moved on. He glares in Caleb's direction. "Is fucking your married boss really the best you can do? Are you that desperate to prove you've still got something anyone wants?"

How the hell does he know Caleb is my boss? And that he's married?

"This is insane," I say, pushing away from the wall. "I'm done listening to you."

I find myself jerked so hard toward him that I stumble. The pain begins in my shoulder and shoots down my arm while threats spill from his mouth, and I barely have time to react before Caleb is there, pulling me behind him and punching Jeremy in the face so hard that he falls to the floor. "You'd better keep your fucking hands off her from now on."

Beck and Harrison jump in the fray, Beck blocking Jeremy from continuing the fight while Harrison turns toward us and groans at the sight of Caleb's arm around me, holding me close to his chest. "Well, if he didn't know you two were together before, he sure knows it now."

Beck wraps a hand around the back of Jeremy's neck, forcing him toward the door. "You just assaulted a female in my bar," he says. "Consider yourself permanently banned."

"You're lucky your friends jumped in," Jeremy says to Caleb as he walks out, rubbing his jaw.

"Let's see if you're so brave outside, asshole," Caleb replies.

"I guarantee you'll regret it when you're searching the parking lot for your teeth."

Harrison pushes a hand through his hair. "No one's fighting in the parking lot. And you and I need to talk. This changes things at the office."

God. Could dating an employee have repercussions for the company, or the merger? Probably.

Caleb's lips press to the top of my head. "Can't it wait?"

"No, Caleb. We need to get ahead of it, in case he presses charges. Which is why you shouldn't have fucking hit him in the first place. What were you thinking?"

"I was thinking that he just wrenched my girlfriend's arm and I was sick of his shit, and you'd have done the same goddamn thing in my shoes."

Harrison's shoulders sag. "Perhaps, but we still need to strategize. *Now*."

"It's okay," I say, stepping away, holding up my phone. "I want to check on the twins anyway."

"Use my office," Beck says. "It's quieter in there."

I open the office door, wandering toward the desks in the corner while I wait for Molly to pick up.

"Hey," I say when she answers, "how are my babies?"

"Your *kids* are fine and asleep, though they knew less about applied physics than I anticipated. How's it going? Have you shown him the lingerie?"

"I doubt I'll be showing him anything. Caleb just punched Jeremy, among several other developments. I assume Jeremy won't try to come by the house tonight and we'll head home soon, but don't let him in, okay?"

"As if," she scoffs. "I didn't want to let him into your house when you still lived with him. But—*ah*—it's so romantic. I wish Michael would punch someone for me. I mean, before your wedding, when it will definitely happen."

I rub my eyes. "No, not romantic. Potentially *problematic*.

And I also learned that Caleb's ex was apparently the world's sexiest human—like Marilyn Monroe, but not dead—so I may have lost the confidence to show him the lingerie."

"If you really want Caleb to prove he cares, have you considered faking your own kidnapping?"

I laugh and let her go just as Beck walks in. He's frowning, worried, but I'm not the object of his concern—it's the photo hanging on the wall just a few feet away, a photo I hadn't even noticed before, one he clearly just remembered was here and didn't want me to see.

In it, Caleb's sitting on a barstool, with Beck standing there waving a dollar bill. And between them, sitting on the bar itself, is a woman who must be Kate.

She has red hair falling nearly to her waist, almond-shaped eyes and a coy smile. Her dress is shirt-length and barely that, showcasing endless legs crossed seductively. She's beautiful, but it's not her beauty I find distressing—it's something else. Some indescribable quality I don't possess—sexuality and *confidence*. In any movie, she'd be cast as the seductive bad girl, the one no man can resist, which is pretty much what Audrey has already told me about her. It's basically what Caleb said too.

"I guess that's Kate," I whisper.

"Don't try to convince yourself that it was some great love story between the two of them," he says, still staring at the photo. "Kate tends to get exactly what she wants, and she wanted him. End of story. They had nothing in common."

"They must have had *something* in common."

"They had *one* thing in common," he says, his voice gravelly, laced with anger, "and without that one thing, they wouldn't have lasted an hour."

I'm sure he thinks he's reassured me, but in reality, he's done the opposite. As I follow him back to the bar, I'm once again fighting the mounting sense that I just can't match up to her.

"You ready?" Caleb asks.

I nod and say goodnight to his friends before we head outside together, his hand on my back the whole way as if Jeremy might be lurking around a corner.

"Ride home with me," he says. "No point in trying to hide it all now anyway."

He opens the door of his truck and I climb in, fighting the desire to burst into tears. He grabs my hand after he starts the engine, but his face is strained.

"Are you really okay?"

That concern in his eyes undoes me. I want this so much, want *him* so much, and it's starting to feel like it's never going to work out. He didn't promise me the fairy tale and between his ex and mine and the fact that he's still planning to move...it's hard to see how we'll wind up with one.

"I'm sorry," I whisper. "I can't believe I got you in a fight tonight."

"You didn't get me in a fight. I *wanted* that fight. I wanted it more than I've ever wanted a fight in my entire life, and I still want it. Are you sure he didn't hurt you?"

"I'm sure."

He cradles my jaw in his hands and kisses me. When he starts to lean away, I grab his collar and pull him to me. His mouth on mine feels like relief, like a cure, but he backs away again, leaning his head against the seat. "Lucie, keep kissing me like that and I'm not gonna be able to stop."

"I don't want you to stop," I tell him. The bar is only thirty feet away, but it's too dark for anyone to see inside his truck. I climb over him. The steering wheel is at my back and my left knee is propped awkwardly on the center console and I couldn't care less. I unzip his jeans, and he lifts his hips just enough for me to shove them and his boxers down. He reaches between my legs and stills.

"Thong?" he asks hoarsely.

"You can't even see it, unfortunately."

"Fuck," he says, pulling it to the side as he thrusts into me. "The idea of it's enough."

I ride him hard and fast. I'm not sure what happened to the girl who always put herself last, because there's no doubt in my mind that I'm doing this entirely for myself.

"Holy shit," he groans. "What's brought this on?"

I say nothing because I can't tell him the truth: that it's starting to feel like the odds are stacked against us. That they've always been stacked against us.

And that maybe we weren't meant to wind up together after all.

32

CALEB

Lucie and I file our disclosure paperwork with HR on Saturday morning. Beck and I search her car for a tracker, and I have her phone wiped for the second time—though my tech guy finds nothing on it.

Harrison can't ask for a restraining order because if he gets one, Jeremy has no reason not to press charges against me for throwing that punch.

It already feels like I'm failing her somehow, and then I get a call Monday morning that *guarantees* I'm going to fail her. It's the call I've been waiting on for weeks—the meeting that will change everything. But it means I have to cancel our weekend away and I'll be gone most of the weeks that would have led up to it.

I text Lucie and ask her to come down to my office.

"Close the door," I tell her.

She takes the seat across from mine with her brow furrowed. "What's up?"

"I finally got invited to Brad Caldwell's compound in Maui."

The light in her eyes grows dim. We haven't discussed what happens after the merger goes through—how soon I'll have to leave, how we'll see each other when we're on different coasts. A piece of me has just been hoping for a miracle, though I don't know what it would be.

"Isn't that a good thing?" she asks quietly. "It means the merger's going forward?"

I nod. "Yeah. That's pretty much the final step of this whole thing. But he wants to meet over Fourth of July weekend, so I'll need to cancel our trip, and I'm going to be gone a lot between then and now. I'm leaving tonight for India and I should be home within a week, but I won't be able to help with Henry's project much."

Lucie flinches. She hasn't even complained, but I already want to remind her that I never promised anything.

"Okay," she says, taking a deep breath. "You'll still come to the show though, right? On the twenty-second?"

I pinch my brow. I'd rather not commit, but I guess I already did. "Yeah." I slide her the phone that just arrived. "That's for you. Jeremy's still tracking you somehow and just because we haven't found spyware doesn't mean it's not there."

She shakes her head. "I can't accept this. And for all we know, he's paying someone to follow me."

"We live out by the lake. You'd see someone behind you on all these back roads. Take the phone. Please. It's the only way I'll be able to relax while I'm gone."

"Okay." She climbs to her feet, and I move around the desk to pull her against me. Her head presses to my chest. "Henry will miss you."

I tug her closer. "What about Henry's mom? Will she miss me too?"

She smiles, reluctantly. "Yes, but thanks to Molly, she owns a vibrator, which will take the edge off."

I groan and press her hand to my crotch. "Just like that, Lucie. I tell you I've got to do nothing but work, and in two seconds, you've got me ready to throw it off to the side."

Her laughter is quiet and forced. She presses her lips to mine. "Have a good trip," she says. And then she walks away, disappointment weighing on her like an invisible yoke.

I sink into my chair as the door shuts behind her and bury my head in my hands. *You can't serve two masters.* That's what my father said to me when my mother finally asked for a divorce.

I heard those words in my head when Kate discovered she was pregnant. We were mostly over by that point—there was the occasional weekend in San Francisco, but we were both more invested in our careers than each other. It was like a game of pretend, deciding to keep the baby and get married, hoping I could be a better father and husband than my dad. I started failing at it all almost immediately. *Beck* was the one who was there for Kate during her pregnancy. He painted the nursery and installed the car seat because I was too busy. He saw Hannah's sonogram photos first because Kate had to show them to someone and I was on a trip. I resented the fact that I'd missed out and also resented the way I came out of it looking like the villain when I was just trying to do my fucking job. And here I am, the villain again, when the actions I'm taking will impact everyone at this company, Lucie included.

TSG is my father's legacy and mine, and we've both sacrificed too much to step off the gas *now*.

But it feels like history is about to repeat. And I'm wondering what we'll lose when it does.

33

LUCIE

Henry's been bright-eyed and eager the whole way home. I didn't want to tell him Caleb's gone just before we got in the car—I didn't want him to crawl inside himself the way he does when he's sad and go to that place where I can't reach him. I wanted to have him in my lap and offer any of a thousand other bribes to keep him happy, but my eyes sting as we get closer to the house because I already know it won't work. There's nothing I can do or say or offer him in Caleb's place. Nothing.

And Caleb's leaving. That's the bigger issue. However difficult I find the next few weeks—they're simply a small taste of what's on the horizon, when he leaves for good.

Henry scrambles out of the car, already looking toward Caleb's house for signs of life. When we enter, Sophie rushes in first, scattering shoes, dumping her backpack out in the foyer to show me the picture she drew and the book she got from the library.

Henry quietly hangs his backpack on its hook by the door and turns to me. "I need to change. It's project night."

I sit on the stairs and reach out my arms for him. He hesitates before taking a seat on my knee. "Sweetie, Caleb had to go out of town. He's not going to be able to come home tonight, but maybe we can go get ice cream instead."

He stares at me, unblinking. "I don't want ice cream. I want to work on the arm with Caleb."

It's as if he's wrapped his little hand around my heart and given it a hard squeeze.

"He wanted to work on the arm with you too. But a really important thing came up and he's going to be gone a lot. Maybe I can help you." I try to pull him close, but he's stiff in my lap, unwilling to hear me, unwilling to accept this outcome.

"You're not good at building," he says.

"If I can't figure it out, Molly will help us. She's good at *everything*."

His shoulders sag. Caleb has brought so much into his life these past months. But as the light fades from Henry's eyes, I'm forced to ask if it was worth it.

I wanted Caleb for my own. I wanted to save him from himself.

But I should have avoided bringing my kids into it...and Jeremy makes it clear he agrees.

"You invited Caleb to Henry's show?" Jeremy screams on the phone that night. "Do you have any idea how bad this makes you look?"

I could point out that I wasn't the one who invited him, but I'm not sure that will help the situation. "Are you through?"

"You've barely been on your own and you're already throwing yourself at someone else," he says. "And if you think *I* was a disappointment as a father, just wait until you're depending on someone who isn't even related to them."

Ah, *there* it is. He's finally managed to say something that hits a little close to the bone. I knew he'd get there eventually. Because that's the crux of it, right? Jeremy owes the twins something, whether he wants to or not. But Caleb doesn't owe them a thing. He can simply walk away as if we never existed, and that seems to be what he intends to do. He hasn't brought up what happens after he leaves even once.

CALEB'S IN INDIA, then Peru, pulling together contracts with support-staff temp firms so that he can prove TSG is ready to expand. I start to lose track of the cities he's in or the reason he's gone to any of them. We've barely spoken since he left, but every time we do, there's almost always someone in the background, someone urging him to get off the phone, to get in the car, to go somewhere else. I hate how exhausted he sounds all the time. I also hate feeling like an afterthought.

Work is going well—the walking program was so successful that we're starting another one, and there's an upcoming TSG Shark Tank event where employees can pitch ideas that everyone's excited about. I even get a call from a recruiter.

But when I get home at night with the twins and Caleb's house looms dark and lonely behind us, I have to ask myself what it will be like when he's gone for good. How often could we possibly see him after the merger happens? I won't be able to jaunt off to New York, but if Kate finishes rehab and wants him back...she can.

He returns on a Tuesday, a week and a day after he left. I get little done at work but manage to check the progress of his flight approximately a hundred times over the course of the morning.

He texts when he's on his way to the office.

CALEB

Almost there. Please have that report ready for me when I arrive.

Where should I leave it?

On my desk.

There *is* no report. I'm grinning like such a fool I'm embarrassed for myself. I walk into his office and shut the door behind me.

"Lock it," he says. The predatory look in his eyes is all the foreplay I need.

I do as he asks, then lean back against the door. "We need to be quick or Kayleigh's going to know."

"Not trying to brag, but I don't think *quick* will be a problem," he replies, stalking toward me.

I meet him in the middle of the room, my hands on the lapels of his jacket. His mouth lands on mine. "I want this too much," he groans, swallowing as I tug on his belt. "I should—"

I slip a hand inside his waistband.

"Fuck," he growls. "Get on the floor."

I drop to my hands and knees. A zipper slides open and then he's behind me, pushing my skirt up and my thong aside, fingers slipping over me and then inside me. He thrusts in abruptly, without warning, and I bite my lip not to make any noise.

"That's so good," he says with a quiet groan.

He reaches around, sliding his hand inside my thong from the front.

The orgasm hits me so fast I can barely warn him. "I'm coming," I whisper. "Cover my mouth."

He does it not a moment too soon, because there is no stopping the noises I'm making right now.

"God, that's hot," he groans, and his body behind me draws tight and tense as he finishes, muffling his final gasps against my shoulder.

It's over too quickly. I need more than a few minutes in his office after a week apart. I need to lie on his chest and hear about his week and have him convince me that we're going to be okay in that way of his...The way in which he never actually says the words.

"When are we seeing you again?" I ask, fixing my skirt while he zips up his pants.

He doesn't entirely meet my eye. "I fly out in the morning, and I've got a lot of shit to deal with here, but I'll try to get home before the twins go to bed."

I kiss him goodbye, guilty and dissatisfied at once. I don't want to add to his plate. But I also don't like feeling as if I'm begging for scraps.

I take the twins to the beach that evening with my stomach in knots. A part of me is dying to tell Henry that Caleb's home simply to watch his face light up, but...I don't actually believe it's going to work out. Caleb has the very best of intentions, but of a long list of priorities...we are last.

The twins are already in bed by the time he calls, and I guess I suspected it would work out like this.

"I'm sorry," he says. "Everything ran late and we're still working. I'm probably going to work through the night and head straight to the airport. I hope Henry wasn't counting on it."

"No." *Because I didn't tell him. Because I didn't quite count on you myself.* "Have a good trip. Don't forget about next Thursday."

"Thursday?" he asks, distracted. The noise of the crowd around him gets louder.

"He's showing the class the robotic arm?"

"Right," he says. "Sorry. It's on my calendar—I swear. Nothing will stop me from being there."

I wish I believed that.

∾

On Wednesday afternoon, I'm showered and ready to see Caleb long before his flight lands. Molly's going to watch the twins so I can sneak next door for our first overnight since we went to the hotel. I bought the black lace garter thing as a surprise— when you've only had quickies for the past month, it warrants a small celebration.

He calls just as we're sitting down to dinner.

"I've got some bad news," he says, and my teeth clench. It feels like he does nothing but call with bad news of late.

I walk toward the front of the house so the twins won't overhear. "Is your flight delayed?"

He sighs. "I wish that's all it was. The COO got held up, so we're getting together tomorrow instead."

The disappointment swings into me hard, like an unexpected door. *But...you promised. Henry was counting on it. This is the kind of thing Jeremy would do, but you were supposed to be different.*

Except he never promised he'd be different. He never said he'd work less. I just wanted to *believe* he would, given the right circumstances. I wanted to believe that when it really mattered, he'd put us first.

"You can't meet with him by video?" I ask, though I already know it's too late.

"Lucie, that's not how a meeting like this takes place. I'm trying to woo these guys. We're having lunch, and I'll catch the five o'clock flight back."

Unless the meeting goes long. Unless the COO decides you should discuss it over drinks instead. "Well, I'd better let Henry know," I say.

"I really am sorry, Lucie, but this meeting—"

"Stop," I snap. "When you say *but* in a sentence, you invalidate all the words you said before it. So please don't."

He sighs again. "I knew this was going to be a problem. I knew my job was going to be an issue eventually."

I can't believe he's using *this* moment to scold me about my expectations. Jeremy's words ring in my head, though I wish they wouldn't: *you think I was a disappointment as a father? Wait until you're depending on someone who isn't even related to them.* "What an excellent time to say *I told you so,* Caleb. Anything else you want to add before I go talk to Henry?"

"I'm sorry," he says. "I'm just tired."

"Me too," I reply.

I'm tired, and I'm lonely, and I'm sick of being unsure where we stand and having to keep it all to myself. I've spent my entire life coming in a distant second or worse to the people who were supposed to care.

I'm not sure I can keep doing it. And I'm not sure I should be setting my kids up for that kind of life either.

~

THE NEXT MORNING, I drive the twins to school. Henry refused to carry the robotic arm that Molly helped him complete, as if it's tainted somehow now that Caleb won't be there. I take it into the school for him, hoping he changes his mind.

The show is small and informal—the parents take seats along the perimeter of the room while the kids sit cross-legged in a circle on the floor.

Henry's classmates attempt to juggle, dance or—in Sophie's case—sing inappropriate pop songs. But when Henry's name is called, he remains still and silent, refusing to even glance at the project I laid on the display table.

"Henry," says the teacher, singing his name the second time, as if that's going to induce him to do anything at all, "it's your turn. Are you going to show us your creation?"

I hold my breath, waiting and praying. Henry stares straight ahead as if she hasn't spoken, and I suspected he would, but when she gives up and moves on to the next kid, I want to weep until I have no more tears left.

The kids are sent home after the presentation concludes, because St. Ignatius assumes that all of us have nannies, or don't work in the first place. I've arranged for Abby, a girl from our old neighborhood, to babysit.

She meets us at the house with a bag full of art projects and ingredients for cookies. I'm grateful and at the same time I hate that I'm paying someone to do things I'd love to do with them myself.

I stall at the front door. "Don't let them go down to the lake without you," I tell her. "And Henry probably won't ask you for things, so anything you give Sophie, just give him the same. And feel free to call at any time. Honestly. There's nothing—"

She smiles reassuringly. "Lucie, they'll be fine. I promise. Go back to work."

I leave with Henry still unwilling to meet my eye. And why should he? I'm the one who let him count on someone who'd assured me he couldn't be counted upon.

I get through planning the retreat for the marketing department, working fast, hoping to cut out by five and get home to Henry—fix things somehow, though I suspect only Caleb can heal this particular wound.

When Caleb texts to say he's boarding his flight, I don't reply. He has a company to run. He needed this meeting and he told me the deal from the start. But I have a son I didn't want to see hurt. I'll do my best to get over it before he lands, but right now...I'm still upset.

I send my last few emails and am just about to close my laptop when the phone rings. *Caleb's flight was cancelled.* I reach for the phone with grim resignation, but it's Abby's name there, not his. I hit the speaker button and when I hear her crying, my stomach drops to the floor. "Abby? What's wrong?"

"It's Henry," she says. "I can't find him anywhere."

My breath stops. "Did you ask Sophie? Maybe they're playing a game."

Abby wails harder. "She said she heard the back door close, but we don't see him outside."

For a half-second, I freeze, my body still, my hand grasping the phone. "Call the police," I whisper. "I'm on the way."

I grab my keys and my phone, and I run down the hall, past Kayleigh, past the small group of employees gathered out front. I call Jeremy, then Molly as I drive, running red lights, driving on the shoulder when necessary. I'm gripping the wheel so tight that my hands ache when I remove them, panicked but at the same time...numb.

This can't be happening. It's a mistake. I'm going to walk in and discover Henry's hiding, that she didn't look carefully. I'll call his name and he'll walk out with one of his wary smiles.

But then I pull into the driveway. The police are here. Abby's crying.

This is happening. This is really happening.

I force myself out of the car and swing Sophie onto my hip. Her head presses to my chest, uncharacteristically silent and still. Her thumb goes into her mouth—a habit I thought she'd outgrown.

"I'm so sorry," Abby says. "My boyfriend came over because we'd had a fight and I came outside to talk to him—"

"How long?" I demand. "How long were they out of your sight?"

"Like, maybe a half hour."

She cries harder, and I turn away when what I want to do is scream, "*I told you! I told you to keep an eye on him and you didn't fucking listen.*"

I blame her, but mostly I blame myself. *This is what I get for trusting a kid with my kids. This is what I get for not being more careful.*

Jeremy pulls up and reaches us just as the chief of police walks over.

"We've got a team combing the woods. Do you have any thoughts on where he might have tried to go? Is there a place he likes to play?"

I hang my head. "He likes to go to our neighbor's house, but he's out of town," I say, pointing at Caleb's. "If we go for walks, it's on the path around the lake."

My voice cracks on that last word.

The captain places a hand on my shoulder. "If he's out there, we'll find him. And the boat is on the way."

I look between him and Jeremy, failing to understand this. "A boat?"

He can't meet my eye. "So we can start dredging the lake."

Dredging.

The second it's out, it feels inevitable—*of course he went to the lake; it's where he would normally find Caleb*—yet at the same time I refuse to accept it. I will comb every inch of this goddamn state by hand before I accept that he went into the lake without me.

"He wouldn't," I whisper. "He knows he's not allowed to go in the lake without an adult."

The chief winces. "Kids don't always listen."

No, they don't. Henry also knew he wasn't allowed to walk into the backyard without me and he does it all the time. Every single time he sees Caleb. *Oh God. Could he have gone into the lake? Could he have gone to check inside Caleb's boat and fallen in?*

Molly squeezes my arm, blinking back tears. I didn't realize she was here. "Why don't I take Sophie inside?" she asks, reaching out. I nod, swallowing hard as I release my daughter.

I start toward the lake. "I'm going to—"

Jeremy gently grabs my arm. "They want us to stay here, Luce. We need to be available if they have questions. Here, you're shivering." He slips his sweatshirt over my head, and I let him. He is not the enemy anymore. Nothing matters except my children, and I can't believe I forgot that for even a minute.

By the time night falls, the yard is full of strangers. News crews are set up along the driveway and I want to tell them to go away, but I don't. I'm just frozen, watching the tiny bouncing dots in the distance where police and volunteers are combing the woods for my son. In an ideal world, it would be Caleb here with me instead of Jeremy, but this is exactly what he wouldn't want anyway, isn't it? The fear, the responsibility, the potential for loss?

Harrison and Mrs. Doherty call. I'm not sure what they say to me. I don't want to hear a single word from anyone unless they've got news about my son. And with every minute that passes, the chance of it being good news fades.

Three hours later, the low murmur of the crowd is broken by a single shout.

We all look at each other. In the distance, there's another shout and then the police chief comes into view.

There's a bundle in his arms.

A bundle the size of a small child.

34

CALEB

I arrive in San Francisco just before eight and turn on my phone the second our wheels hit the tarmac. I wait for my texts to load as if they are a death sentence. Lucie's mad that I missed the thing with Henry this morning, but what was I supposed to do?

I head toward the exit, torn between irritation and worry. *You cannot serve two masters.* My father was right. I have a company that needs me. I have hundreds of people who rely on me for the check that puts a roof over their heads, that puts food in their kids' mouths. And I have the capacity to create something great—to build software that could change a child's entire educational experience. I'd have loved to be at Henry's thing. Doesn't Lucie realize I gave something up today too?

Harrison calls just as I climb into the waiting Uber.

"Thank God," he says when I answer. "Where are you? I've called a thousand times."

"Airport. I'm on the way home. What's up?"

His swallow is audible. "Caleb, it's Henry. He's missing. He disappeared this afternoon from the house."

The driver's eyes meet mine in the rearview mirror. I blink, too shocked to find words.

"Have they—"

"They've done everything. But Lucie needs you. They're... they're dredging the lake." He clears his throat. "She's going to need you when they find him."

It's exactly like the moment Beck called to tell me Hannah had died. I never thought history would repeat itself so precisely, but it is.

The car is still moving, but I feel like I'm suspended in time. I see every streetlight, notice the way the sign over the bakery flaps in the wind, a single corner blown loose.

"He can't be dead." My voice is hard, businesslike. But I'm far from calm. My stomach is about to swallow me whole.

"I hope not, man," Harrison says, but his voice is full of doubt and pity. And I remember that too...that same sort of pained, exhausted certainty in Beck's voice when he told me about Hannah. I'd thought the same things then, didn't I? I told Beck that I'd seen her three days before on an ultrasound. That she'd been sucking her thumb—that she couldn't just be *gone* without warning.

I can't. I can't go through this. I can't lose him. I can't watch Lucie lose him. I can't.

I can't believe this is happening all over again.

THE FLASHING blue and red lights of police cars are visible from a block away. A barricade is in place halfway down the street, so I grab my bag and run—into the cul-de-sac and over the crest of the hill—stopping only as the house comes into view.

Lucie's on the ground, holding something in her arms. I freeze in place. "Oh, God."

"They just found him," says the man beside me.

My knees go loose, my stomach swimming.

"That family got lucky," he adds. "Should have been watching their kid better."

"He's okay?"

The guy shrugs. "Far as I know. Found the kid somewhere off in the woods. Got lost on the path or something."

I sprint down the driveway and don't stop until I reach them. Lucie is clutching Henry and Jeremy has his arms around them both.

I realize they had children together, but the sight of them like that after all the shit he's done to her infuriates me. For now, though, I ignore it and drop to the ground. "I'm so sorry. I got here as fast as I could," I tell her. I brush a hand through Henry's hair. "Hey, bud. You okay?"

Henry nods. He's the only one of the three of them who will even look at me.

"So what happened?" I ask Lucie.

She buries her face into Henry's hair. "The sitter wasn't watching, and he walked out the back door. It took three hours to find him."

"Three *hours*? Where did he go?"

"Where do you think, asshole?" sneers Jeremy. "He was looking for you."

I glance at Lucie to confirm this, and she can't meet my eye.

"You were looking for me?" I ask Henry, swallowing down the bile in my throat.

He blinks. "I wanted to show you the arm. You always come around the path after a trip."

He walked around the lake because I fucking promised him something, and he just couldn't believe I wouldn't deliver.

It makes me want, simultaneously, to promise him everything—that it will never happen again, that we will build a fucking airplane in my front yard to make up for it—and at the same time I want to get in my car and drive away. This feeling—

this sick, fucked-up feeling—is exactly what I wanted to avoid. I have a job that requires everything, and I had nothing to give on top of that, but I went for it anyway.

"Come on, Henry," Lucie says, rising and lifting him into her arms. "Let's get some dinner and go to bed."

I watch, numb, as she starts walking toward the house with Henry. Jeremy looks me in the eye and then turns to follow her. Like he belongs, and I do not.

And that's just it...I don't. I knew all along that I didn't belong here.

I never wanted to live through what happened with Hannah again and tonight I nearly did. I shouldn't have been a part of this in the first place.

35

LUCIE

For all the tears I've shed tonight, there are more inside me. Those hours I spent thinking my son was dead have taken a decade off my life. They've also put everything in perspective. I have decisions to make, later on, though I sense I've already made them. The way Caleb jerked backward when Henry said he'd been looking for him—as if we were too much trouble, more weight than he was willing to carry—told me everything his half-in, half-out stance has not.

If we're too much baggage for him, fine. I've got a little boy to take care of. I will not waste an ounce of energy trying to convince a grown man we're worth his time.

Jeremy stops to shoo away a reporter, and I'm nearly to the door when a bespectacled guy who's been hovering for hours stops me. "Lucie?" he begins.

"We're not giving interviews right now," I say for the tenth time, my jaw tight. "I need to get my son inside."

"Oh, right. I'm not...I work with Molly. I drove her from the office because she was so frantic, I didn't trust her behind the wheel." He gets a soft smile on his face. "To be honest, I'm not sure I *ever* trust her behind the wheel, but especially not today.

Can you just tell her Michael is here? I'll drive her home whenever she's ready to leave."

I stare at him blankly. This can't be the *same* Michael, can it? This sweet, quiet guy with his painfully obvious crush on Molly is *nothing* like the hot, Christian Grey-style billionaire Molly's been describing for the past two years.

"Michael her *boss*?"

He blinks in surprise. "I mean...technically, sure. I own the company, though I don't think *anyone* tells Molly what to do. How did you know?"

Henry snuggles sleepily against my chest as he looks up at him. "Molly wants to marry you. She talks about it all the time."

Michael's eyes widen and before he can hide it, there's hope there too.

I manage a smile. "It's true, actually. She does. I'll tell her you're waiting."

Tears spring to my eyes as I walk inside. My fairy tale is ending, but maybe Molly's will begin in its place.

Henry's too sleepy to eat more than a bite or two. I rinse him off, and Jeremy and I tuck the twins in—both of us still too shell-shocked for it to seem weird. He's quiet and respectful and walks downstairs without being told to leave.

"Lucie," he says, his voice rough as we reach the door, "they can't keep living here. This isn't me trying to control you, but my God, I never want to go through a night like this again. I'll pay for it. I saw a rental over in Idlewild. Nothing fancy but nicer than this. If you're interested, go take a look. I'll pay for the next year, and we'll figure it out after that."

I nod, trying to hold myself together. "Yeah, okay. I'll call tomorrow."

He opens the door. "I'm sorry. I'm so fucking sorry about all of this. Let's try to clean up our shit for them, yeah?"

Under other circumstances, I'd be inclined to say it's not *our* shit that needs to be cleaned up, but that inclination of mine to argue all the time probably isn't helping either. "Yeah, okay."

He leaves, and I go upstairs and stare at Henry, unable to shake off the terror of the last few hours. Unable to forget every image that carved itself into my head while we waited for news —his body, face down in the lake; him shivering in the woods overnight, or wandering, calling for me, getting more and more lost with each second that passed.

There's no version of this story where the ultimate blame isn't on my shoulders: I left him with Abby, and I allowed him to count on someone who told me at the outset he couldn't be what we needed. I didn't listen to Caleb because I didn't want to hear what he said...but I'm listening now.

The twins are sound asleep, and I'm still sitting next to Henry in bed when Caleb texts to say he's waiting on the back deck.

What happened tonight wasn't his fault, but I'm too raw for any conversation we are likely to have—one that will probably involve some weak apology on his part accompanied by the reminder that he told me he didn't have time for this.

I find him outside pacing. His gaze flickers to Jeremy's sweatshirt, which I never removed. Jesus, as if that could possibly matter right now.

"Is he okay?" he asks, but the question sounds like a formality. *Business Caleb* asking the polite thing to get it out of the way.

I hug my arms around me. "Yes. He's fine."

He swallows, hands in pockets, staring at the deck. "I'm sorry if it bothered Henry that I wasn't around," he says stiffly. The words are flat and reluctant—it's the apology of someone who doesn't think he should have to offer it.

"Are you?" I ask. "Because you don't sound sorry."

His jaw shifts. "Look, I told you when this began that I'm trying to make this merger happen—"

I pinch the bridge of my nose. "Stop. Just stop. You're right.

You told me you didn't have a lot of time. But this has been the worst night of my life, and I don't need to hear you justify the fact that you made a promise to my son you didn't keep."

"So you're blaming me," he says, and my stomach sinks. I still haven't recovered from watching a boat dredge the lake for my son—I'm not sure I will *ever* recover from it entirely—and I can accept that it's my fault. But Caleb's defensiveness is *really* poorly timed. "I'm not blaming you for anything."

A vein throbs in his temple. "I think you were expecting something from me that I just can't give."

"I'm not expecting anything from you, believe me," I retort. "And we're moving, so allow that to ease any lingering fears about our *expectations*."

"Moving?" he repeats blankly. It's the first thing I've said that seems to have knocked a brick out of this wall he's suddenly got up. "Where?"

"Some place Jeremy saw in Idlewild. He said he'd pay our rent for a year, so I agreed. This house is too old, and the yard isn't fenced. We can't keep living here."

His eyes narrow. "Oh, you and *Jeremy* agreed? Suddenly he's the good guy?"

"Do you have any idea what we just went through?" I demand, my voice cracking. The agony of the entire night is catching up with me at once, compressed into a single moment. "I don't give a *shit* where we go or who found it for us. I need to make sure my kids are safe."

"He's playing you," Caleb snaps. "How can you not see this? He's been awful to you and them for years, but one little thing and it's all good?"

I take a small step back. *One little thing? Are you fucking kidding me?*

Caleb's failure to grasp what occurred tonight, how devastating it was, is this whole situation in a nutshell. When you love someone deeply and you nearly lose them, everything else is so fucking trivial that you're shocked it could ever matter to you in the first place. Jeremy, for all his flaws, managed to put everything aside—his grudges and selfishness, the squabbling —when Henry went missing. Caleb isn't able to do the same.

It still feels as if he's who I was meant for, and maybe it would have worked out if my life had gone a different way. But it didn't, and I have two children who need to come first.

My chin lifts and I swallow hard. "I've loved you since I was six. I used to watch out that back window for you and only you, dreaming up these crazy scenarios that would make you see me." My voice cracks and I have to stop talking.

"Lucie—" he begins. "I'm sorry. I just can't be respons—"

I hold up a hand because if I don't say this now, I never will. And because if he's about to offer yet another fake apology, I'm going to lose it.

"You've got a company to run that comes first for you. Maybe I didn't want to accept that, or maybe I thought once you fell in love with us, you'd choose to change. But I spent my entire life as the kid no one wanted, and I'm not doing that to my own children. For their sake, Caleb, I need to stop waiting on you to figure it out."

His eyes are wide, his mouth is ajar, and I don't give him a chance to reply as I turn to walk into the house.

There was no point in waiting—he wasn't going to promise to change. He was just going to apologize and continue proving with his inaction and his defensiveness that he doesn't feel the same way I do.

I'm someone no one has ever wanted quite enough and I put my kids in the same position.

But at least I know how to make sure it stops happening.

❧

I WAKE on the floor between the twins' beds. I tried to sleep in my own room, but I couldn't do it. I needed to be able to hear them breathing.

I sneak out to go in search of my cell phone, which I left downstairs last night after the conversation with Caleb.

My stomach sinks, remembering how it ended. But it had already ended for me, in a way, the second Henry admitted he'd been looking for Caleb when he got lost. I wanted to save Caleb from himself. I wanted my fairy tale. But those are goals for someone who doesn't have two children depending on her.

The phone shows that I already have a missed call from Molly—at six in the morning.

I dial her back immediately. "Hey, is everything okay?"

"Michael asked me out!" she screams so loudly I have to hold the phone away from my ear. "Oh, wait. Henry's okay, yeah? I guess I should have asked that first."

I smile. "He's fine. So how did this happen?" I think I'll keep our potential role in this to myself for the time being.

Molly goes on to describe how she completely lost it as he drove her home and couldn't stop crying. "And so he hugged me and somehow we were kissing and then, you know—"

"You slept with him?"

"No, Michael was all annoyingly honorable about it and saying he didn't want to take advantage of me in a vulnerable state, which goes to show that a lot of my plans that involved him rescuing me from traumatic situations would not have ended as sexily as I thought. But anyway, he said he's had a crush on me since the day I interviewed but never wanted to put me in a weird position and we're going out tomorrow night!"

I tell her how happy I am for her and agree to help her shop for lingerie for their date, though she's been buying lingerie for this date for years now.

"Now he won't have to punch one of Caleb's friends at your wedding," she replies with a laugh.

It stings—because yes, there was a ridiculous part of me that really believed there'd be a wedding—but I don't correct her. What happened between me and Caleb can wait.

This is Molly's moment. I got my moment too. I just hope hers lasts a little longer than mine did.

I call in sick and keep the kids home from school too. Henry's teacher phones later in the morning to tell me she feels awful about what happened yesterday and wants to give him another chance to demonstrate the robotic arm. Kindergartners aren't normally a part of the school-wide end-of-year show on Friday, but she's convinced them to make an exception for him. To my utter shock, he agrees, though I doubt he'll go through with it.

There are other calls too, because the whole world, it seems, has heard about Henry going missing. Even the moms at St. Ignatius, women who've never said a word to me, call or text. *God, you must have been so scared,* I hear again and again. As different as we are, there's one thing we have in common: the terror of loving someone so much—someone we could lose.

The one person I don't hear from all day long is Caleb. He's already back at work and moving forward, while I'm the one with this wound in my chest reopening every time I look at his house. *I'm* the one fighting this childish hope that we can be salvaged, when the sight of Henry looking out our window for him should be enough to remind me it can't.

I did this to myself, and I did this to my kids, and now I'm going to undo all of it. The sooner we get out of here, the better.

36

CALEB

I do what I've always done when shit's gone wrong: I head to the office and bury myself in work, and then I get on another goddamn plane and travel back to the east coast.

Budgets, contracts, the merger. None of it really matters anymore. I should be ecstatic, but even yesterday, when the last piece was set in place for the weekend at Caldwell's estate, Henry's potential disappointment was eating at me, ruining it.

I land in New York to discover texts from my friends *about* Lucie, but nothing at all from Lucie herself, which I guess makes sense. *'One little thing and it's all good?'* I demanded. I was referring to Jeremy's offer of assistance, but when she took it the wrong way, I didn't stop her. I guess a part of me thought it seemed like the easiest way to cut this whole thing off. And then she cut it off herself, and she was absolutely correct to do so.

BECK

Just checking in. How's Lucie?

I assume she's fine.

> Please tell me you didn't end it.

> It wasn't going anywhere. It's for the best.

> You fucked things up with Kate and now this.
> How many chances do you need to be given?
> You let her go and you're going to regret this
> for the rest of your life.

"It's better for them in the long haul," I say quietly.

It's the truth. I'm not sure why it feels like a lie.

When I finally fall asleep after forty-eight hours awake, it's a nonstop montage of my worst memories. It's coming over the hill to see Lucie clutching Henry's body. It's walking into the hospital to find my wife singing to our dead daughter with tears rolling down her face. It's holding Hannah for the one and only time, her little rosebud mouth pursed as if asleep—so tiny, so helpless and so failed by me. It's Henry saying, '*I wanted to show you the arm*,' and Kate's screams when I let the hospital staff take Hannah away. It's Lucie with her eyes full of tears, saying, '*I've loved you since I was six*' and telling me she'd given up. It's my father's agony over failing the company as he died—a situation I could have prevented if I'd come back here after grad school—and my mother weeping as we left the lake house for good.

It's an entire night spent dreaming about the death of various people's dreams, deaths I'm responsible for.

Harrison comes by my room when his flight lands. We have corporate lawyers here for the negotiations, but I brought him in as a backup. He catches shit no one else does, and he'll put my interests—and TSG's—first.

He perches on the edge of my bed. "This isn't what you need to hear right now, but Kate took off again. The process server couldn't find her for a while—she'd left rehab and was in a halfway house—but she was gone the day after the papers were served."

"Okay."

I stare out the window—Central Park is in full bloom this time of year, and the whole damn city appears to be out there enjoying it. Couples stroll hand in hand, parents chase errant children. They are the living...and I don't know what I am. I'm not a ghost, but I'm not one of them, either.

"You all right?" Harrison asks. "Ready for tomorrow?"

"Yeah." The negotiations should be straightforward, which means this merger is pretty much a done deal assuming the trip with Caldwell goes as planned next weekend. I've worked for years for this, yet here I am, imagining another life entirely. I'm imagining myself as one of those parents chasing a kid. As the old guy helping his wife.

"I talked to Beck," Harrison says slowly. "He said you and Lucie ended things."

I move away from the window. "If you're planning to tell me I fucked everything up with Kate and I'm fucking this up too, save your breath. Beck already said it."

He sighs. "Kate wasn't your fault. Beck's always...He's always defended her, even when she didn't deserve it."

None of us ever discuss it aloud—Beck's thing for my ex-wife. I'm pretty sure Kate's the reason he stopped dating, the reason he just fucking gave up on life.

"But Lucie's different," Harrison continues. "The two of you make each other happy. She turned everything around."

No, she turned my well-organized life into fucking chaos. I was happy before, or if not happy, I was...used to things. And now I'm daydreaming about a life I don't have instead of figuring out how to exist in the one I do.

Maybe I'm a ghost after all.

37

LUCIE

I take the twins to see the rental Jeremy mentioned. It's nicer than the cabin but unfurnished. I guess it's lucky that Caleb and I are no longer going away next weekend so I can get it set up.

"It's so fun, moving to a new place, isn't it?" the agent asks.

I give her a polite nod, and the kids don't respond. But no, it's not fun at all. Moving to an empty, new house with my two sad children feels less like the start of something good than the end of it.

Just after we arrive home, a call from my mother flashes on my phone. I strongly consider not taking it because this day's been hard enough, but relent at the last second.

"I just heard about what happened to Henry," she says. "I can't believe I'm only hearing now."

I roll my eyes. *Because you've been such a devoted, involved grandparent? The kids don't even know who you are.* "What do you want, Mom?"

"I'm extremely concerned. This wouldn't have happened if you hadn't left Jeremy. You know that, right? You should have been watching them yourself."

I laugh. "The way you watched *me* growing up? Should I have watched them like that?"

"I had no choice. You do."

I'd worried that adversity might turn me into my mom. That I'd become the sort of person who bullies everyone around her as a form of self-protection. I feel fairly certain, now, that I won't—but I can definitely put a bully in her place when necessary.

"I'm a better parent on my worst day than you were on your best," I reply. "If I ever need advice, you'll be the last person I seek it from."

And then I hang up.

~

WHEN I ARRIVE at work on Monday—both relieved by Caleb's absence and emptied by it at the same time—there's an email waiting from Mark:

Congrats. Knew I was right about you.

I click the article he's linked to—*"Five People Changing the Workplace."* There, in bold lettering, is my name, followed by a description of the walking program and team retreats, giving me way more credit than I'm due for the improved retention rate.

It's bittersweet, this moment. I've done things here, good things. Growing up in the shadow of Robert Underwood and his aunt provided me with skills no legitimate job could have. It just took putting them to use to understand it for myself. That doesn't mean I can stay, however. If you want to let an old dream die, you've got to stop dreaming it first. And how am I supposed to do that if the old dream is a guy I still work for?

I walk out and run into Mark, who's scrubbing a hand over his face and doesn't even seem to see me. "Oh, Lucie," he says, narrowly avoiding me and appearing a decade older than he did last week. "Sorry. Congrats on the article."

"Thanks. Are you okay?"

He gives me a tired smile. "Just got off the phone with Caleb. He's in a mood."

He starts to walk past me, but there's a question I've wanted to ask nearly since I arrived here, a question I've tiptoed around for too long. "Hey, Mark? Why did you guys close the seventh floor before?"

His eyes widen, and then he frowns. "Well, Caleb was concerned about the utility costs."

I shake my head. "Except the utilities are minimal relative to the rest of the budget. Did something happen there?"

He looks over his shoulder before he answers. "This stays between us," he says, "but the last event we held up there was a baby shower for Caleb and his wife. Make of that what you will."

I flinch. It's an even worse answer than I expected, one that simultaneously makes me wish I could spend my whole life fixing Caleb's while recognizing that he has wounds no one can fix until he admits they're there.

I search my email for the recruiter who reached out a few weeks ago. Caleb never wanted me here in the first place and it'll be easy for my replacement to pick up where I've left off if they actually *want* to fill the position. My guess is that after the merger, it will be someone in New York overseeing both companies anyway.

"I'm so happy you called," the recruiter says. "I actually have a client who's asked for you specifically. I'm sure you're familiar with Underwood Industries?"

After a half-second of startled silence, I simply sigh. I have no idea if it's a coincidence or my father perhaps trying to offer me some high-salary job to buy my silence, but it doesn't matter. "Yeah, I've heard of them. Except I wouldn't work for

Robert Underwood if my life depended on it. Please tell them I said so."

She gives a small, awkward laugh. "Okay. But are you open to other possibilities if I come up with something?"

I swallow. "Yeah. I'm open. I'm looking to leave here as soon as possible."

ON FRIDAY MORNING, Molly comes over to watch the twins for me since kindergartners have a delayed start—St. Ignatius once again assuming all students have a stay-at-home mom or nanny at their disposal.

She's glowing with excitement when she arrives—the date with Michael last weekend went spectacularly well (she screamed, '*Five times, Lucie. Five times!*' into the phone so loudly that Sophie demanded to know what had happened) and they're going away together this weekend as soon as I return to pick up the kids.

"I'm going to do your makeup," Sophie announces.

Molly raises a brow. "I was going to teach you about derivatives."

"Then we're at an impasse," Sophie replies.

Molly chokes on a laugh. "You win, simply for being a six-year-old who uses the word '*impasse*,'" she says, but she has her concerned face on as she walks me to the door.

She knows I'm about to see Caleb for the first time in a week—news about the merger leaked, so he's called an emergency staff meeting to quell any anxiety. That alone would be hard enough, but I've also got Henry's doomed presentation, followed by the twins going to their grandparents' for the holiday weekend. The prospect of it all requires more grit than I may have.

"Are you sure you're okay?" she asks. "You can always come

with me and Michael. He rented a house. There's tons of space."

I smile. "That's nice of you, but I might get in the way of all the sex on the kitchen table you'll be having."

"You wouldn't get in the way," she says with a grin. "I don't mind an audience."

I laugh. "I'm a bit worried about that as well."

Molly glances at Caleb's house, which is dark again, though I saw a light go on late last night. Her smile fades. "Just get through today, yeah?"

I swallow hard. "Yeah." Simply surviving the day seems like the best I can hope for.

I get to work and set up bagels and coffee in the auditorium with my stomach in knots. As the room begins to fill, I take a seat toward the back since I'll probably need to cut out early to get the twins.

Caleb enters just a minute or two before the meeting begins, cleanly shaven, new haircut and new suit, more handsome than ever. He searches the room—not even trying to hide it—until he finds me. His gaze holds mine for longer than it should. He looks exhausted. He looks broken.

If it wasn't for the twins, I'd have clung to him forever, content with the scraps he was willing to give me. Because it's always been him for me, since the moment I first saw him. Maybe I'll meet a nice guy someday, someone who cares about my kids, someone it's nice to come home to. But it won't touch what he and I could have had if life had taken a different path. No matter who I'm with, a part of me will always wish it was him.

The meeting begins. Mark does a little housekeeping, and then Caleb admits that a merger is in the works. There was worry in the air before, and now it's shifting closer to panic.

Someone asks if the merger will mean jobs are cut. My father would make some grand, sweeping promise assuring everyone their jobs are safe even if he was about to lay off half the workforce. But Caleb won't do that, though I'm sure Mark —currently wincing—wishes he would. He tells the truth, no matter how hard it is. He told me the truth, too, I guess. I just didn't want to hear it.

"I hope not," Caleb replies. "I'll do my best to make sure everyone has a position, but I can't say anything for sure."

He answers a few more questions, then sits while Mark tries to reassure everyone. My phone, resting on my thigh, vibrates with an incoming text.

CALEB

We need to talk.

I glance up at the stage to find him watching me again. It's the text he might send before telling me we can't keep working together. What it definitely is *not* is the text he'd send if he wanted to work things out.

My fingers hover over the screen, but instead of replying, I lock the phone and slip out of the room to go get the twins. Today is hard enough without hearing Caleb deliver the final blow.

I get home and pull up beside Molly's BMW, my gaze on Caleb's house instead of my own. There's a car in the driveway. I can't imagine Caleb having visitors, given the current state of his home and the fact that he's about to leave for Maui.

We need to talk, he'd said. Was it about this? This mysterious visitor he was worried I might run into?

When I get inside, the twins are still not in their uniforms and Molly's got way more makeup on her face than normal.

I send Henry and Sophie upstairs to change and turn to Molly. "Have you looked in the mirror, hon?"

Her eyes widen. "No. Is it that bad?"

I hitch a shoulder. "That depends on your taste. You've got a circle of lipstick on each cheek, however."

She rubs at her cheek and stares in dismay at the lipstick on her fingertips. "Fucking kids," she says. "Are you in a rush? I need to fix this."

"No, we've got plenty of time. There's makeup remover in my medicine cabinet."

She heads upstairs, and I wander, as always, to the back window where I've spent my entire life hoping to find Caleb on the dock, though I know he won't be there today.

Someone *is* there, however—a woman, stretched out and basking in the sun. She's long and lean, her red hair fanned out around her.

Kate.

Kate is here.

I don't realize I'm walking toward her until the door closes behind me.

The noise rouses her, and she pushes up on her forearms, watching me approach. Kate, in person, is a thousand times more beautiful than any picture of her led me to believe. Even the way she assesses me is cool, *sultry*—the way a girl in a rock video might, as if she's never experienced a moment of self-doubt, as if she already knows she's won.

I reach the dock and I still have no excuse for why I'm down here.

"Hi," she says. Her voice is a purr, slightly smoky. A bedroom voice. I do not have a bedroom voice—I sound like I'm six when I'm excited about something—and it's a minor thing, but it speaks to the infinite differences between us. That I'm someone who'd rather stay in and bake cookies than go out to a bar, while this girl probably shoots straight whiskey, doesn't blink twice at threesomes, and is game for things I don't even know exist—things she probably did with Caleb.

Standing five feet away from her, it's hard to imagine how he *wouldn't* choose her over me. And it sort of seems as if that's exactly what he's already done.

"Hi." I want to retreat without explaining myself. Say *sorry, wrong dock*, and make a run for it. "I'm Lucie. I, uh, live next door."

There's a hint of sympathy in her gaze. She's clearly accustomed to women with a crush on her husband. "I'm Kate. Caleb's wife."

His *wife*. Not his ex-wife. And she certainly doesn't give any impression that this is merely a visit.

I blink, thinking of his face as I sat at that meeting today. His serious, worried face. He couldn't take *me* on a business trip to Maui, but I bet he could take a brilliant, beautiful MBA.

We need to talk, he said.

Oh, God. Was it this? Of course it was this.

I was so certain he was mine when I was small, and I assumed, because the feeling never went away, that it meant something. That I was meant to save him and he would save me at the same time.

But no one is going to save me.

And Caleb never wanted that from me in the first place. He just wanted his wife to return, and now she has.

38

CALEB

My chest aches when I reach my desk. I have a thousand things to do before I go home to pack, and I don't give a shit about a single one of them.

This was supposed to be the most important weekend of my life, but it'll be entirely meaningless without Lucie there at the end—without her laugh, her smell, that soft skin at the base of her wrist, the arch of her foot, and her head resting on my chest. It's meaningless without the kids too. Without Henry's slow smiles, without Sophie's crazy vocabulary and sentences spoken in code.

I miss all of those things and I've *been* missing them, but it wasn't until I saw her in the auditorium this morning that I wondered how I'd survive without getting them back.

Beck calls and I answer reluctantly. He's probably going to yell at me again. At least now we're on the same page.

"You gonna see Lucie before you leave town?" he asks.

I sigh. "I told her we needed to talk at the meeting today, but she didn't wait."

His laugh is short and unhappy. "Let me guess. You said you needed to talk without ever suggesting you were sorry, but you're shocked that she wasn't waiting with bated breath to hear from you."

His words grate. In part because he's being an asshole and in part because he's right. I didn't apologize. I didn't tell her I haven't been able to eat or sleep or function since I saw her last. That I forgot my laptop as I walked through airport security and then tried to board the wrong plane because I'm so out of it. That when I got home, I stayed awake for hours, staring at her house and trying to figure out how to fix this.

I'm completely fucking lost without her. I have no idea how to get through the coming weekend leaving things the way they are, but it looks like I don't have a choice. She didn't wait.

"I went by her office and she was gone—she had something at her kids' school, apparently." I run a hand over my face, fatigued by this day already. "Swearing I'll work less when I'm on my way out of town for *work* seems like it might fall a little flat. I'll get through this meeting and try again when I'm home."

"Caleb," he says slowly, "that's not good enough. You fucked up, dude. Like, you really, really fucked up. She thought her kid was dead last week and you basically shrugged like it wasn't your problem and left town."

"That's not what—"

"I know," he says, cutting me off. "That's not what you meant to do, but ever since Hannah died, what you *intend* and what you actually do are not the same thing. Which brings me to my point...telling Lucie you'll work less isn't going to solve anything. It's probably not even true."

My temper is starting to fray—I'm operating on very little sleep, I'm pissed that I didn't get a chance to talk to Lucie and the only thing keeping me from hanging up is that he's right again. Why would Lucie believe a promise that I'll work less? I don't even believe it myself. I'll be good for a few days or a week, and then I'll start to backslide. "Okay, since you know so much, what the fuck am I supposed to do? Quit my job? Wait tables at your bar, morning shifts only?"

He sighs. I can picture him pushing a hand through his hair out of frustration. "Caleb, the issue isn't how much you work. It's that you blame yourself when anything goes wrong, and you abandon the people who need you most when it happens. You abandoned Kate because you felt guilty about Hannah, and what happened with Lucie last week sure seemed to follow the playbook, didn't it? Until you deal with your guilt, I'm not sure how you fix anything."

I push away from my desk, grabbing my keys. "Thanks for the armchair psychology, Beck," I snap, walking out of my office and ignoring Kayleigh entirely. "You haven't had a single relationship in at least five years, yet you're able to diagnose all my problems, it seems."

"Diagnosing your shit doesn't require a degree, asshole," Beck says as I push through the front doors. "*Everyone* knows what's going on with you, except for you. *Everyone* knows that you freaked out after Hannah died and acted like it didn't matter in the first place. You're forgetting we were all there. You kept her ultrasound pic in a frame on your desk. You had her car seat professionally installed *twice* because you were worried it wasn't secure enough. You fucking cared, and you're the only person in the world who doesn't know it. Go to Hannah's grave for once in your life and then come tell me I'm wrong."

He hangs up and I keep walking to my truck, my jaw grinding.

Why the fuck would I go to the grave? I can't bring her back. What good would it do to remember how it all was? To remember everything I hoped for and how it ended?

But when I reach the turnoff for the lake...I keep driving. The cemetery isn't far from here, though I've only been once. Beck thinks I can't go to her grave? Of course I can. I'll go and it will be every bit as meaningless, as performative, as I knew it would be.

I park in the cemetery, and there's an odd, leaden weight in my stomach as I climb out. The last time I was here was at the burial. We didn't have a ceremony. It was just me and Kate. She wrapped her arms around the tiny casket, choking on her sobs, and the longer it went on, the more dead I felt inside. I was removed and robotic as I pulled Kate away.

She couldn't eat and she couldn't sleep, and all I wanted in the entire fucking world was to go to the office, which I did as soon as humanly possible. Beck was right. I abandoned her. I fucking abandoned her.

I walk toward the grave, which sits at the top of the hill because Kate demanded Hannah have a view. Kate had been the most rational person I'd ever known until Hannah died, and after that...she was barely sane. I'd catch her in the middle of the night, trying to go to the cemetery. I'd find her online researching meconium aspiration, as if she could find a way to change what went wrong.

And I...did nothing. I spent a few days assuring her things would feel better and ran off to work. And soon there were nights, then weeks, when she didn't come home, and I was worried, but I was also fucking relieved. Relieved that someone else was helping her because I didn't feel like I could. Relieved she was crying to someone else because I couldn't stand to hear her reference Hannah one more time, couldn't stand to have her ask me if I thought Hannah knew we loved her, if she was cold now, and alone.

I reach the grave at last, crouching low and brushing a long-dead bouquet away to stare at the plaque.

Hannah Jane Lowell. October 24, 2020.

And I don't want to remember, but suddenly I do. I remember how tiny she was in my arms, tiny but solid, and how some bizarre part of me thought that maybe the hospital had made a mistake.

That was the first and last time I ever held her. And the nurse reached out and I knew what she wanted—that she wanted me to hand Hannah over because Kate wouldn't—and I wasn't ready.

I wasn't fucking ready, and I didn't know what to do, so I chose to believe it didn't matter. That I couldn't have cared all that much because if I had, I'd have been there sooner, and that one of us had to be rational and it would have to be me. So I handed Hannah over, and when Kate screamed and tried to lunge from the bed, I was the one who kept her from following.

I was wrong. I'm not sure what I should have done. But I should have done more than I did.

"I'm so sorry, Hannah," I whisper. I'm surprised by how rough my voice is. I'm surprised by the way my hand shakes as I reach down to press it flat to her grave. "I'm so, so sorry I wasn't there. I really wanted to be your dad."

There. It's out. I did want the things we lost, and it was harder than I ever let on, but admitting it doesn't leave me feeling like a weight has been lifted as I return to my truck. It's more as if one's been added...as if a piece of me I shut off a long time ago is back again, and it fucking hurts. I'd have given anything, done anything, just to have my daughter back. I still would.

I turn toward the lake, cursing Beck for suggesting it in the first place. I don't need this shit right before I head to Hawaii, and I somehow have to get my head back in the game.

Take another shower, I command as I crest the hill to my house. *Change clothes, get a stiff drink the second you're on the plane, and get your head in the—*

I hit the brakes, staring at the car in my driveway, unfamiliar, with out-of-state tags.

Somehow, I already know it's Kate.

I climb from the car and walk into the backyard, my dread growing with every step. She's on the dock in shorts and a t-shirt, smiling as her head turns my way. It's her old Kate smile —confident, on top of the world. Until she started doing drugs, there was no one alive surer of herself than Kate. She climbs to her feet and bridges the distance between us, throwing her arms around my neck.

I step away as quickly as I can. "You should have told me you were coming."

"I was worried you'd run in the opposite direction."

I try to smile, but honestly—yeah, if I'd known, I'd have asked her not to come *here*, at the very least. I look over my shoulder—thank God Lucie and the twins aren't home. "I guess you got the papers?"

Her smile fades. "Yeah," she says quietly. "Can we talk?"

God, this is the worst possible time for this. I run a hand through my hair. "Sure. Of course. I've got a flight to catch but —"

"I've been clean for three months, Caleb," she says, cutting me off. "I know I fucked up and I shouldn't have left rehab in the first place, but I went back. For you. For us. I want us to start over."

A chasm opens in my stomach. I don't want to hurt her sobriety, and I'm so sorry that I didn't do a better job of helping her when she fell apart, but...it's far, far too late. In some ways, it was too late even before she left. We weren't necessarily wrong together, but that's very different from being with the *right* person, the person you were meant for. Something I didn't understand until Lucie reentered my life.

"Kate, you were gone for a year," I reply. "I had no idea where you were or if you were *alive* until a few weeks ago. I had to move on. I *did* move on. I'll help however I can, but anything between us is over."

Her eyes widen, as if it never occurred to her that I might

find someone else. "Look, I know I need to re-earn your trust," she begins. "I'd feel the same way if I were you. So if you want me to take a urine test every hour on the hour, I'll—"

"Kate, stop," I whisper. She's a born negotiator. I don't want to hurt her, but she never thinks the door is closed and she'll keep right on asking to be let in unless I give her the entire truth. "I'm with someone now. Lucie. I wasn't looking to move on, but we share the dock and it's just—"

"*Her?*" Kate demands, her face bleached of color. "You're with *her?*"

My stomach tightens. "You saw her?" My voice is flat, utterly emotionless, the opposite of how I actually feel.

"She came out here about twenty minutes ago and took off. You can't be serious. What could you and that girl possibly have in common?"

Fuck, fuck, fuck. I can see it all from Lucie's perspective: I tell her I need to talk, and she discovers Kate here, lying out on the dock as if I invited her. "We have everything in common. Fucking everything that matters. What did you tell her?"

Kate wraps her arms around herself as if she's been hit. Her mouth opens, then closes, and I'll probably wish I'd been more diplomatic later on, but I really need to know how much damage was done so I can fix it.

"Nothing. I just told her who I was and she took off. Is it serious?" Her voice is so muted it's barely intelligible.

No one has asked me this question. Not even Lucie. We danced around it because I was scared where the conversation would lead, but the answer comes easily now, clear as day:

Lucie and the kids come first. I failed Hannah and I failed my wife. I'm beginning to understand why it happened, and I'm also beginning to understand that there's something worse, more unbearable, than responsibility and risk. It's the idea that someone you love is in pain, and you're its cause. Even the vaguest possibility that Lucie thinks I chose Kate over her has me ready to give up everything in order to set the record straight.

I *want* the responsibility, and I want the risk. I want everything that comes with having them in my life, the good and the bad.

"Yeah," I reply. "As soon as this is done, I'm going to marry her." I hate that I've been so blunt, but I've spent too long not quite committing to the things that matter.

I'm ready for that change. But first I have to find Lucie.

"I'm so sorry, but I've got to go," I tell her. "I think we'll need to file the divorce paperwork differently now that you're back, but I'll give you a call?"

"Sure," she says. "I'll be around."

I hesitate. "You're not staying with that dealer, are you?"

She shakes her head. "No. Don't worry about me."

I take her at her word, mostly because I'm too freaked out about Lucie to do anything else.

I call Mark on the way back to my truck. "Can you tell Caldwell I can't make it this weekend?" I ask.

"Can't make it? Are you insane? This weekend means everything!"

Yeah, I thought so too, but I was wrong.

It turns out what means everything was sitting next door, waiting for me. And I don't want them to wait even a minute more.

39

LUCIE

I've just gotten a seat near the front of the school auditorium when Mrs. Kroesinger comes to find me. "We have a little problem," she whispers. "Henry isn't sure he wants to go on."

I expected as much, but I follow her to the left of the stage where Henry sits on an overturned milk crate with his chin in his hands, a truculent set to his face. He isn't *unsure*, as his teacher suggested—he's already decided. I kneel in front of him. He won't admit he's scared, but it's there in his wide, lost eyes. "What's going on, buddy?" I ask, pulling his hands into mine.

"I don't want to do this."

I nod. "Everyone gets a little stage fright. Tell me exactly what you're worried will happen."

"People could laugh. Or it might not work."

"Has it ever not worked before?" I ask.

He stares at his tiny knees, pressed tight together. "No."

"Why would people laugh?"

"If I mess up."

I take a seat on the step beside him and pull him into my lap, pointing to the ladder built onto the back wall. "You know how they build a ladder like that?" I ask quietly. "By nailing the first rung and then climbing on that rung to nail up the next. And life's a little like that ladder. A good life is made up of all these brave moments. And you use the confidence you get from the first brave moment to move on to the bigger and better ones. But how are you ever going to get there if you won't take that first step?"

His eyes meet mine. I have no idea if he's gotten the analogy. "Is Caleb coming?"

There's a pinch in my chest. "I'm sure he'd have wanted to. I didn't invite him."

He frowns. "Why not?"

There are so many answers on the tip of my tongue. Yes, Caleb couldn't have come. He'll be heading to the airport soon, perhaps with his wife. But Henry's asking a bigger question. He wants to know why we no longer talk to Caleb or talk *about* Caleb and why I've stopped saying *'maybe'* or *'I hope so'* when Henry asks if we'll see him soon. And I have answers for that too, but I'm not sure they're entirely truthful.

Can I honestly say Caleb didn't want us? Can I honestly say it was never going to work out?

I can't. Because I was too scared to push for the answer. Caleb is terrified of repeating what he lived through before, but I was terrified too. I worried that I'd keep trying and he'd say, *'no thanks,'* the way both my parents did at various points—Jeremy as well. That I'd let my kids love him and he'd say *'no thanks'* to them too.

I didn't reply to his text today. I didn't even ask him about Kate after I met her. I just ran away, so scared of wounding us that I denied us the very small chance we could have been healed.

"Because I wasn't brave," I admit to Henry.

He raises his eyes to me, questioning, waiting for me to make the same concession I am asking of him.

It's not going to change anything, I long to argue. But I guess I can let Caleb say what he's going to say. I guess I can let him tell me he's moved on.

Henry rises, pressing his lips to my forehead—the way I kiss him at night. And then he points over my shoulder. "Okay. Caleb's over there. If you'll be brave now, I'll be brave too."

"*What?*" I stare at him, wondering if this is some metaphor I don't understand or a game of pretend. But I follow his gaze...and see Caleb in the corner, talking to one of the teachers and watching us with that anxious furrow between his brows.

He has a plane to catch. I can't imagine why he'd be here unless something disastrous has happened.

I rise slowly and walk to him, my heart beating so fast in my chest that it's hard to breathe.

"Lucie," he says, pulling my hands into his. "Can I...can we—?"

He looks around and then pulls me behind a pillar, where we are hidden from view.

My mouth opens, but he stops me. "Let me go first, okay? I'm not with Kate." He binds my wrists with his large palms, begging me to meet his eye. "I had no idea she was coming, but I'm not with her. I love you, and I'm so fucking sorry it took me this long to say it. I'm so fucking sorry I freaked out last week. But if you'll just take me back, I swear to God—" his voice cracks. He stops, swallowing. "I swear to God, I'll do better."

I press my face to his chest, and it all comes out—the pain I've held in for the past hour and the past week and the past month. His hold on me tightens.

"What about your flight?" I ask, wiping my eyes.

"I'm not going."

"But—"

He shakes his head. "It's done. You guys come first now, and

I'm not putting it off until Monday or next year or when the twins have left for college. It wouldn't have worked anyway...How the hell could I have you and the twins on the west coast when I was working in New York?"

I swallow hard to keep from bursting into tears again.

"I've been waiting to hear you say that since I was six," I whisper, laughing and crying at once. "Maybe not the twins part."

He pulls me closer. "I'm so glad you waited. I promise I'm going to make it worth your while."

His lips press to mine, and then we walk out the side-stage door and reenter the auditorium from the back, sliding into seats just as the lights are lowering.

When the curtain rises, Henry steps up first and his robotic arm works without a hitch.

Sophie jumps to her feet before he's even done. "That's my brother," she announces to the kids around her, loud enough that we can hear her all the way in the back, "so you all need to stand up and clap."

And they do.

We walk outside once the show concludes to meet Jeremy, who theoretically got held up at work and is only arriving now. Caleb has remained in the school lobby at my request—Jeremy's mom will do most of the parenting this weekend, but I want this tentative peace with him to last at least until the twins are home safely.

"Great job, buddy!" Jeremy says, thumping Henry on the back as if he was there. "Did you crush the other kids?"

"It's not a competition, Daddy," Sophie scolds. And while his father mutters something along the lines of *that's what losers say*, Henry looks at me and gives me that secret smile of his—

the one that rests entirely in his eyes and makes me think he might already be wiser than his father and I put together.

I hand Jeremy their weekend bags.

"So what are you doing while we're gone?" he asks. "You could come with us, you know."

I stare at him, incredulous. "I'm not sure your girlfriend would appreciate that."

"I think that's over. She wasn't coming until tomorrow and I can tell her to stay home."

Oh my God. The fact that Jeremy never seems to realize he doesn't still have a chance should no longer shock me, but it does. I shake my head. "I don't think that's a good idea."

"Well, think about it. I can send a car for you if you change your mind."

I drop to my knees and pull Henry and Sophie into my arms, praying the conversation hasn't given them some renewed hope about me and their father.

"Remember," Henry whispers. "You promised to be brave."

I laugh and kiss his cheek. He doesn't want me and Jeremy together. He wants Caleb in his life, and that's what I want too.

I return to the lobby, where Caleb is typing on his phone. My stomach tightens, waiting for him to tell me some new emergency is calling him away.

But when I reach him, he puts the phone in his pocket and rests his hands on my hips. The parents milling around do double takes—let them. I've moved on and I want the whole world to know. Especially the Toms of the world, who are likely to get punched in the face if they manhandle me henceforth.

"It occurs to me," he says, "that we both have the weekend free. What if we went away?"

"You don't need to talk to Kate?"

He frowns. "I said everything I needed to say. She knows I'm with you and that it's serious. The divorce will need to be refiled, but that can wait a few days. Let's just go. We can buy whatever we need on the way."

He's so certain about this, about me, that he doesn't understand why I'm asking the question.

"Yeah, okay," I say with a grin. "Let's go away. If we can even find a place...It's a holiday weekend, so—"

"I might have already booked something," he says with a grin.

He wasn't on his phone dealing with work. He was booking us a place. After more than twenty years of waiting for him, we're finally on the same page.

IT TAKES two hours to reach our mystery destination. After running into one store for bathing suits, t-shirts and shorts, and another for toothbrushes, he pulls up in front of a massive wrought-iron fence and consults his phone for the gate code.

"I thought you said it was a *cottage*?" I ask as he punches the numbers in.

"It's only three bedrooms, therefore a cottage." He grins at me. "But I wanted to make sure we had some privacy."

My nipples tighten under his darkening gaze, and there's a flutter between my legs. It's only been two weeks, but it feels like months since I was last beneath him.

We head down a long driveway and park in front of the 'cottage,' which is larger than his house and mine put together. I follow him through the front door and stare wide-eyed at the place he chose. It's perfect—a daydream of black-lacquered hardwood and crisp white furniture.

He hits a button and the entire glass back wall of the house slides open to the long rectangular pool. Beyond it, a sweeping backyard leads to the sea.

"Holy shit, Caleb," I whisper, walking toward the back. "For a guy who once complained about a nearly free walking program, you've really done a one-eighty."

"Claiming the walking program was 'nearly free' doesn't make it so," he says with a playful growl, climbing into a lounge chair facing the ocean and pulling me into his lap. "You do realize that, right?"

I press a hand to his chest. "I bet it cost less than renting this place for an entire weekend."

"Key difference: the walking program didn't involve you naked part of the time."

I look at the high hedges surrounding us on both sides. "I suspect I could be naked for *all* of it if you'd like."

He nuzzles my neck, his large hands palming my ass. Beneath me, he is already hard. "Let's start now."

"Should we go upstairs?" I suggest, turning to straddle him. His cock is pressed between my legs, so engorged it must be painful.

"Or," he says, slipping his fingers between my legs, pulling my panties to the side, "I could just fuck you right here. Jesus, you're so wet already."

I glance over my shoulder. The hedges block most of the view but not from the beach. "Someone could see."

His hand slides up the front of my blouse and he groans as his palm covers one breast. "I'll risk it if you will."

He unbuttons my shirt and tugs the bra low, and when his mouth tightens around one nipple, then the other, I no longer care who sees. They can film it and play it on a Jumbotron at local games for all I care.

He lifts his hips as I drag his pants and boxers down.

I grasp his cock and slip it between my legs, letting it press to my entrance, drawing out the delicious tension.

"You're killing me," he grunts, and I lower myself onto him, burrowing into his neck to muffle my groan.

His hands go to my hips, a silent plea for more, and I begin to move, clenching each time I rise up. Clench, release, clench, release. The breeze blows cool against my bare back, while inside me he is hot and slick and perfect.

His head falls back against the chair. "I can't get enough of this," he says, almost to himself, looking up at me through hazy eyes. The sun dances lazily over my forehead, my cheekbones. The world grows Technicolor, like a child's drawing—the hedges the most verdant green, the pool the deepest blue.

His lips pull fiercely on my nipple, too rough, his abandon the surest sign that he is losing control. He dwarfs me in size, he commands the respect of hundreds, but right here he is all mine—this man who takes orders from no one, a slave to my slow, drawn-out movements.

I sink down again, squeezing as I reach his base. My nerves fire a warning.

"I'm close," I whisper. I can feel it coming, with the clamor of a freight train, and I chase it, no longer worried about slowing down for him. "Oh God, I'm so close."

When it hits me, I clench one last time, like a fist, and he lets go at last.

"Oh fuck," he hisses, his head thrown back, the tendons of his neck taut.

I slide over him a few more times for good measure, and his eyes open heavily, as if drugged. "Jesus." His voice is slurred.

I climb off him at last, resting my head against his chest as we both catch our breath.

"I have no words, Lucie," he says. "It's going to be hard to top that this weekend."

"It was okay," I tell him, smiling.

"You think I can't tell how hard you came?" he asks, standing and lifting me with him, tugging his pants up as he walks us toward the house. "I'm happy to try again if you insist, though."

He carries me to a bedroom, where he does, indeed, show

me one more time. We fall asleep and he shows me again and then we swim and start the process anew.

And as I doze off against him just as night begins to fall—naked, damp, sandy—I realize that I wound up with a better version of the fairy tale than I ever could have dreamed of as a child. One with my twins and him, and a future that now appears endlessly bright.

It took two decades, but I wouldn't change a single thing.

ON SUNDAY AFTERNOON WE LEAVE, both of us rosy-cheeked and sated and suspiciously free of tan lines, and I'm so relaxed that I'm melting as I curl up beside him in the car...until Jeremy calls.

My hands fumble in my panic as I hit *speaker* on the phone.

"Mommy?" asks Sophie. "The password isn't working. To buy stuff on the iPad."

Caleb and I exchange a glance, and I groan in relief. "Sophie, I already told you no more games and no more gems this week."

"I know," she says. "Daddy made me call."

I stiffen. So does Caleb. I'm not even sure what's triggered us here, but...something's amiss.

"He *made* you call?" I repeat.

"He said the passcode wouldn't work and I should ask you."

When I hang up, Caleb slaps a hand over his face. "Jesus, I'm an idiot. How did it not occur to me you'd be sharing your password with them?"

"Is that how he's been tracking me?"

"He's been able to see anything that goes to the cloud from via your Apple ID if you don't have multi-factor authentication set up—your location, your texts. All he had to do was download it onto a new phone."

We call Harrison, and once he's done gloating over the fact that we're back together, we tell him about the phone issue and he gives us the reply I expected: there's nothing to be done unless we can *prove* Jeremy was tracking me, which we probably can't.

"But," he adds, "you've won the battle that matters."

"We have?" I ask.

"You're together, right? As long as you've got that, you can wait for everything else to sort itself out."

Caleb's fingers twine with mine, and he gives me a small smile.

Yeah, Harrison's right.

This won't be my last fight with Jeremy. There will be plenty more ahead.

But we've won the battle that matters, and whatever happens in the future—I won't be facing it alone.

40

LUCIE

The air is mild, the skies are cloudless—a perfect day to learn to surf, if we can just get out of the house.

"You've got enough sunscreen, right?" Caleb asks, leaning over to peek into my tote. He worries about the twins as if they're newborns. "And snacks? There won't be much there. Goldfish and apples aren't gonna cut it if the kids want to stay."

I laugh. "For the third time, yes. They'll be fine. I promise. Isn't it a forty-minute drive? We'd better get going."

"Henry can't find his flip-flops," Sophie announces, heading toward the door. "But that's on him."

Caleb and I exchange a grin over her head. I've got no idea where she gets this stuff.

"I think we should install tracking devices in the soles of your shoes, bud," Caleb says, ruffling my son's hair.

"Can we?" Henry asks. "Can we do that instead of surfing?" The idea of balancing on a board atop a moving wall of water terrifies him. I get that—it terrifies me too.

"You're going to love it, Henry," Caleb says, and I restrain a wince. Today is not only about teaching the twins to surf. It's also about saying goodbye to a major part of Caleb's childhood.

Harrison's dad's place just went under contract, and today he'll be meeting his friends there for the last time. In typical fashion, he's acting like it doesn't bother him when it must, and is entirely focused on how surfing will change the twins' lives.

He hasn't parented long enough to understand that basing your happiness on that of your kids is a recipe for disaster—even the most fun day has a fifty percent chance of ending in tears or tantrums.

And trying a new, difficult sport doesn't sound all that fun in the first place. As we climb in the car and begin our journey, Caleb's the only one of the four of us who's even vaguely enthusiastic. It's only when we get to the beach and turn onto Harrison's street that his serenity takes a hit. "It's so weird to be back here."

This isn't simply the last visit. It's also the first visit since their friend Danny jumped off a nearby cliff eight years prior, the event Audrey described to me at the bar...one that sent all of their lives in a downward spin for varying reasons. Beck suggested today's outing, jokingly, as an attempt to 'break the curse,' but I think a small piece of them actually hopes it will work.

I squeeze his hand. "It's okay to be sad, you know. You're saying goodbye to a part of your childhood."

He shakes his head. "It's the beginning of something life-changing for the kids, which is even better."

"We'll be lucky if one of them is willing to *try* it," I warn. "It's definitely not going to be '*the beginning of something life-changing.*'"

"You'll see," he replies.

He pulls into a driveway behind Harrison's Range Rover, and as I climb from the car, I get why he referred to that place we stayed over the Fourth of July as a '*cottage.*'

"*This* is where you vacationed as a kid? I was expecting a surf shack. It's a mansion."

Caleb pops the trunk and reaches for the wetsuits he insisted on buying the twins, wetsuits they'll *never* be willing to wear. "It set the bar pretty high."

"It must be hard for you now, vacationing now without a butler to serve you caviar," I reply, taking the wetsuits. "No wonder you were so worried about my snacks."

He walks under the carport and hoists two surfboards overhead as if they're light as air. "It's not *that* fancy."

We follow him onto the wooden walkway. "Just because there's not *currently* a butler here doesn't make it any less fancy. I bet it had a staff."

He laughs. "Okay, yeah, there was a staff."

"And did they bring you snacks on the beach?"

He grins over his shoulder. "Not *caviar.*"

"Finally," Harrison says as we walk up, tugging Sophie's ponytail before he gives me a hug. "The fun has arrived."

In the weeks since Caleb dropped plans for the merger, we've seen a lot more of Harrison, but nothing of Audrey. It's pretty clear he's ready to be a dad. It's also pretty clear there's some tension with his wife over it.

Caleb looks around. "Where's Beck? This was his idea."

"Something came up," Liam replies, not quite meeting Caleb's eye before he glances at the twins. "You guys ready for this?"

Henry doesn't answer. "We want to build sandcastles," Sophie says, and Henry nods. They reach into my bag for buckets and walk to the shore.

"Why don't you guys surf a bit?" I ask Caleb. "Let the twins see how fun it is."

He hesitates before giving me a reluctant nod. Harrison and Liam head to the water, while Caleb tugs his t-shirt overhead. I've seen him naked more times than I can count, but I don't see him undressing in public that much. I have a renewed appreciation for the long, lean lines of him, for the broad shoulders tapering to narrow hips, for that tattoo on his shoulder, which I recently learned is some surf thing and not an homage to Kate.

He grins, tiny smile lines forming around his eyes. "Keep looking at me like that, Lucie, and I won't make it into the water at all."

My gaze drifts from the kids down near the water's edge and back to Harrison's dad's house. "I'd be okay with that. I bet he's got Frette linens on every bed."

He swoops down and throws me over his shoulder in a fireman's carry. "Let's go see."

I laugh. "Sure. Should I put Henry in charge of Sophie, or vice versa?"

He allows me to slide back to the sand, continuing to hold me close, pressing a kiss to the tip of my nose. "Henry would blow it off and giving Sophie that much power would be dangerous. I guess it'll have to wait."

He finishes pulling on his wetsuit and dives into the water while I venture down to help the twins make a castle, which we garnish with shells and plants. My attention, however, is only partly on the job, because Caleb surfing is a particularly distracting sight—he carves into a wave with as much ease as he complains about work expenditures. It's even hotter than I suspected it might be. And I already expected it would be really, really hot.

In my only real relationship prior to this, things went dramatically downhill the moment they were official. With Caleb, it's been the opposite. He's wonderful with the twins, but also wonderful with *me*. He provides things I didn't even know I needed until they're presented to me. He knows Jeremy's cheating left a mark, so when he's traveling, he sends me his itinerary. After he met with Kate to discuss everything, he called me and reported back every word. The part of me that is still fragile and shaken gets a little less so every day, entirely because of him.

The twins and I make a series of sand birthday cakes, but their interest is waning. They both watch Harrison pop up on his board and ride a moderate wave. Like Caleb, he makes it look effortless.

"What happens if they fall?" Henry asks quietly, just as Harrison dives off and reemerges, laughing.

"You're the science guy," I reply. "What happens when you fall into water?"

Henry doesn't answer, but continues to watch, as does Sophie, though her glances are less curious than they are irritated. "I don't want to wear a wetsuit," she announces, rising.

"The water's pretty cold, Sophie. You wouldn't be able to stay out long without it."

"*Fine*," she says angrily, stomping back up the beach, where she proceeds to put on the wetsuit alone, howling in frustration with how tight it is around the legs. Caleb comes out of the water to get her and within minutes she's balancing on one of the big foam boards. "Mommy!" she screams, "look! Henry! Henry! Look at me. You're not look—"

She goes over the side and Caleb is next to her in seconds, lifting her back onto the board.

"Henry!" she yells. "Did you see me?"

He turns away and I laugh. "Henry, throw her a bone. Tell her you saw her."

He glances at me and, wordlessly, marches up the beach for his wetsuit and brings it back so I can help him put it on. I bite my tongue as I tug it over his legs, holding in the desperate way I want to encourage him: *You're going to love this, Henry; I'm so proud of you; You're going to do great.*

I don't say a fucking word, because Henry's like a timid animal at times like this—even the smallest errant movement can set him off. If he's going out there solely to keep Sophie from bragging about it for the rest of the day, so be it.

Caleb seems to sense that he needs to tread lightly. He puts

Sophie in the care of Liam and Harrison, gets the second board and approaches without too much fanfare, catching my eye and raising a brow. I give him the tiniest nod and he reaches for Henry's hand.

"Hop on and I'll push you out," he says.

Henry swallows, staring at the board, not moving. And then, in the distance, Sophie shouts his name again and he moves forward, lying down just the way she did, his jaw set with grim resignation.

"Here goes nothing," I say to myself, watching Caleb paddle him out to the break.

Sophie goes whizzing past them, sure-footed and proud of herself, yet another thing that's come naturally to her. It could easily set Henry off, but Caleb simply pulls the board away from Liam and Harrison so that Henry won't be discouraged by his sister's success.

Once they're in position, Caleb waits for a small wave and pushes the board, but Henry lies flat, making no effort whatsoever to stand. Through the next few waves, he progresses to his forearms, then his knees and my breath holds, waiting for the moment he'll get discouraged and quit, waiting for Caleb to grow impatient—because even I'd be growing impatient by now.

On his fifth wave, Henry stands. It lasts only a second, but Caleb is thrilled.

"Hell yeah!" he cheers, as ecstatic as the father of an Olympic medal winner.

On his sixth wave, Henry gets up and stays up. His balance is shaky—he doesn't make it look easy, the way Sophie does. And it doesn't matter in the least.

"Mommy! Caleb!" he shouts. "Look at me!"

He's smiling as he goes over the side.

My eyes cloud with happy tears, and even from this distance, I can tell Caleb's have too.

EPILOGUE
CALEB

W e meet with the developmental pediatrician, Dr. Stein, just before the new school year begins. He brings us back while Henry plays in the waiting room—Jeremy hasn't shown up, of course.

Lucie squeezes my hand as we follow him to his office, and I thank God I came. Life at work is a lot calmer than it was, but it's still not calm: Caldwell was furious about my failure to show up in Hawaii, and even more furious when I told him I couldn't move to New York. We're back to square one, but I've hired someone to find us investors and promoted Mark to Chief Operations Officer. His first job as COO was to fire Kayleigh after I caught her telling Lucie off, which had apparently become a routine occurrence.

I don't always work nine-to-five, and it was tempting to stay at the office today when Lucie assured me she'd be fine.

I came in case she needed me, and it's pretty clear she does.

We sit together on a couch while Dr. Stein discusses Henry's evaluation. Nothing he says is a surprise: Henry is smart as hell and a very nice kid. He's also on the autism spectrum.

Lucie's fingers twine with mine and squeeze tight.

"I know that's not what any parent wants to hear—" the doctor begins, and she cuts him off.

"Henry's exactly who he's meant to be," she says, though her eyes are bright, "and he's exactly the son I want. We're going to be fine."

We leave the appointment with Henry between us, each of us holding a hand. She glances at her watch. "Do we have time to go to lunch before you head back to the office?" she asks.

Henry glances up, waiting for my answer.

"Why don't we all just take the day off?" I ask, and for the first time since we entered Dr. Stein's office, he smiles.

She was right. He's going to be fine. We all are.

ON A KID-FREE SUNDAY A MONTH LATER, Lucie and I leave Liam at the lake house to work on renovations—I wanted to do them myself originally to prove I was a different man than my father, but part of being a different man is not wasting time that could be spent with Lucie and the kids—and I take her to look at a place down at the busier end of the lake.

It's a new build, twice the size of my house. Lucie's eyes are wide when we walk in, and just keep getting wider. It's not quite the house we rented over the Fourth of July, but it's a hell of a step up from any place either of us have lived before, with six bedrooms upstairs.

We tour every floor and then leave the agent inside while we walk onto the screened porch overlooking the lake. At the house next door, a little boy is playing alone in the backyard, building an elaborate structure out of sticks. Already, I can see the friend we both want for Henry. And the future we *both* want, I hope.

"Wow," she says quietly. "This house is something else."

I swallow. "Yeah? So you might want to live here?"

She turns toward me. "Hypothetically?"

I pull her hands into mine. "No. Not hypothetically. With me. You and the kids."

She exhales. "It's a big step."

I'd hoped for slightly more enthusiasm. We haven't discussed it yet, but I can already picture the day when we might add a kid or two to the ones we already have. I assumed that's what she wanted too.

I tug on her hands. "What is it that you're thinking but don't want to say?"

She stares at the floor between us. "I feel weird discussing it."

"Is it dirty?" I ask. "You can whisper it in my ear."

She laughs. "No, pervert. It's not dirty. It's just...I don't know. It might be a bigger step than I'm ready to make."

"Okay," I say, struggling to master my disappointment. "Is it too soon? Or is it something you don't think you'll even want to do eventually?"

"Neither one," she says hastily, squeezing my hand. "I'm just not sure about the twins. Not everyone's as liberal as we are. So, on the one hand, I don't really care how it looks, but on the other, I'm worried about what kids will say to them and—"

"So you're saying you want to get married."

She blushes. "No. That's exactly why I didn't want to discuss this. Because it *sounds* like that's what I'm saying and I'm not. I mean, obviously I'm not. Neither of us is even divorced yet, so—"

She's babbling. Nervous. There's a laugh bubbling in my chest, one I struggle to hold in. "So you're saying you *don't* want to marry me."

She groans. "No. I'm just saying there are other things to consider and, well, I—"

"You aren't *sure* you want to marry me."

She huffs an irritated laugh. "You're *trying* to annoy me, aren't you?"

"Just answer the question. Are you not sure you want to marry me?"

"Yes," she mumbles, looking away. "I'm sure."

"And did you honestly think I would expect you and the kids to move in without making some kind of commitment first?"

"Well, yeah...I mean, you're not a fan of marriage, and I get that, I really do—"

"I never said I wasn't a fan of marriage," I reply. I pull out my phone. "Hang on. I need to send a text."

She frowns at me. "Right *now*?" And then she hears her phone chime and I glance at the text I just sent.

> ICWTMY

She pulls out her phone, continuing to frown as she reads before a small smile plays around her mouth. "I can't wait to... maul you? Muffle you?"

"Try again, Lucie."

She smiles wider. "I have no idea. Oh, wait. Masturbate you? I don't think that's grammatically correct."

"Don't think I won't spank you right here, even with the agent watching. You know what the 'M' stands for."

"Yeah," she says, typing into her phone. "I think I do."

LUCIE

> ICWTSY

I can't wait to say yes.

I can't wait til she does either.

THE END

Can't get enough of
Elizabeth O'Roark?

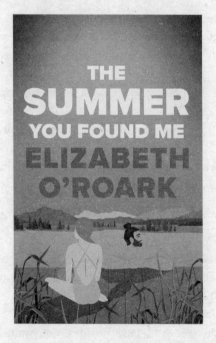

Keep reading now for a sneak
peek of Beck and Kate's story in
The Summer You Found Me.

Coming soon!

PIATKUS

THE SUMMER YOU FOUND ME

COMING JANUARY 2024

Beck's cabin is deep in the woods, and straight out of every horror movie you've ever seen. You catch a glimpse of this house during any film—*Saving Private Ryan, High School Musical*—and you know someone is about to die. The seedy motel I stayed in last night last night is looking better and better.

He isn't home yet, which isn't a surprise. Beck rarely sleeps in his own bed. I wait on his front steps, my legs stretched in front of me, and it's not long before I hear the roar of a motorcycle in the distance.

As wheels rumble over the gravel lane, my heart begins this weird, tripping rhythm—nerves, I suppose. I could take or leave most of Caleb's friends, but Beck was different. I've thought of him a lot this past year, his image often resting behind my eyes like the screensaver on a dormant computer—the black brows that make him look like he's glowering any time he isn't smiling, the wavy dark hair falling to his shoulders. And his eyes, that strange light brown, glimmering as if backlit by a fire.

The bike purrs to a quiet halt in front of me. Even seated,

the sheer size of him is overwhelming. His arms, his chest—all the parts I've seen firsthand—are double the size of a normal human's. I wonder, as always, about the parts I *haven't* seen.

He pulls off the helmet and raises a brow at me as he rises. My pulse speeds up in response. There's something dark and slightly predatory about him, like a housebroken tiger—maybe he plays along but that thing inside him is always one step removed from violence. It appeals more than it should. He's got a beard now. That appeals too.

He tucks the helmet under his arm. "I heard you'd come back."

God, I hate small towns. I should have known they'd all be gossiping.

"I'm about to start my period. Were they talking about that too?"

Beck's smiles are rare and even then, barely noticeable, but his mouth moves slightly upward as he passes me to walk up his front steps. It feels like a victory, that *almost* smile.

He unlocks the door and I follow him inside without waiting to be invited in. Nothing has changed in the year I've been gone. Aside from the bathroom and two bedrooms off to the right, it's just a small kitchen in the back and a tiny living area so empty you'd think he was in the process of moving out. There's a table with two old chairs and a shitty, ancient couch facing the TV; not a single vase, photo, or lamp.

I grin. "I love what you've done with the place."

He acts as if I haven't spoken, tipping his chin toward the couch and grabbing a chair for himself, sitting astride it to face me. "Why are you here?" he asks.

I deflate a little at his tone. I knew I wouldn't be welcomed back by *everyone*, but I sort of thought it would be different with him. It used to be.

"Aren't we going to make friendly chit chat first?" I ask,

curling up on the couch. "You ask where I've been and I tell you what a good girl I am now?"

He raises a brow. "You? *Good*? Unlikely. Tell me why you're in Elliott Springs."

"My husband is here," I snap. "We aren't divorced yet. Nothing's been done that can't be undone." If he won't feign civility, why should I? I've never had to play nice with him anyway.

"I fucking knew it," he mutters, running a hand through his hair. "Kate, let it go. She's a nice girl. They're good for each other."

I roll my eyes. "*Girl* is the key word. She looks like a Disney princess, just waiting for her magical first kiss."

There's a glimmer of amusement in his gaze. "And that makes you...what? The evil queen?"

He thinks that's an insult but I warm to the analogy. Caleb *wants* an evil queen, whether he admits it or not. He appreciated my ruthlessness and he loved my filthy mouth, while Lucie's the kind of girl who can't resist a photo of kittens in a basket and couldn't utter the word *cock* if her life depended on it. Caleb will be bored any minute now.

"I'm the one he married," I begin. "I know I fucked up. I know I lost his trust. But if he sees I've changed he'll—"

"It won't matter." His voice is knife-sharp. "He loves her and she makes him happy."

I let my head fall to the back of the couch with an aggrieved sigh. "He *thinks* he loves her. There's a difference. And I made him happy once too." Though it's been a long while since I made Caleb happy, and it sure didn't last long. Beck is kind enough not to point this out.

"So why are you here, at my *house*?"

My heart restarts its nervous, tripping pattern. I'm comfortable arguing. I'm comfortable demanding. But asking...*begging*? It's not my forte. "I was hoping I could stay with you."

"It's probably not the best idea," he says, prodding his cheek with his tongue.

My stomach sinks. I really thought Beck would be the one person who wouldn't turn me away. I knew he'd worry about Caleb's reaction, but he's always handled moral ambiguity well.

"Fine." I climb to my feet, shrugging with an insouciance I don't at all feel. "There are other people I can stay with."

This is largely untrue. There's only one person who'd welcome me right now, and he's the last person I should stay with. Beck knows it as well as I do.

"Stop," he says, and I fight the desire to smile. "You can stay. Just until you're back on your feet. But there are conditions."

I run my thumb over my lower lip. It's so cute, the way he thinks he's in charge.

"Condition one, no drugs." My mouth opens to argue but he waves me off. "Yes, I know you said you're clean, but I've heard that out of your mouth about twenty times before."

My fists clench. This is what I'm in for here—a thousand reminders about how much I've messed up in the past. "You have no fucking idea how hard I worked to get to this point so don't you dare act like I'm incapable of improvement."

His expression remains flat, *bored*. "I don't think you're incapable of it. But it doesn't mean you're incapable of failure either. None of us are. So no drugs."

None of us are incapable of failure but you, Kate, are particularly susceptible to it. That's what I hear and the fact that he's right doesn't lessen my irritation. "Fine," I reply, blowing my hair off my face, trying to be Good Kate. I'm only a few hours in, and being Good Kate is already tedious as hell.

"Condition number two: you don't fuck with Caleb and Lucie."

Anger steamrolls over Good Kate in a second. "Why are you taking her side?" I demand. "You've known me for years. You've known her for what, a *month*? A *week*?"

"I'm not taking her side. I'm taking Caleb's." He rises slowly from the chair. "Do we have a deal or not?"

I click my tongue. "Whatever."

He appears to accept this as agreement, which it really was not—Lucie doesn't get to *keep* my husband just because I need a place to stay—and gestures toward the spare bedroom.

I cross the hall to peek in. I've never seen any of the bedrooms in Beck's house—it's oddly thrilling even if there's nothing in there but a bare mattress laying on the dusty floor and a light bulb that swings eerily from the ceiling. "This looks like the room you'd hold a captive in," I tell him.

His lips twitch. "I'll have to keep that in mind for the future."

I picture it before I can stop myself—Beck holding someone down on that mattress—and electricity surges through my blood. If I'm being honest, it's not the first time Beck has had that effect on me. I remind myself—as I have before—that it's probably the effect he has on everyone. I bet even innocent little Lucie fantasizes about Beck holding her down once in a while.

"I've gotta get in the shower," he says, rising from the chair. "I'm already running late."

A tiny echo of disappointment pings in my stomach. Even if Beck and I mostly argue, I sort of wanted him here. "You're already going back to work? You just got home."

He gets this dirty almost-smile on his face. "I wouldn't call what I was doing this morning *work*. I'll try to get back here, but the bar doesn't close until two tonight."

It's kind of him. There's this weird cavity in my chest anyway. Is it envy, loneliness? I'm not sure. I fought my way back from the dead, but I still don't have a life.

"Don't worry about it. I love staying alone in creepy, isolated houses straight out of a horror movie."

He tilts his head. "You're the evil queen, remember? This place is made for you."

I smile. "Nothing wrong with being the evil queen. Most men appreciate a little bad with their good."

Caleb *definitely* appreciates a little bad with his good.

I just have to remind him.

ACKNOWLEDGMENTS

It took a village to get this book out of the gate.

Thanks so much to all the people who cheered me on and read and gave me feedback: Jen Wilson Owens, Jodi Martin, Katie Friend, Katie Meyer, Laura Pavlov, Maren Channer, Meagan Reynoso, Michelle Chen, Nikita Navalkar, Nina Grinstead, Samantha Brentmoor and Tawanna Williams.

On the editing front, thanks to Sali Benbow-Powers, who read an earlier (discarded) version, Sue Grimshaw who read the next version, Anna Bishop (editing), and Christine Estevez and Julie Deaton (proofreading).

Lori Jackson—thanks for an amazing cover and I promise I'll never put you through that again. Samantha and the team at Brickshop Audio: thanks so much for your flexibility and for being consistently wonderful.

To the dream team at Valentine PR: I adore all you all. Christine, Kelley, Kim, Meagan, Nina and Sarah—thank you for making my life easy and for taking care of all the things I'd do poorly or forget to do at all. (Nina is thinking "Like putting on deodorant before a book signing?" and yes, that's exactly what I'm talking about.) When I look at where I was two years ago versus now, it's an understatement to call you all life-changing.

Thanks so much to Kimberly Brower and Piatkus for getting my books read outside of the United States at last.

And to the members of Elizabeth O'Roark Books, thanks

for reminding me why I do this when I'm longing for a 9-5 job. I love you guys.

Can't get enough of the Summer Series?

Go back to the beginning and meet Luke and Juliet.

Turn the page for the first chapter of *The Summer We Fell*.

1

NOW

It wasn't that long ago that I could get through an airport without being recognized. I miss that.

Today my sunglasses will remain on. It's one of those obnoxious *"I'm a celebrity!"* moves I've always hated, but that's better than a bunch of commentary about my current appearance. I slept most of the way from Lisbon to San Francisco, thanks to my handy stash of Ambien, but I'm still fucked in the head from the call I received just before I got on the flight...and it shows.

Donna has always been a ball of energy, cheerful and indefatigable. I can't imagine her any other way. Of all the people in the world, why does it have to be *her*? Why is it that the people who most deserve to live seem to be taken too soon, and the ones who deserve it least, like me, seem to flourish?

I've been promising myself that I just need to hold it together a little longer, when the truth is that I've got three straight weeks ahead of holding it together with no end in sight. But if I think nothing of lying to everyone else, I'm certainly not going to quibble over lies to myself.

I duck into the bathroom to clean up before I head for my

luggage. My hazel eyes are bruised with fatigue, my skin is sallow. The sun-kissed streaks the colorist added to my brown hair won't fool anyone into thinking I've spent time in the sun lately, especially Donna. Every time she's visited me in LA, she has said the same thing: "*Oh, honey, you look so tired. I wish you'd come home*", as if returning to Rhodes could ever improve anything.

I step back from the mirror just in time to catch a woman taking a picture of me from the side.

She shrugs, completely unashamed. "Sorry. You're not my taste," she says, "but my niece likes you."

I used to think fame would solve everything. What I didn't realize is that you're still every bit as sad. You just have the whole fucking world there to watch and remind you you've got no right to be.

I walk out before I say something I'll regret and head down the escalator to baggage claim. It wasn't until I started to date Cash that I understood the kind of chaos that can descend when the public thinks they know you—but today there's no crowd. Just Donna waiting near the base of the escalator, a little too thin but otherwise completely fine.

She pulls me into her arms, and the scent of her rose perfume reminds me of her home—a place where some of my best moments occurred. And some of my worst.

"You didn't need to pick me up. I was gonna Uber."

"That would cost a fortune," she says, forgetting or not caring that I'm no longer the broke kid she was once forced to take in. "And when my girl comes home, I'm going to be the one to greet her. Besides...I had company."

My gaze follows hers, past her shoulder.

I don't know how I didn't see him, when he stands a foot taller and a foot broader than anyone else in the room. Some big guys go out of their way to seem less so—they slouch, they smile, they joke around. Luke has never done any of those things. He is unapologetically his unsmiling self, size and all.

He looks older, but it's been seven years, so I guess he would. He's even bigger now, harder and less penetrable. His messy brown hair still glints gold from all those hours he spends on the water, but there's a full week's beard on a face that's normally clean-shaven. I wish I'd been prepared, at least. I wish someone had said, *"Luke will be there. And he'll still feel like the tide, sucking you out to sea."*

We don't hug. It would be too much. I can't imagine he'd be willing to do it anyway, under the circumstances.

He doesn't even smile, but simply tips his chin. "Juliet."

He's all grown up, even his voice is grown up—lower, more confident than it was. And it was always low, always confident. Always capable of bringing me to my knees.

It feels intentional, the fact that I'm only learning he's here *now*. Donna knows we never got along. But she's dying, which means I'm not allowed to resent her for this tiny manipulation.

"He offered to drive," Donna adds.

He raises a brow at the word *"offered"*, arms still folded across his broad chest, making it clear that's not *exactly* the way it happened. It's so like Donna to attribute far kinder qualities to us than actually exist.

"How many bags do you have?" He's already turning toward the carousel, manning up to do the right thing, no matter how much he hates me.

I move in front of him. "I can get it."

It irks me that he walks to the carousel anyway. I press a finger to my right temple. My head is splitting, finally coming off everything I took yesterday. And I just don't feel up to polite conversation, especially with him.

I swallow. "I didn't know you'd be here."

"Sorry to disappoint."

I see my bag coming and move forward. "That's not what I

meant." What I really meant was *"This is the worst possible situation, and I don't see how I'm going to weather three weeks of it."* I guess that's not much better.

I glance over my shoulder. "How is she?"

His eyes darken. "I just got in this morning, but...you saw her. A strong wind could knock her over."

And with that there's really nothing left to be said. Not easily or comfortably, anyway. The silence stretches on.

We both reach for my bag at the same time, our hands brushing for a moment.

I snatch mine back but it's too late. Luke is already in my bloodstream, already poisoning me. Making me want all the wrong things, just like he always did.

Do you love contemporary romance?

Want the chance to hear news about your favourite
authors (and the chance to win free books)?

Kristen Ashley
Ashley Herring Blake
Meg Cabot
Olivia Dade
Rosie Danan
J. Daniels
Farah Heron
Talia Hibbert
Sarah Hogle
Helena Hunting
Abby Jimenez
Elle Kennedy
Christina Lauren
Alisha Rai
Sally Thorne
Lacie Waldon
Denise Williams
Meryl Wilsner
Samantha Young

Then visit the Piatkus website
www.yourswithlove.co.uk

And follow us on Facebook and Instagram
www.facebook.com/yourswithlovex | @yourswithlovex

PIATKUS